THE PACT

THE PACT

A Rich Coleman Novel

Volume 1

BY

William Manchee

Top Publications, Ltd.

The Pact
A Rich Coleman Novel
Volume 1

Top Publications, Ltd.

ISBN 978-1-7333283-9-5

TABLE OF CONTENTS

The Pact

Do you love me?
You say you do,
but there can be no doubt
if I'm to die for you.

I must be sure, absolutely.
You must be tested.
Life is too precious to waste
on but a shallow infatuation.

If we cannot live together
we should not live at all.
It's cruel, but it is our fate.
This is your test.

For I cannot will your death,
because I do love you.
But you must prove to me
your absolute love and devotion.

Remember that fateful day we met.
You looked up and smiled at me.
For a moment, I forgot how to breathe.
You must have felt it too as you
blushed, then quickly looked away.

Our love was forbidden,
unthinkable–a felony.
Yet, we were mere mortals
without the strength or the will
to resist our tragic destiny.

Those first few months before
our secret life was revealed,
I felt only joy and happiness.
A perfect life awaited us
until that fateful day.

A cruel and hateful woman, your aunt.
The world is now a better place
but soon it will be without us too.
Was it you or I, or a conspiracy?

The DA doesn't know
nor does he care as long
as he has a neck for his noose.
Will you pass the test?

Cyanide–quick be death.
If you truly love me
you won't even flinch.
Will you pass the test?

If you do, I will confess
But if you fail, I'll run,
leaving you to swing
by your neck.

1
Last Will and Testament

It all started on a cold day in January 1979, the same day the Shah of Iran was forced to flee from the country he had ruled for thirty-eight years. I remember listening to the news reports of his departure on my way to work and wondering what impact it would have on oil prices. I had been a finance major in college and liked to think I knew something about stocks and commodities. In fact, a group of us at UCLA had formed a fantasy investment club which we called the Wall Street Wizards. We used to meet once a week to discuss market trends and strategies. Then we'd all make fantasy purchases and keep track of how they did. We would have preferred to make actual trades but none of us had extra money. Coming from middle-class families, just making enough money for tuition and expenses each semester was a major chore. Law school was even worse. I managed to rack up nearly seventy-five thousand dollars in student loans in those three years.

According to my calculations, though, had I actually made all of the trades that I had carefully noted in my journal, I would have earned roughly sixty-two percent on my money. Starting with just a modest investment of ten thousand dollars, I figured I could have had nearly three hundred thousand dollars on the day I graduated from SMU Law School. Everyone told me when I actually started investing it would be different, but I couldn't imagine why.

The office was dark when I stepped out of the elevator precisely at seven. Since Paula's death a year earlier I usually didn't linger around the apartment in the morning. Given any amount of idleness, I would invariably daydream about her and end up with a bad case of melancholy. It also made sense to go in early since the traffic was much lighter. Traffic jams tended to induce daydreaming too, so I tried hard to avoid them. I know it sounds like I needed therapy, but I was actually getting along okay, at least I thought I was.

After picking the Wall Street Journal off the floor and unlocking the door, I turned on the lights and looked at the big letters on the wall that spelled out Rogers, Phillips & Coleman, P.C., Attorneys at Law. It's not that I was an ego freak or anything, but I did get a little twinge in my stomach each morning when I saw that sign. During law school, I had clerked for a large Dallas law firm and had been awed by how the firm's partners were treated. Their time was so precious that no one dared interrupt them unless it was a matter of utmost importance. Most of them wielded enormous power and they all pulled down incredible salaries. But of all the partners only a few had their names as part of the firm's official title. This was the epitome of success. I prayed someday I'd reach that lofty position. My prayers were answered more quickly than I ever imagined.

During law school, I had a job selling life insurance for Prudential Life Insurance Company. It was the only job I could find at the time. They gave me extensive training in estate planning and marketing which proved to be invaluable once I graduated. The small firm of Rogers and Phillips hired me to handle their client's estate planning needs but when I discovered they didn't have a marketing plan, I volunteered to develop one for them. It was a brash move on my part since I knew little about marketing a law firm, but I figured something was better than nothing.

After careful thought, it occurred to me that the problem with lawyers was that most clients would only come in to see them when they were in trouble or thought trouble was lurking on the horizon. Obviously, going to the lawyer under these circumstances was dreaded and avoided if at all possible. Consequently, it was common for a client to see his attorney only once or twice during his lifetime, if he were lucky. I had to do something about that. My plan envisioned bringing clients into the firm's offices on a regular basis so that a close relationship with them could be developed. A client on a first-name basis with an attorney in the firm, wouldn't be so reluctant to call him if the need arose. We brought clients in for parties, seminars or just to ask for their advice on how to better serve them. The clients loved being pampered and consequently, my marketing plan was a big success. It was so successful, in fact, I was made a partner in less than three years.

After stopping by the kitchen for some coffee, I headed for my office where I sat down and began scanning the financial section of the paper. Unfortunately, I still hadn't accumulated any money to invest. With big monthly payments on my student loans, the wedding, the unexpected funeral, food, clothing, and auto insurance to name just a portion of the outflow of cash, I was lucky just to break even. I took a deep breath and contemplated the bonus that had been promised to me once I made partner. Thirty-five thousand dollars was a lot of money, more money than I could imagine having at one time. It didn't seem possible that in less than ten days I'd have it in the bank. Soon I could discard my fantasy portfolio of securities and actually play for real.

At eight o'clock I was glad to hear my secretary, Suzie Hoffman, rummaging around in her desk. I needed a cup of coffee and I knew she'd be bringing me one soon. Suzie was a great secretary. Not only was she competent and dependable but she was always in a good mood, laughing and joking about everything and everybody. It was hard to be depressed around her because she was always smiling and would invariably have me laughing at her silly jokes and antics. I can't imagine how I'd have survived that first year after Paula's death without her. Suzie walked into my office gingerly carrying a cup of coffee so as not to spill it.

"Hi, Boss," She said. She wasn't a woman's libber like some of the girls in the office, thank God. I liked being pampered. We chatted for a minute like we did every day until it was time to get down to business.

"So, what's on tap today?" I asked.

"Oh, you don't know. Today's your lucky day, Franklin Fox is coming in to see you at nine."

"Who's he?"

"He's an old client, a high roller who blew his daddy's fortune. He acts like he's a billionaire, but I seriously doubt he's even solvent."

"I take it by the tone of your voice, you don't like him much?" I said.

"Don't get me wrong. I wouldn't mind having his children. He's a great-looking guy, but he's a little on the flaky side."

I laughed. "If he's a typical rich kid, he probably doesn't appreciate money or have a clue how to make it."

"Well, he does know how to spend it. You may end up doing his bankruptcy one of these days."

"So what am I doing for him today?"

"He needs to do some estate planning. We did his divorce last year and he's just finally getting around to changing his will and setting up a trust for his daughter."

"Oh, part of the divorce settlement?"

"No. He got custody of his daughter," Suzie said.

"That's unusual."

"I don't remember exactly what happened, but I don't think his wife Carmen asked for custody."

"Why did they get a divorce?" I asked.

"Franklin came from a rich family and Carmen was poor. She was a waitress at Franklin's country club if you can believe that. That's where they met. From what I heard, she never fit in. Franklin's family did everything they could to sabotage the marriage. Divorce was inevitable."

"Do we have financials for him?" I asked.

"Sure, we have his divorce inventory, but it's a year old, and whether or not he listed everything is anybody's guess."

"Well, it will be a start. Bring it to me."

Suzie left and I started searching my form files for an estate planning questionnaire. When she returned with the file, I began looking through it and started transferring information. According to the divorce inventory Mr. Fox had separate property of about a half-million dollars which I assumed was left from his inheritance. Community assets had been sparse consisting of a little equity in a homestead, household furnishings, and a couple cars. Besides losing custody of her daughter, Carmen got little from the divorce. It seemed a little odd, so I decided to go talk to one of my partners, Peter Phillips, about it. It was already eight forty-five, so I hurried down the hall to Peter's office. Peter was reading a letter when I walked in. He looked up.

"Good morning," Peter said. "What's up?"

"I'm sorry to bother you, Peter, but I'm seeing an old client of yours this morning, Franklin Fox."

"Oh really? To change his will, I hope."

"Right."

"He should have done that a year ago. Be sure he changes the beneficiary on his life insurance too," Peter said.

"I'll check into that, but what I was curious about was the divorce. I know you're a great attorney, but poor Carmen didn't get a dime. Is there something I should know?"

He thought a moment and then said, "Yes ... if I

remember correctly, Carmen got pissed off one day because she found out about one of Franklin's affairs. Shortly after that, she took off without letting anyone know where she was going. After searching for her for some time, Franklin finally gave up and filed for divorce. Not knowing where she was, we got service by publication. Since she obviously didn't show up for the trial, we got a default."

"How can a parent just up and leave like that?" I asked.

"You've got me. It was all kind of bizarre, totally unexpected."

"Did she say goodbye or give anyone any indication that she was leaving?"

"No," Peter said.

"Huh. ... Suzie was saying Franklin got some big inheritance from his mother and father, but I only saw maybe a half a million in assets and quite a bit of debt on his financial statement. Is there a trust or foundation or something that didn't show up in the divorce inventory?"

"No, he inherited about four million but most of it's gone. Franklin's got some bad habits-gambling, women, expensive cars, to name a few. I think he even sponsored a NASCAR racing team at one time."

"Oh, God. No wonder he's broke." I laughed. "I think I've got a handle on it now."

"Have Franklin come back and say hello when you're done," Peter said.

As I was walking back to my office, I noticed a middle-aged man and a pretty young girl in the waiting room. When I went by Suzie's desk, she told me it was Mr. Fox and his 17-year-old daughter, Erica. After putting on my coat and straightening my desk, I told Suzie to show them in. Erica walked in, surveyed the office, and then smiled at me. She was a knockout in her maroon plaid skirt and white cotton blouse. Franklin followed right behind her and extended his hand. After a little chit-chat, we got down to business.

"So, I understand we need to do a little estate planning?" I said.

"Yes, Peter told me to come in six months ago, but I've just been too busy," Franklin said. "Erica and I are going skiing in Switzerland next week, so I thought it would be smart to get my affairs in order, you know, for Erica's sake."

"Yes, it's a good idea to review everything periodically, especially after a divorce. Where in Switzerland are you going?"

"Zermatt," Franklin said.

"Oh, I've never been there. I went to St. Moritz once when I was a teenager but that was a long time ago."

"The Alps are spectacular this time of year," Franklin said. " I try to go there at least once a year. This is the first time I've taken Erica though. She's pretty excited about it."

"I bet. Do you do a lot of skiing, Erica?"

"Uh-huh, we go to Aspen every year," she replied.

"We'll be careful. I had a client in here last week on crutches as the result of a brush with a tree."

"Don't worry," Franklin said. "If I know Erica, she'll be spending most of her time in the club flirting with all those European hunks that are sure to be there."

Erica smiled and shook her head. "Come on now, Daddy. You're going to give Mr. Coleman the wrong idea. You know I'm going with you to catch up on my reading."

"Yeah, sure," he chuckled. "So, do you ski, Mr. Coleman?"

"No, I used to, but my wife didn't like skiing much, so I haven't done it for some time."

"Are you divorced?" Erica asked.

Franklin frowned at Erica and said sternly, "That's none of your business, young lady."

"Well, he said she didn't ski," Erica said seemingly unconcerned about her father's reprimand.

"It's all right," I said, a little embarrassed by the

exchange.... "No, I'm not divorced. Actually, my wife died last year in a car wreck."

"Oh, Lord, I'm so sorry," Franklin said frowning again at Erica.

Ignoring Franklin, Erica looked at me intently with her big brown eyes. I smiled at her wondering what she was thinking. Had the revelation of my wife's death reminded her of the loss of her mother? She did look a little sad. I guess I looked at her a little too long as Franklin lifted his hand to his mouth and faked a cough.

"Okay, I need to ask you some questions," I said as I picked up my questionnaire and gave it a once-over. "Have you acquired any new assets since the divorce?"

"Ah, let me see," Franklin said, "Erica got a new 911."

"Oh really? A sports car. Lucky lady," I said.

Erica nodded. "Daddy promised he'd get me one if I went to college."

"And Daddy always keeps his promises," Franklin noted. "She deserved it."

"I bet she did." I said, "Anything else?"

"No," Franklin said.

"Do you still have the AT&T stock?" I asked.

"No, it wasn't going anywhere. I went ahead and sold it," Franklin replied.

"Okay, what about the Houston Port Authority Municipal Bonds."

Erica said, "I hate bonds. I don't know why my daddy ever bought them. They only earn five or six percent."

"So, did you sell them?"

"Yeah," he said. "I took the money and put it into a restaurant."

"Oh, so you own a restaurant now?" I asked.

Franklin shook his head. "Well, I did, but we had to put it into Chapter 11."

"Chapter 11 bankruptcy?"

"Yes."

"I see. So, is it still operating?"

"No, it was losing about eight thousand a month, so we finally shut her down and converted to Chapter 7."

"Oh. That's too bad," I said. " So, you don't have any securities then?"

"I'm afraid not," Franklin said and then looked over at Erica. "I have a big life insurance policy, though, just in case something ever happened to me. I want Erica to have plenty of money."

"Is that the million-dollar policy with Metropolitan Life?" I asked.

"Right," Franklin said.

"What's this twenty-five-thousand-dollar policy?"

"Oh, that's something I got on my American Express card. I figured it should just about pay off my Platinum bill if I kicked the bucket."

"Who is the beneficiary?" I asked.

"Probably Carmen. I suppose we ought to change that."

"Yes, I think so. I'd suggest a life insurance trust own the policy and be the beneficiary. That way you could provide for someone to manage the insurance proceeds for Erica until she gets a little older, and the policy proceeds wouldn't be taxable in your estate."

"That's exactly what I was thinking. I've got to have someone to look after Erica when I'm gone, and I sure as hell don't want Uncle Sam getting any of my money."

"Well, if you were to die, the trustee would collect the million dollars and invest it for Erica's benefit. It would be his responsibility to take care of the money for her until she got old enough to handle it."

"When should that be, do you think?"

Erica gave me an intense stare as I contemplated the question. It was awkward making this kind of decision with her present. After carefully choosing my words, I said, "You know your daughter better than anyone. When do you think she would be mature enough to handle a million dollars?"

Erica looked at her father with no less intensity. He smiled.

"I guess when she's about fifty-five," Franklin said.

"Oh, thanks a lot, Daddy," Erica said and then looked at me and smiled. "I'm more mature than he is most of the time."

I didn't reply.

"You're right, honey," he said, "but a million dollars ain't as easy to handle as you might think. You'd have half the male population of Dallas after you if they knew you had that kind of money."

"I doubt that," Erica replied.

"He's right, Erica. It would be a tremendous burden on you, and it would be a lot safer to have a professional take care of it for you, at least until you're older."

'How much older?"

"Well, I usually recommend twenty-five or thirty."

"Okay, twenty-five," Erica said.

"Hey, little princess, it's Daddy's decision, not yours. We'll go with thirty."

I smiled at Erica feeling a little guilty. Here I was a perfect stranger meddling with her life. It was my job, but I could feel her resentment. I hoped she'd realize I was just looking out for her best interest. She stared at me a moment, shrugged, and then returned the smile seemingly content with the decision. I felt relieved.

"The trustee, of course, will have the discretion to invade corpus if the income isn't enough to take care of Erica," I said.

"What's corpus?" Erica asked.

"That's the property in the trust or the assets the trust owns."

"Oh."

"Okay," I said. "Who's going to be the trustee?"

"Gee, I don't know. Who do you suggest?" Franklin asked.

"Well, usually you appoint a family member whom you trust implicitly. And, of course, it should be someone who's good with money."

"There's nobody like that in my family," Franklin said. "The only family I've got left is my sister, Martha, and I wouldn't trust her with my junk mail."

I laughed. "That bad, huh?"

"She's a witch," Erica said.

"She's just a little bitter," Franklin said.

"Why?"

"My father disinherited her. When she was seventeen, she wanted to get married to a guy in the Navy. My father refused to give her his permission, so she eloped. She figured after thirty years he would have put her back in his will, but he didn't. Oh God was she pissed when she found out I got everything. She threatened a will contest but nothing ever became of it."

"I can imagine she would be a little bitter."

"After dad died, she asked me to give her half the money, can you believe that?" Franklin said.

"So, what did you say?"

"Kiss my ass."

We all laughed. "Okay, then how about a bank?"

"You're joking, right?"

"Well, no. What's wrong with a bank?"

"You haven't known many bankers, have you?"

"Not many," I said.

"Those sorry sons of bitches would just as soon slit your throat as give you the time of day. The only time they want to loan you money is when you don't need it. If it wasn't for the bank calling our note the restaurant may not have gone under."

"Well, there are trust companies that do nothing but manage trusts and pension plans," I said.

"I don't think so. I don't want some stranger taking care of Erica. She'd just be a number to them. Erica needs special attention, she needs someone who cares about her, someone she feels comfortable with."

"Well, they wouldn't be taking care of her. That's the guardian's job. They would be taking care of her money."

"Same difference," Franklin said and then looked me in the eye. "How about you?"

"Huh?" I said. "Me?"

"Yeah, why don't you be Erica's guardian?

"You mean trustee?" I said.

"Right."

The idea of being Erica's trustee hadn't crossed my mind. Before that day I hadn't even known she or her father existed. I looked at Erica and noticed a slight grin on her face. It wasn't unusual for a client to ask their attorney to be a fiduciary and the prospect of seeing Erica on a regular basis was not unpleasant. I was flattered at the request, but being her trustee wasn't a good idea.

"Well, it's not usually appropriate for your attorney to be the trustee. Our insurance carrier frowns on it," I said.

"You know more about me and my affairs than anybody. I'd really like you to be the trustee," Franklin said and then looked over at Erica. "Don't you think Rich would be a good choice, honey?"

Erica was playing with the rubber band on her ponytail. She glanced over at her father and replied, "Yeah, that would be fine."

"You sure, honey?" Franklin said.

Erica continued to play with her ponytail. Finally, she looked at me, smiled, and replied, "Yes, I'd be most delighted to have Mr. Coleman manage my money." She laughed. "That is until I'm thirty and then I get to blow it."

"You better not blow a million dollars, honey."

Erica looked directly at Franklin and replied, "Why not? You blew four million."

"Hey!" Franklin said. "That wasn't nice, little lady. Maybe I should do to you what my daddy did to Aunt Martha."

"You can't, there's nobody else to leave it to."

"There's always the Salvation Army, right Rich?"

"True," I said.

"Ah, you love me too much to give it to anyone else."

Franklin smiled but didn't say anything.

"I think she's got you there," I said. "I'll have to check with Peter to see if the firm will let me act as the trustee. It's not that I don't want to be trustee but there are a lot of legal issues involved in something like this."

"Well, go find Peter and tell him to get his sorry ass in here."

I laughed. "Okay."

I got up, smiled at Erica, and went to find Peter. As we walked back to my office, I briefly told him the situation. When we entered the room, Franklin stood up and Peter shook his hand. Erica, who had gone over to the window to look at the Dallas skyline, turned and walked toward them. Peter looked at her and did a double-take.

"Boy, you're so grown up and getting more beautiful every year. What are you eighteen now?" Peter asked.

"Seventeen and a half," Erica said.

"Really, so it's off to college, huh?"

"Yes, I've already been accepted at SMU next fall."

"Congratulations," Peter said.

"Thank you."

"So, what's this about Rich being your trustee?"

"Well, you know how I hate banks and we don't have anyone in the family capable of doing it. So, Erica and I figured Rich would be our best bet," Franklin said, "unless you want to do it."

Peter laughed. "No, I don't think so. That's not my area of expertise. I'm lucky if I can balance my checkbook."

"So, that leaves Rich."

Peter thought a moment. "Well, ordinarily I would say no. We don't usually allow attorneys in the firm to act in a fiduciary capacity since there is a lot of risk to the firm, but there have been a few exceptions. It just so happens Rich does have a good financial background and considerable talent in managing money. He would definitely be qualified."

"He'll do a good job, I'm sure, and I can tell Erica likes him already," Franklin said. "That's the most important thing, Erica needs to be comfortable with the man who's handling her money."

"Thank you," I said wondering what I had done to garner such trust in just fifteen minutes. I looked at Erica to get her reaction. She looked away.

"Okay," Peter said. "It's settled then."

"Good," Franklin replied.

By eleven we had pretty much finished our meeting. We scheduled a time to sign everything before the ski trip and then Franklin and Erica left. This was my first appointment as a trustee, so I was feeling somewhat flattered by the gesture. I got out a legal pad and started thinking about how I would invest a million dollars if I had it. Under trust law, I knew I couldn't do anything the least bit risky, and I had to diversify my holdings. That meant no commodities, trading on margin, selling short, buying options, or other risky investment techniques that had intrigued me so much over the years. Without these tools and techniques, I figured I'd be lucky to earn ten percent on Erica's money. It was a shame I couldn't just invest the money without restriction and really watch the portfolio grow.

A few days later, Franklin stopped by and signed the trust, beneficiary, and ownership changes on the life insurance policy and all the other estate planning documents we had prepared. Suzie and I wished him a bon voyage and made him promise to send us a postcard. That was the last time I saw him.

I quickly forgot about Franklin and Erica as Peter had set up a luncheon for the members of the firm to give out annual bonuses. I was obviously very excited. The luncheon was held at the Landmark Club and Peter had invited all the wives and most of the firm's VIPs. When everyone was seated, Peter got up to say a few words.

"Good afternoon. I want to thank you all for taking time out of your busy day to join us for lunch today. As you know Rogers, Phillips, and Coleman was formed five years ago by Paul Rogers and me, and thanks to all of you we're the second-fastest-growing law firm in Dallas with seven new associates this year."

There was a round of applause, and then Peter said, "You all know Paul who's seated next to me here with his lovely wife, Alice. As you know Paul and I struggled the first few years. We were only modestly capitalized and starting a new law firm in such a competitive marketplace as Dallas was tough. Fortunately, Richard Coleman came along with a new perspective on running the firm. A lot of our success has been due to his hard work and skill. As you know, we rewarded him by making him the first associate at Rogers and Phillips to make partner."

The crowd gave me a round of applause, and I smiled and nodded my thanks. Peter continued, "It wasn't until Rich came that we learned how to market the firm's business effectively and we really began to grow. Many of you are here today because Rich taught us that our clients were the most important members of the firm and they should always be kept informed as to what we were doing and invited to participate in the firm's activities. Rich, we thank you for your contribution and look forward to another great year of growth and innovation."

"Thank you, Peter," I said.

Once Peter got going it was tough to shut him up. He went on for another twenty minutes or so before he announced the firms' fourth partner, Rudy Wells, and handed out the annual bonuses. I was happy about having a thirty-five-thousand-dollar check in my hand at long last, but not having anyone to share it with left me feeling empty inside.

On the way home I stopped by the offices of Bear Stearns & Company to see my friend, Joe Weston. Joe had been my college roommate and closest friend. We were both finance majors and were in the Wall Street Wizards together. After we graduated from college, he went to work for Bear Stearns, and I went to law school. He was my best man when Paula and I were married and a pallbearer at her funeral. I was excited to tell him the news.

"That's a pretty sweet bonus," Joe said.

"Tell me about it. So, what should I do with it?"

"You're asking me? As I recall you got the Wisest Wizard award four years in a row."

"True," I said. "But that was for fun. Now I'm talking about real money. You're the expert now. I haven't been on top of the markets like you have. They must be smothering you with in-depth reports and inside information, right?"

"Yeah, but I'm not as good as you were at cutting through all that shit," Joe said. "You're the only person I know who could hold a prospectus up to his nose and tell whether the investment stunk or not."

I smiled. "Well, my sense of smell's not so good these days. Just put me into something relatively safe."

"Safe? Are you feeling okay?"

"Yeah, I'm doing fine. Maybe some muni bonds so I don't get killed on income taxes."

Joe shook his head. "What is it? Paula?"

"I guess. I still think about her a lot."

"Hey, maybe I should fix you up with somebody? You need to start thinking about the future and forget about what happened. We just hired a new secretary. I know you'd love her. She's hot as a jalapeno."

"Thanks, but I can't imagine another woman in my life right now. I'd be a lousy date."

"I doubt that. Wait till you see her. She'll make the past nothing but a blur, I promise."

"I doubt that, but thanks for giving a shit."

Joe shrugged. "Well, if you change your mind, let me know. There's a new club on Greenville I want to take you to."

"I'll let you know," I said and pulled my bonus check from my coat pocket and handed it to him. "Put this to work for me, okay. I'm gonna go home. It's been a long day."

"I'll take care of it.... Hey, the firm's got a half dozen season tickets to the Rangers. You want to catch a few games?" Joe asked.

"Absolutely, that would be great."

"Good, I'll give you a call when the tickets come in."

On the way out, Joe made a point to introduce me to Renee. I'll have to admit she looked very tempting, but just thinking about asking her out engendered such a flood of guilt I quickly dismissed the idea. I knew there would have to be a time when I got over Paula and got on with my life, but my heart told me that time had not yet come. I wondered how long it would be.

2

Rude Awakening

It was early the following Saturday morning when I got a phone call. I hated phone calls in the night because they almost always meant trouble, somebody was dead, sick, or in jail. I hesitated before picking up the phone.

"Mr. Coleman, this is Jean-Paul Moitz with the American Consulate in Berne."

"Where?"

"Berne. Berne, Switzerland."

"Switzerland? You sure you dialed the right area code?"

"Yes, you are Richard Coleman, am I right?"

"Yeah ... okay. What can I do for you?"

"I have a young lady here who is quite distressed and asked me to call you."

"Huh? ... What's her name?" I asked.

"Erica Franklin. She says you are her guardian."

"Erica Franklin?"

"Right. Are you her guardian?"

"Ah. ... Well, not really, I'm her trustee. What's going on?"

"Her father, Franklin Fox, died early this morning in a skiing accident?"

"Oh, Lord!"

"She said she doesn't have any relatives so I should call you," he said.

"She told you to call me?"

"Yes."

"Huh. ... Well, is she there? Can I talk to her?"

"Yes, hang on."

"Mr. Coleman?" Erica said.

"Yes, hi Erica," I said. "I'm so sorry to hear about you father."

"Thank you. I'm sorry to bother you but I don't know what to do. I need some help and I didn't know who else to call."

"It's all right, I'm glad you called me. When did this happen?"

"Just a few hours ago," she said.

"Are you all right?" It was a stupid question, and I quickly regretted asking it.

"No," Erica said as she began crying. "Why did this have to happen? It's not fair. What am I going to do without Daddy?"

These were all tough questions. I took a deep breath while I rummaged for something comforting to say. "I'm so sorry. I know how terrible you must be feeling, but you've got to be strong."

"I know, I'm trying to be. Now I know how you felt when your wife died."

It surprised me that she remembered my brief mention of Paula and had related my experience to what was happening to her. It seemed extraordinary for a teenager to be so perceptive at a time of such personal tragedy. "I guess you do," I said. " Listen, I'm going to hop on the next plane. I don't know how long it will take me to get to you exactly, but I should be there within twenty-four hours, I would imagine. Can you stay at the consulate until I get there?"

"I don't know, I'll ask."

The phone went dead for a moment. I couldn't believe this was happening. While I was holding, I tried to remember what I had going on the next few days. Could I just cancel everything and run off to Europe? I took a deep breath and waited.

"They said they'd take me back to my hotel at Zermatt until you get here. They said they'd alert the local authorities, and I can call them if I need anything."

"Good, what hotel?"

"The Victoria-Jungfran."

"Okay, you hang in there. I'll see you tomorrow."

After hanging up the phone I looked at the clock. It was 4:35 a.m. My body wanted to go back to sleep but I knew if I wanted to catch an early flight I had better get going. I leaned down, picked up the yellow pages from under the bed, and began flipping pages searching for the number for American Airlines reservations. Once I found it I called and was advised the next flight to London was at 7:27 a.m. After taking a quick shower I pulled my suitcase down out of the closet and started packing. By 5:45 I was ready to leave so I called a cab to take me to the airport. After a forty-five-minute trip to Love Field, I checked in and then decided I better call Suzie at home and advise her what had happened. I called her and told her to cancel all my appointments for the next few days.

Luckily, I had a current passport, and a visa wasn't required for Great Britain or Switzerland. At 7:15 I sat down in my seat on Flight 221 to Geneva, Switzerland via London. As soon as we were in the air, I closed my eyes and fell asleep. When I awoke, we were over Tennessee. The flight attendant asked me if I wanted some breakfast, but I declined as I usually didn't eat before noon.

An hour later, as the big jet headed out over the Atlantic, it suddenly dawned on me that I would soon be collecting over a million dollars in life insurance proceeds. Even though the money wouldn't be mine, the thought of managing such a large sum excited me. For several minutes I imagined myself wheeling and dealing with Erica's money.

I could see her joyful face as I handed her a big check and she rewarded me with a grateful kiss. Then suddenly I was stricken with fear. What if I screwed up and lost money? What if the stock market crashed and I lost everything? Shit. If I lost my own money that was one thing, but if I lost Erica's money that would be unbearable.

By the time we were mid-way to London, my daydreaming had inevitably turned to Paula. She had been the perfect wife, always so attentive and full of love. We had been high school sweethearts at Santa Barbara High School. She had waited patiently for me to graduate from UCLA and then SMU law school. It had been difficult for us living so far apart but our love had been strong enough to survive that long ordeal. Our wedding took place at the old Santa Barbara Mission. It was a magnificent place for a wedding. While standing at the altar waiting to take the vows of marriage, I had wished that our marriage would be as enduring as the fortress in which it took place. I could see her in her wedding gown, so happy, so vivacious coming down the aisle.

Then we were driving south on Central Expressway near Campbell Road. From nowhere a car began weaving in and out of traffic. It veered in front of us, so I slammed on the brakes to avoid a collision. The car spun around and smashed into the center median. It bounced back in front of an eighteen-wheeler and that's all I remember. I woke up in Richardson General Hospital. I was in intensive care with tubes running up my nose, IVs in my arms, and electronic sensors taped to my chest. "Nurse, where's my wife?" I said as I looked around the stark room.

The nurse's face dropped like ice in a tall glass. She turned away, I could see the pain in her face. She turned back toward me, looked me in the eyes, and replied, "She's dead."

Tears began to well in my eyes. I began to shake, I couldn't breathe.

"No! ... Please God, No! Not Paula.... No! No!" I cried.

"She died this morning. She put up a good fight but the damage to her spinal cord was too extensive."

My eyes were wet and swollen when I pulled myself from my bitter memories. The flight attendant stopped and gave me a hard look. I wiped away the tears and forced a smile. She asked if I was okay and if I wanted anything. I asked for some water. She nodded and went to get it for me.

As I looked out the window at the vast ocean passing beneath us, I wondered how Erica was doing. She must be devastated. First the divorce, then her mother's disappearance, and now her father's death. God, what she must be going through. I looked down at my watch and saw it was nearly two. It wouldn't be long until we landed in London and then in another few hours I'd be in Geneva. I wondered how I would get from Geneva to Zermatt. When the flight attendant showed up with my water I decided to ask her.

"No problem," she said thoughtfully, "there's a bus. As a matter of fact, I have a few days off, so I'm taking the bus to Zermatt this afternoon. I'd be happy to show you to it."

"Oh, would you?"

"Sure, it will take me about fifteen minutes to check out and clean up after the flight, and then we can leave."

"Thank you. That's very nice of you."

"My pleasure."

"What's your name," I asked.

She smiled and extended her hand. "I'm Kathy Conley."

I introduced myself as we shook hands, and then she went back to her duties. I couldn't believe how lucky I had been to get an escort to Zermatt. I knew that would save me a couple of hours of travel time and Erica a few hours of loneliness. The remainder of the flight went quickly. We landed in London briefly and then were back in the air on our way to Geneva. As the Alps appeared beneath me, I suddenly realized I hadn't packed for cold weather. It was sixty-nine degrees in Dallas when I left so I forgot all about the freezing weather I would be facing in Switzerland. Finally, the plane made its descent and landed in Geneva. After deplaning I sat down to wait for Kathy to finish up her work so we could leave. When she emerged from the ramp, I stood up and smiled.

We walked through the lobby area towards a big sign that read Customs. We went through some glass doors and then got in one of the long lines to have our passports checked.

"So why are you in a hurry to get to Zermatt? Are you a skier?" Kathy said.

"No, this isn't a vacation. Unfortunately, a client of mine died yesterday. I'm an attorney."

"Oh."

I explained the situation to Kathy in the cab on the way to the bus station. The bus was filled with a boisterous bunch of skiers anxious to get onto the slopes. The route to Zermatt was extraordinarily beautiful as we traveled through majestic snow-capped mountains, magnificent forests, and numerous quaint little villages. As I watched Kathy, I began to feel a little guilty, but I didn't know why. Then I realized Kathy was beautiful, and I was attracted to her. Sure, I was single, but it had only been a little more than a year since Paula had died. I hadn't even thought about another woman until Joe had brought it up. I felt ashamed. My shame, however, couldn't quell the emotions that were rising inside me.

"Are you a good skier?" I asked.

"No, not really, but I have fun anyway."

"It's so beautiful here it would be difficult not to have fun."

"Do you ski?" Kathy asked.

"Yes, but I haven't done it for a while?"

"How come?"

"My wife, she-"

Kathy frowned. "You're married then."

"I was. She died a year ago."

"Oh. ... I'm sorry. I didn't—"

"It's all right. It was a car accident." I told her about Paula's death.

"So how about you, are you married?" I asked.

"Divorced."

"Oh, that's too bad."

"It was the best thing that ever happened to me."

"Really? Do you have any children?"

"No, being a flight attendant doesn't leave much time for a family. My husband was an architect and didn't have much extra time either. We hardly saw each other."

"Is that why you split up?"

"No, it was due to his secretary, Rita."

"He cheated on you?"

"I'm afraid so."

"I can't imagine that."

"Why?"

"If you were my wife, I doubt I'd be looking at other women." Kathy smiled and turned away. Another cringe of guilt overcame me. What was I doing flirting with a woman? It wasn't right I told myself ... but I couldn't stop. "Men just don't appreciate what they have nowadays. Paula was the most wonderful woman in the world, and I knew it. When she died, I was devastated. Your husband was an idiot for letting you get away."

"I'm lucky to be rid of him," Kathy said.

When the bus finally arrived in Zermatt, I was a little sad. I hadn't had a serious conversation with a woman in over a year. Talking to Kathy had felt good and brought back memories of the wonderful conversations Paula and I had enjoyed during our brief marriage. After Kathy said goodbye, I caught a cab to the hotel where Erica was staying. An aide from the consulate was waiting there for me. She briefed me on the procedure for getting Franklin's body shipped back to the U.S., then we went upstairs to Erica's room. She opened the door on the first knock.

"Mr. Coleman, oh thank God you're here," she said as she put her arms around my neck. She held me tightly for a moment, sobbing intermittently. I smiled at the aide who was watching us intently. Finally, I eased her into the room, and we sat down. I looked at the aide and said, "Thanks' so much for your help. I think she'll be all right now. I'll call over to the Consulate in the morning and make an appointment to come in and take care of everything."

The aide left and I turned my attention to Erica. Her eyes were swollen and bloodshot. She obviously hadn't slept since she'd called me. Her clothes were soiled and wrinkled, and she couldn't keep her hands from shaking.

"Have you been all right?" I asked.

"Yes, the people at the hospital and the Consulate staff were so nice," Erica replied.

"That's good. Did you sleep?"

"No, I couldn't."

"I didn't either the first night. I know it must have been tough for you. The first night is the worst."

"I can't believe Daddy's gone. We were having such a good time. Why did this have to happen?"

"No one has an answer to that question except God. Maybe someday you'll understand."

"I'll never understand what I did to deserve this. It's not fair." Erica sobbed. "Isn't losing a mother enough?"

"This isn't a punishment thing. It's just fate. There's nothing you could have done to prevent your father's death."

"How do you know how God punishes people?"

"I don't. It's just an opinion."

"But you made it sound like it was a fact," Erica said.

"You're right, I'm sorry for getting into religion. I don't even know what religion you are. Listen, are you hungry? I bet you haven't eaten today."

"Mom and I were Catholic. Dad was Episcopalian but he never went to church."

"Oh. ... Are you hungry?"

"Not really, but-"

"Come on, I saw a little café down the street."

Erica went to the closet and got a heavy coat. As we were leaving, she looked at my light jacket. She frowned. "You're going to freeze to death."

"It didn't occur to me to bring warm clothes. I kind of left in a hurry."

"I'm sorry," she said and then went back to the closet and returned with a heavy jacket. "This was Daddy's jacket. You can use it."

"Oh, thank you," I said and then put it on.

We left the room, took the stairs to the hotel lobby, and then went outside. I quickly felt the icy chill of the north wind and was glad I had a warm jacket. The sky was dark, and light snow was falling. As I looked around the bustling little village I thought, what a nice place to die. I mean, if you have to pick the spot, Zermatt was certainly a beautiful place. We walked two blocks and then entered the Restaurant Seilerhaus where we were welcomed by the warmth of a raging fireplace. The waitress took us to a table, and we sat down.

I said, "Tomorrow I'm going to the funeral home to arrange for transportation of your father's body. I'm going to need a death certificate too so we can collect the death proceeds from the insurance policy. I'm afraid we're going to have to stay a day or two to get it."

"Why don't you just have them mail it?"

"If we don't get it before we leave it might take weeks or even months to get it. The insurance company won't pay without a death certificate."

"So, I'm rich now, huh?" she asked.

"Well, I guess you could say that, but a million dollars isn't what it used to be. You'll need every penny of it to maintain the standard of living you're used to."

"How long until I get it?"

"Usually just a few weeks," I said.

Erica looked around the room nervously, took a deep breath, and smiled.

"You okay?" I asked.

Erica nodded and then asked, "Where will I live?"

"Where are you living now?"

"In Daddy's condo."

"Why don't you go live with your aunt?"

Erica lowered her head and replied, "Get real."

"What's wrong with your aunt?"

"Besides being a bitch, she lives in Odessa for godsakes. I've already lost my parents, isn't that enough. What now, I get exiled?"

"No, you're too old to be told where to live. I'm just trying to discuss options."

"Why can't I stay by myself at Daddy's condo?" she asked.

"I don't know. We'll have to give that some thought."

"It's not that big. Daddy and I were pretty cramped. It's really perfect just for me."

"Well, when we get back, I'll check the feasibility of you staying there. Since you're not eighteen yet, technically you should be under the custody and control of an adult. Logically that would be your aunt."

"I'll be just fine on my own. Besides, if I need anything, I can come to you, right?"

"Of course, I'll help any way I can, but I'm not your guardian or a substitute parent."

Erica smiled and replied, "Well, I should hope not."

After dinner, I took Erica back to the hotel and we went to our rooms. The next day I took care of the transportation arrangements and then thought about how Erica and I should spend the remainder of the weekend. I wanted to keep Erica occupied so she wouldn't be dwelling on her father's death. After explaining my dilemma to the concierge, he suggested we go to an ice-skating exhibition that night and attend a hockey game on Sunday afternoon. Erica seemed appreciative and was very pleasant company. On Sunday morning when we went to church, Erica looked much better. She had gotten some sleep, taken a hot bath, and put on a black dress purchased for her by one of the secretaries at the consulate.

"This is the most beautiful church I have ever seen," Erica said.

"Isn't it, though? They don't build churches like this back in Dallas," I said.

"Do you think Daddy is watching us?"

I took a deep breath to keep from laughing. "I don't know. It's possible, I guess."

Erica looked up and scanned the ceiling. "Wouldn't it be funny if he were floating up there right now looking down at us?" Erica waved her hand and whispered, "Hi, Daddy." She looked at me and laughed, "Everyone's going to think I'm crazy, huh?"

"No, you may be right. Who knows?"

"Do you believe in the tunnel and the bright light?"

"Huh?"

"You know how people who have had near-death experiences claim to have been drawn down a tunnel to a bright light. Do you believe that's what happens when you die?"

"Well, it's kind of hard to believe, but then again there have been so many people with that same experience it's kind of hard just to dismiss it as nonsense."

"Well, I believe it," Erica said. "Can we go to the chapel and light a candle for Daddy after mass?"

"Sure, I'd like to light one for Paula, too," I said.

"Were you mad at God when Paula died?"

I thought for a minute. "I don't know if I was mad at God so much as I was with the asshole who was driving after downing eight beers."

"Well, I'm pissed. Daddy never hurt anybody; he was a good man. There was no reason for him to die."

"I know. It makes no sense, and we will never be able to understand it fully. So, just try not to think about it."

"Like you don't think about Paula?"

Luckily, the service began before Erica broke out in tears again. It was a beautiful ceremony. When it was over, we went to the chapel, lit two candles, and prayed for our lost loved ones. After lunch, we went to the hockey game which turned out to be quite exciting although we didn't know one team from the other. Early on Erica determined that we should back the red team as they had prettier uniforms. Although I didn't see the logic in that, I didn't feel like challenging her at this point. That night we went to dinner at Restaurant Stochorn which was highly recommended by the concierge. When we were done, we ordered coffee.

"Thank you, Mr. Coleman, for helping me get through these last few days."

I hated when people called me, "Mr. Coleman." It made me feel old. "It's been my pleasure and I think we can cut the formality. Why don't you call me Rich? That's what all my friends call me."

"Does that mean we're friends?"

I smiled. "I hope so."

Erica smiled back. "Good."

"I've really enjoyed being with you. Your father must have loved you dearly. You're a wonderful girl. I think it's going to be interesting being your trustee."

"You like handling money?"

"Well, as a matter of fact, I do. It's kind of a hobby of mine," I said.

"Really. Are you any good at it?"

"Well, on paper I've done pretty well."

"How well?"

"Oh, sixty percent or so annually in the last ten years," I said.

"Oh, my God."

"But to be honest, I never really bought any stock, they've all been fictitious trades."

"What do you mean?"

I explained the Wall Street Wizards to her.

"But if you would have actually had the money, you would have made the same trades, right?

"I would assume so."

"How do you know when to buy and sell?" she asked.

"You've got to follow the stocks closely, research the companies and keep an eye out for good buys. Then you've got to leverage yourself by trading on margin and when the time is right, selling short. I'm pretty good at commodity trading too. You can make a killing in a hurry in commodities if you can anticipate important market swings."

"So, do you get paid for doing this?"

All these questions caught me off guard. It made sense, though, that Erica would be curious about my duties as trustee now that her father had died. No doubt she paid little attention when she and her father had first met with me because it didn't seem important to her father alive and well. Now suddenly I would be controlling a million dollars of her money. So my duties were quite important to her future well-being. She deserved some answers.

"Do I get paid for being your trustee?"

"Uh-huh," she said.

"Yes, of course."

"How much?"

"The trust provides that I get the greater of five percent of earnings or $5,000 a year. Why? Does that bother you?"

"No, you should get paid, I was just curious," she said.

"I want you to understand everything that's going on. If you ever have any questions about anything just ask me, okay?"

Erica laughed. "I will, believe me, I will."

After standing in line for two hours I was able to get Franklin's death certificate. With our business concluded we went to the station and took the last bus to Geneva. We stayed overnight in Geneva and boarded our American Airlines flight Tuesday morning. Erica had a middle seat, and I was seated on the aisle. As I was easing back into my chair getting ready for our take-off, I heard a familiar voice. It was Kathy.

"Hey, I was hoping I'd see you on your return flight," she said.

"How are you?" I asked.

"Fine."

I introduced Erica to Kathy.

"Oh, I'm so sorry about your father, Erica," Kathy said.

"Thank you," Erica replied and then turned her head away.

"Well, we can talk later. Enjoy your flight," Kathy said.

"Thanks, Kathy. I'm so glad to see you."

"Me too."

Erica watched Kathy as she walked down the aisle. Then she turned to me and said, "You didn't tell me you made a friend on the way to Switzerland."

"I didn't know you'd be interested," I said.

"I'm not, I just thought in all the hours we were together you would have told me."

"I only saw her for a couple of hours and when I got to Zermatt I forgot all about her."

"Do you like her?"

"Yes, I do. She's very charming, and I think she'd be fun to be with."

"Are you going to ask her out?"

"Maybe."

Erica's line of questioning amused me. I couldn't believe she cared about my social life. The funny thing was it felt good to have someone care a little about me. For the first time since Paula's death, the emptiness inside began to wane. It occurred to me that whether I liked it not, I was destined to become Erica's surrogate father. What a strange and wonderful feeling it was to suddenly be responsible for another human being. I almost felt like passing out cigars.

3
Death Claim

It wasn't easy getting out of bed on Wednesday morning as I was suffering from a bad case of jet lag. The thought of facing the office after a three-day absence didn't help either. There would be a stack of phone messages capable of producing instant depression, and the in-box would be stacked halfway to the ceiling. Finally, I dragged myself out of bed and hit the shower. The hot soothing water felt so good I lingered longer than I should have. Eventually, I got dressed and left for the office. As I was driving south on Midway Road towards LBJ, I felt an unusual hunger pain. I attributed it to overeating in Switzerland. My stomach must have been stretched, and now it was accustomed to more food than it needed. The thought of stopping at Denny's crossed my mind but luckily the memory of a childhood weight problem resurfaced, and I drove on by.

When I got to the office, Suzie greeted me with her usual gleeful smile and went to get me some coffee. As I walked into my office, I shuddered at the sight of my desk. It was even worse than I expected. Before I got my coat off and had a chance to sit down, Peter walked in.

"So, how is Erica?" he asked.

"It was really tough on her. She took it pretty badly."

"I can imagine," Peter said. "Losing two parents in a year must be hard to take."

"It was, but she seems to be a tough young lady."

"So, did Franklin sign his trust before he left, I hope?" Peter asked.

"Yeah, he did, so I guess I've got my work cut out for me. In fact, she's already presented me with an interesting problem."

I explained Erica's aversion to living with her aunt.

"But she's a minor."

"I know, but we can't force her to move to Odessa. Besides, she'll be eighteen soon."

"So, what are you going to do then?" Peter asked.

"I suppose I'll petition the court to emancipate her, so she'll have the rights of an adult. She seems mature enough to handle it."

"Good idea. That way she'll be responsible for her own actions, and we won't have to worry about any potential liability exposure."

"That's true, I hadn't thought about that," I said.

"You better start thinking about covering your ass now that you're her trustee."

"What do you mean?"

"I mean now you have a fiduciary duty towards her. You better dot all your i's and cross your t's, my friend," Peter warned. "If you screw up, she'll own you."

"She's a nice girl. I'm not worried about that."

"If I were you, I'd worry about it," he said. "Money has a way of bringing the worst out of people."

I shook my head. "I think we really bonded this weekend. It's going to be fun being her trustee."

"Fun? I know she's a knockout, but you're not supposed to have fun. You're just her trustee, remember?"

"I'm talking about the money. Having a million bucks to play with."

"Oh ... that, well actually it's two million, isn't it?"

"What?" I said.

"Double indemnity. Accidental death."

"Oh yeah, you're right. Oh my Lord."

"You better be careful. Don't even think about doing any of the exotic securities trading you've told me about."

"What do you think, I'm stupid?" I said.

"No, but it's a lot of money, so I just want you to be extra careful."

"Trust me, I will be very careful."

"Good," Peter said.

After Peter had left, Suzie showed up with my coffee and an exuberant smile. The anxiety Peter had momentarily created vanished as I told Suzie about my trip.

"So, ole Frankie boy really did it this time," Suzie said.

"What do you mean?"

"He managed to screw up Carmen's life, then his own, and now Erica's."

"How did he screw up Carmen's life?" I asked.

"He married her."

I laughed. "Was he that bad?"

Suzie nodded. "He was a real bastard. I hated him the first day I met him."

"Well, he can't do any more damage now. Hopefully, Erica will come through all of this with some semblance of sanity. At least with two million dollars money won't be a problem."

Suzie left and I started answering phone calls. By lunchtime I had reached everyone that I could, so I put my briefcase on my desk and opened it. Franklin's death certificate lay on top of an assortment of legal documents. Seeing it reminded me I needed to file a death claim. I hit the intercom button and asked Suzie to bring me Franklin's estate planning file. After she brought it to me, I found the insurance policy and called information, and got the number of the insurance company's home office. I called and advised a young lady in the claims department of Franklin Fox's death. She put me on hold and went to get the policy file.

"Let me see here," she said when she got back on the line. There was a moment of silence. I began to get nervous.

"What's wrong?"

"This policy seems to have lapsed."

"Lapsed?"

"Yes, nearly a year ago."

"You've got to be joking!"

"No?" she said. "I'm sorry but that seems to be the situation."

"Oh, Jesus. Are you absolutely sure about this?"

"Yes, there are several lapse notices in the file, and there's a note we called Mr. Franklin but, I'm afraid he never sent in the delinquent premium."

I got up and started pacing behind my desk. "Oh my God. I can't believe this. ... Damn it. ... Two million dollars! Oh shit!"

"I'm sorry, Sir. I'll double-check with my supervisor, but the policy has definitely lapsed."

"Can you send me copies of the lapse notices?"

"I'll send you a claim form. You can file a claim, but I'm sure it will be denied."

"Okay," I said too stunned to think clearly.

"I'm terribly sorry," the lady said.

"So am I."

I leaned back in my chair and rubbed my forehead to ease the headache that had suddenly developed. How was I going to break the news to Erica that she was penniless? I hit the intercom button and yelled for Suzie to come in.

"What's wrong!" she said with a bewildered look on her face.

I told her the bad news.

"How am I going to tell Erica? Oh God, I can't believe this!"

"It's not like it was your money, Rich."

"Erica's going to be devastated."

"Well, there's still the group insurance."

"What group insurance?" I said.

"Didn't Frankie have an American Express Life policy for twenty-five grand?"

"That's true, he did."

"So, if he paid his American Express bill it'll still be in force," Suzie said.

"And if it had double indemnity it'll pay off $50,000," I said.

"That's not two million but it's better than a chisel up your ass."

I shook my head. "Come on, Suzie. This isn't funny. How would you like to give Erica the bad news?"

"If you'll swap salaries with me, I'll do it," she replied.

"Don't tempt me. Right now that doesn't sound like such a bad deal." I took a deep breath and tried to calm myself. "I guess it could be worse. Fifty thousand dollars ought to keep her off the streets a couple of years."

"Well, I don't know about that, she's used to living pretty lavishly," Suzie said.

"She'll have to change."

Suzie laughed. "Fat chance."

"You better call her and have her come see me right away. I don't want to keep something like this from her for too long. It's best to just get it over with so we can start figuring out how to deal with the problem.... Oh, God. This is terrible."

On Friday Erica was scheduled to see me. At nine-thirty, Suzie advised me that she had arrived. I hadn't slept all night, so I felt like crap. I cleared off my desk, put on my coat, and stared out the window for a few moments trying to figure out what I was going to say to her. Getting no inspiration, I finally told Suzie to send her in. I'd just have to ad-lib. As she entered my office, she gave me an exuberant smile. When I didn't reciprocate, she frowned and immediately asked me what was wrong. She sat down, and I briefly explained the situation.

She swallowed hard. "You mean I won't get the money?"

"I'm afraid not. There was no insurance coverage when your father died."

She jumped up and began pacing. "That can't be right. Daddy always paid his bills."

"Not this time, apparently."

She glared at me. "I know he must have paid them. He promised me I'd be taken care of if anything happened to him. There must be some mistake."

I stood up. "There's no mistake, Erica. The policy lapsed."

She closed her eyes and put her hand on her temple. "Oh shit. What am I going to do without money."

"Well, you're not destitute, there was a fifty thousand dollar policy in effect."

She opened her eyes. "How much?"

"Fifty thousand," I said and sat down.

"Fifty thousand, that's nothing! In a year I'll be broke. SMU costs $25,000 a year just in tuition. What am I going to do?"

I took a deep breath. "I don't know, I'm really sorry."

She began biting her fingernail. "Isn't there anything you can do? Can't we sue them?"

"Not really, they're sending me proof that the policy cancellation was justified. We wouldn't have any grounds for a lawsuit."

"What am I going to do? This can't be happening. How could Daddy let the policy lapse?"

"I'm sorry. I'm really sorry, but we'll figure out something. Don't worry."

Erica gave me a scathing look. "Don't worry? What in the hell am I going to do? Shit!" She went to the window and paced back in forth. Finally, she stopped and turned to me.

"Rich, you've got to do something."

"Come sit down. We need to do a budget for you. You'll have to curtail your lifestyle a little bit to make the money last."

Erica looked at me. "But I don't want to do that. Daddy promised he'd always take care of me. Now, I'm going to end up on the street."

Erica began to cry. I got up and went over to her and put my hand on her shoulder.

"You're not going to end up on the street, but you may have to get a job," I said.

Erica pushed me away. "What? And make four bucks an hour. That will do me a lot of good."

I shook my head. "A lot of people make just four dollars an hour."

"Not me. I'm not doing that," Erica said as she folded her arms and glared at me.

I laughed. "What choice do you have?"

"You're my trustee. Can't you do something?"

"I'm your trustee, not a magician," I replied. "I can't make money out of thin air."

"You could have checked and made sure the premiums were paid."

"My job didn't start until your Daddy died.... Besides, the policy lapsed over a year ago."

"Great. You've got an excuse for everything, don't you?"

"What?!"

"I can see picking you was another one of Daddy's screw-ups."

After Erica stormed out of my office, I became panicky. I suddenly realized when we sent in the change of beneficiary and ownership forms to the insurance company, they should have advised us the policy had lapsed. What had gone wrong? When I went to the file room and located Fox's estate planning file, I quickly discovered the problem. Somehow the beneficiary change request had been punched and filed rather than sent to the insurance company.

"Damn it!" I said as I slammed the file drawer closed. I went back to my office and collapsed in my chair. Then I started rationalizing. Even if the change form had been timely filed there is no guarantee the insurance company would have notified me of the lapse in time to do anything about it. Since Franklin and Erica had left almost immediately for Europe it's not likely I could have done anything to avoid the catastrophe that Erica now faced. Although my analysis made sense, I didn't feel much better. I felt partially to blame for what happened to Erica. Somehow, I had to rectify the situation, but how could I ever possibly do that?

4
Quiet Desperation

After Paula's death, I felt a vast loneliness, particularly on the weekends. Sundays were the worst. Paula and I used to go to church together every Sunday morning. Except for going to Mass with Erica the previous week, I hadn't set foot in a church in over a year. Depression sank in quickly after my altercation with Erica. I realized then that letting myself be talked into being her trustee had been a big mistake. The idea of resigning crossed my mind. It was unlikely anyone would ever realize that I had screwed up. I could walk away on the premise that Erica obviously didn't want me as her trustee anymore. No one would blame me after what she said to me. But it seemed like everyone was bailing out on Erica and she didn't need that right now. Besides, if I was partially to blame for what had happened, I couldn't run away from the problem. It wouldn't be right. Somehow, I had to ease Erica's financial bind. I didn't know how that could be done, but if there was a way, I had to find it.

The thought of being alone all weekend disturbed me. My depression would only get worse. The excitement of the past weekend with Erica made me remember what companionship used to be like. Then I thought of Kathy. She had been quite friendly on the plane, and we seemed to hit it off on the bus to Zermatt. I called her.

"I'm glad I caught you in. I was afraid you would be off in some far distant continent."

"Well, as a matter of fact, I'm leaving on a four-day trip to South America Sunday morning," she said.

"Really? ... Well, I thought maybe we could do something this weekend."

"Gee, I don't know."

"I'd really like to see you. I've thought a lot about you since we met. As a matter of fact, you're the first woman I've even considered dating since Paula died."

"Are you sure you're ready?" she asked.

"Yes, I think so."

"Well, okay. I'm free tomorrow if you promise to get me home early so I won't be exhausted Sunday morning."

"I promise."

"So, what did you have in mind?"

"Do you like the theater?"

"Sure."

"Good. We can have an early dinner and then go to the Majestic and see Runaways," I said.

"Oh, that would be nice."

"I'll pick you up at 5:15 on Saturday, okay?"

"Okay, see you then."

It felt strange asking a woman out on a date. It had been three or four years since I had done it last and I had forgotten how scary it was. Kathy had made it easy for me though. She hadn't played hard to get and for that, I was much relieved. The thought of seeing her soon took my mind off of how I was going to deal with Erica's situation. The sick feeling that had been lingering inside me began to fade a little.

By the end of the day on Friday, I had cleaned off my desk and finally felt like I was back in control. Once I left the office, I started to plan my evening with Kathy. When I got home I called and made reservations at the Mansion. I wanted to make the evening memorable, so Kathy would want to go out with me again. On my way home I picked up the tickets to the Majestic Theater. The only thing left was to buy Kathy some flowers and go by the cleaners and pick up my dry cleaning. When I went to bed Friday night everything was set. It was just a matter of time now before Kathy and I would be together.

On Saturday, I worked until two o'clock and then went home to get ready for the evening. On the way home I went to the florist. The lady who helped me suggested a corsage rather than flowers. It made sense as she would be gone for several days in South America and wouldn't be able to enjoy a bouquet. So, I bought her a corsage made of beautiful white and purple orchids. I prayed Kathy would like it. When I got home, I showered, shaved, and got dressed. At five o'clock I drove over to Kathy's apartment in the Village just off Northwest Highway. It took me a while to find her apartment in the huge complex but nevertheless precisely at 5:15 I knocked on her door. A few seconds later the door opened, and a girl I had never seen before smiled at me.

"You must be Rich," she said.

"That's right. Is Kathy here?"

"No, she told me to tell you that she got a call from work. One of the other girls got sick and she had to fill in for her. She's probably in Mexico City by now. She really felt bad. She tried to call you this morning, but nobody answered."

"You've got to be kidding. I've got reservations at the Mansion and tickets for the Majestic Theater. I can't believe this."

The girl's eyes lit up. "You said the Mansion?"

"Yeah, the Mansion."

She smiled. "Well ... I was going to the movies with a friend ... but I could cancel it if you need someone to stand-in for Kathy."

I laughed as I briefly considered the offer, but quickly decided a night with a stranger would be awkward. Besides, I really liked Kathy, and she might not approve of me going out with her roommate. "Thanks, but that's all right. I guess it wasn't meant to be."

"Sorry. She said to call her on Tuesday."

As I walked to the car, I wondered if Kathy had really been called away or she had just changed her mind about dating me. That sick empty feeling returned with a vengeance. When I got back to my car I got in and pulled out the theater tickets. "Damn it!" I said tearing them in half and tossing them in the back seat. I started the engine and took off like a cork out of a champagne bottle. When I reached Northwest Highway, I screeched around the corner and sped west to Central Expressway. I heard a siren behind me. I looked in the rearview mirror and saw a patrol car closing in on me.

"Great!" I said as I pulled over and stopped. I closed my eyes and took a deep breath. "I must be cursed."

The officer got out of his car and approached me. I rolled down the window as he came up beside me. He said, "What's the big hurry?"

"I'm sorry, officer. I've had a really bad day. I was just anxious to get home."

"You know you could have killed someone driving recklessly like that."

"You're right. I apologize. I don't usually drive like that. I just got stood up for a date and-"

"Can I see your license please?" the officer asked unmoved by my explanation.

"You're going to give me a ticket?"

"That's what happens when you break the law," the officer said as he started writing.

"Great! That's just great."

The officer filled out the ticket, made me sign it, and then left. When I got home, I tossed the corsage in the garbage, got a beer, and turned on the TV. I picked up the channel changer and began flipping between channels. There was nothing decent on, so I shut off the TV and looked for a book. Everything I could find I had already read, so I opened my briefcase to work on a project I had brought home. As I was glancing through the file, the doorbell rang. Not expecting anyone, I hesitated a moment. Finally, I got up, went to the door, and opened it. It was Erica all dressed up like she was going to a party. She had on a tight black sleeveless dress, black stockings, and a pearl necklace. I took a breath and could smell the sweet scent of gardenias.

"What are you doing here?" I asked.

"I need to talk to you a minute," she said. "Can I come in?"

I hesitated, then said, "Yeah, I guess, come on in."

Erica walked in and stood in the hallway while I closed the door. I turned and looked at her amazed at how much older she looked all dressed up. My depression quickly vanished when she gave me a sweet smile.

"Come in, sit down. Boy, you sure look nice tonight. You got a date?"

She laughed. "No, I just decided to look decent for a change. You've never seen me dressed up."

"You've always looked nice," I said. "Would you like something to drink?"

"A beer would be great," she said.

I went to the refrigerator and got another beer, poured it into a glass, and brought it back to her. Then it occurred to me she wasn't old enough to drink.

"Oh. I shouldn't be giving you a beer, should I? You look so much older dressed the way you are. I'm sorry, what an idiot."

"Don't worry about it," she said. "I've had two today already."

"Well, that's a lot of alcohol. How about a coke?"

She sighed. "Whatever."

I put the beer down on the kitchen sink and got her a glass of coke.

"So. What's on your mind?" I asked extremely curious as to the purpose of her visit.

"I came to apologize ... for the other day."

I shrugged. "Oh ... that. Don't worry about it. It's okay. You're under a lot of stress. I understand."

"No, I said some terrible things, and I feel bad about it. You're the one thing Daddy did do right, and I feel so rotten about what I said. You must think I'm terrible."

"Attorneys have thick skins. Don't worry about it. I forgive you."

"You've been so wonderful," Erica said. "I don't know what I would have done if you hadn't shown up in Switzerland. I've never been so lonely as I was that first night. Just hearing your voice and knowing you were coming gave me such great comfort."

"I'm glad I was able to help," I said. "I think coming to your rescue was good therapy for me too. It's so difficult when you lose someone you love."

She sighed. "You know I think the shock of losing Daddy is just now setting in. I've been so depressed and lonely I can hardly stand it. I hope you don't mind me coming by."

As I listened to Erica, memories of the torture I felt after Paula's death came rushing back to me. For weeks I stayed alone in my apartment, eating nothing but drinking everything in the liquor cabinet. On one particular weekend, Joe called me, and when I didn't answer he came overlooking for me. He found me unconscious in my room. After that, he insisted I get some counseling and I eventually learned to cope with the loss. When I looked at Erica I could feel her pain. It occurred to me that she was in a very vulnerable state. It would be easy for her to turn to alcohol or drugs to ease her suffering. I couldn't let that happen.

"No, not at all. I know exactly how you feel. ... Hey! I've got an idea. Are you hungry?"

"Yeah, as a matter of fact, I'm famished," she said.

"I've got reservations at the Mansion. You want to come?"

She raised her eyebrows. "The Mansion? ... Oh yes, but–"

"I know this is weird, but what the hell," I said. " We both need a night out on the town."

She laughed. "What are you talking about?"

"Do you like the theater?"

"Of course," she said. "I'm going to be a drama major at SMU. You know that."

"Good, I've got theater tickets."

"You do?"

"Am I good, or what?" I said feeling like a knight saving a damsel in distress.

Erica responded by shaking her head in disbelief.

"Oh, I've got you a corsage too."

Erica laughed again. "Am I missing something here?"

"Oh, you didn't know I was psychic, did you?"

"No, you didn't mention that."

"I'm just kidding. I'll explain all this later. For now, let's just say you picked a good day to visit."

"I guess so."

I took the corsage out of the trash without Erica seeing me and brought it over to her. I noticed she had traded the coke I had given her for the beer I'd left on the counter. I didn't say anything, although I guess I should have.

"Oh! Thank you. It's so beautiful. The orchids go well with my dress," Erica said as she held the corsage up against her bosom. "Would you pin it on for me?"

"Sure," I said and then slid my hand behind her dress so I could fasten the corsage. She smiled at me as I worked. When it was securely fastened, I stepped back and took a good look at it. Erica stood up straight as if posing for a camera.

"Boy, that looks good on you."

"Thanks."

I looked at my watch. "Well, we better hurry we've got reservations at six. It's nearly ten of so we better go. We don't want them to give our table away," I said.

After recovering the torn-up tickets from the back seat of my car we took off. As we drove towards our destination, I started to have second thoughts about what I was doing. What was I thinking when I invited Erica out? It wouldn't look good if someone saw us. I glanced over at her and she smiled. Obviously, it was too late to cancel the evening. I'd just have to be discreet and get her home early. It wasn't likely anyone would see us. When we arrived, it was a little after six so we didn't have to wait long before we were seated. The waiter took our cocktail order and then disappeared.

"I love this place. Daddy used to bring me here all the time," Erica said.

"He did? This is only the second time I've been here."

"Yes, I think they have a seat with his name on it at the bar," she said.

I laughed. "Is that right?"

Erica sighed. "I feel so much better than I did an hour ago."

"Me too. I thought I was destined to spend a lonely night working."

"So, you're glad I stopped by?" Erica asked.

I looked at her not knowing how I should respond. I was very happy she had stopped by, but I didn't want her to know it. I had to keep my professional distance.

"A little companionship is always nice," I said.

She smiled. "The condo is so quiet at night. It's spooky sometimes. With Daddy there, I never gave it a thought. But since I've been back from Switzerland I've been on edge. Every noise I hear scars the shit out of me."

It occurred to me she might want to reconsider staying

with her Aunt Martha in Odessa, but I kept that thought to myself. "Don't you have any friends you can invite over?"

"Usually I have my best friend, Monica, over on the weekends, but she had to go to a wedding."

"Oh. Don't you have a boyfriend?" I asked.

Erica seemed startled by the questions. "No, nothing serious."

"Well, that's hard to believe. A girl-" I stopped myself afraid she might think I was hitting on her. "I mean . . . ah . . . you just strike me as someone who would have men falling all over you."

She laughed, "Oh, sure a lot of boys ask me out, but most of them are so immature I can hardly stand it."

"Well, girls mature more quickly than guys," I said thinking it was time to change the subject. "So, what are you going to do this summer when school's out?"

"I guess I'm going to get a job since Daddy left me penniless."

"That's a good idea," I said, impressed by her sudden display of maturity.

The waiter brought our drinks and took our orders. I cringed at the prices of the entrees. I knew it was an expensive restaurant, but this was unreal. Erica noted my alarm and said, "Don't worry, you're on duty, you can charge it to my trust fund."

I laughed and said, "No, this is on me. ... What do you want?"

"Let's see. I think I'll have the lobster."

The waiter noted her order and then looked at me.

"I'll take the filet, medium," I said.

The waiter finished up the order and left.

"So, what did you and your Daddy usually do on the weekends?"

Erica smiled and thought a moment. "I don't know. Sometimes he'd take me to Six Flags. That was always fun.

We loved Judge Roy Scream and the Texas Twister."

"Paula and I used to go to Six Flags every once in a while, too. We always enjoyed it a lot. The River Raft ride was my favorite ride, particularly on a hot summer day."

"Oh, I loved that one too. We'd always get soaking wet. I remember one time Daddy's watch got wet. It was one of those fancy sports watches with an alarm. I guess the water short-circuited the mechanism which caused the alarm to go off constantly. It was so funny. It wouldn't stop. Everybody kept looking at us as we walked through the park. Daddy stuck it in his pocket, but it was still just as loud as ever. He tried like hell to get it to stop but it wouldn't. He was so embarrassed. Finally, he threw it away in a trash can. You could still hear it beeping as we walked off.

"Twenty minutes later we happened to be walking back through the same area where we left the watch. Much to our shock, the bomb squad had been called and a half dozen men were carefully examining the trash can."

I laughed. "Oh no. What did you do?"

"We just turned around and got the hell out of there."

We both laughed. The waiter showed up with our orders and a bottle of wine. He filled our glasses never questioning Erica's age. I didn't want to embarrass her, so I kept my mouth shut. Everything looked and smelled wonderful, so we dug in eagerly. As I watched Erica eat, I couldn't help but think how incredibly beautiful she was. It felt so good to be out on the town with such an elegant young lady. We talked and laughed as we enjoyed the incredible cuisine that was placed before us. It was nearly seven when we finally left and drove to the Majestic Theater.

I'd had enough wine that I was feeling pretty carefree. The usher looked at me rather oddly when I handed him the torn-up tickets, but luckily, he didn't say anything to humiliate me. We got to our seats just as the show was about to begin. As we were being seated, I suddenly became concerned that someone I knew might see me with Erica. I looked around, but all I saw were strangers which made me feel better. After a few minutes, the lights went out and the show began.

As I was watching the play intently, Erica snuggled up to me and put her head on my shoulder. My instinct was to gently push her away even though it felt good having her so close to me. Then I thought perhaps this was something she did with her father. It was probably just an innocent gesture that didn't mean a thing. I certainly didn't want to embarrass her. But then she slid her arm on top of mine. Startled, I looked over at her. She smiled and then took my hand in hers and gripped it tightly. I became aroused, and I could hardly breathe. She began playing with my hand, running her fingernails gently back and forth and squeezing it tenderly. It felt so wonderful I couldn't move. Then she lifted my hand to her mouth and kissed it. I pulled it away.

"Erica, what are you doing?" I whispered. She gave me a hurt look and then sat up straight and turned toward the stage without responding. I felt horrible. I took a deep breath and tried to concentrate on the show. I wondered what she was thinking. On the way home, she acted as if nothing had happened, so I didn't press the issue. We talked about the show, the dinner we had enjoyed together, and how much she loved her new Porsche. She told me about what classes she would be taking next semester at SMU and how she wanted to be an actress or a model when she graduated. Erica suggested I take her home rather than to my place to get her car as she was too tired and intoxicated to drive.

It was nearly midnight when we arrived at her condo. She asked me to walk her to the door as it was dark, and she was afraid. When we got to her front door, she asked me to come in and see the place since I had never been there before. I said no, but she took my arm and pulled me inside. Once inside she put on some soft music and then excused herself to go to the bathroom. While I was waiting, I checked out some pictures displayed on the TV. I noticed one of Franklin and Carmen Fox before a tennis match. They looked so happy. He was very handsome and athletic. Suddenly I felt another rush of guilt. What was I doing in Erica's home? It wasn't right, I had to get out of there. I heard the bathroom door open. I turned and there was Erica in a pair of lilac satin pajamas with boxer shorts. She had let her hair down and had only bothered to button one of four buttons on her pajama top. My eyes were drawn to her long, luscious legs. They were smooth and finely tanned.

"Did you make us a drink?" she said and then moved to the sofa and sat down.

"No, we've both had enough, don't you think? You shouldn't be drinking at your age anyway."

"Daddy didn't care. Why should you?"

I smiled politely. "Listen, it's been a wonderful evening. I've really enjoyed your company, but I better be going."

"Don't go yet. Let's relax and talk for a while. Come sit down."

"No, you look like you're ready for bed. It's late. You must be really tired."

"Do you like my pajamas?" Erica asked.

I gave her a good look. She made a little move like she was a model. "Yes, they're really cute."

"I'm glad. I bought them especially for you."

"What?" I said suddenly realizing Erica's behavior all night had been less than innocent.

"I was looking at a short black nightgown, but it didn't feel right," she said. "I didn't think you'd go for the slut look."

I blinked just to be sure I wasn't dreaming. "Really?" I said as my pulse quickened.

"Why don't you take off your coat?" Erica said with a seductive wink.

I lingered a moment considering her suggestion. Then I came to my senses. "I don't think so," I said and then turned to leave." I'll see you tomorrow when you're sober. Call me when you want to retrieve your car and I'll come to get you."

Erica frowned as I walked to the door. I gave her one last smile and left. My heart was pounding as I got into my car. I couldn't believe I had actually considered having sex with her. I closed my eyes and thanked God that I had been strong. I nearly jumped out of my skin when Erica started pounding on my window. I rolled it down quickly.

"What the hell?"

"You left so quickly; I didn't have a chance to ask you if you'd take me to church tomorrow."

I couldn't believe Erica was standing out at the curb in her pajamas. I looked around to see if anyone had seen her. Luckily, nobody was around.

"Erica, go back into the house. Someone might see you."

"I will, but first tell me. Will you take me?"

"To church?"

"Yeah, remember the last time we went to church. We had a great time."

"I don't think so."

"Come on, it will be good for both of us."

I saw the lights of a car coming up the street. I looked in my rearview mirror to get a better look. "Okay, okay. I'll take you to church. Now get in the house, someone's coming."

Erica put her arms around my neck and thanked me with a passionate kiss. Then she scampered back into the condo. I quickly drove off before the occupants of the approaching car could identify me or see my license plates clearly. I couldn't believe Erica's behavior. She obviously had some kind of teenage infatuation with me. Now, what was I going to do? How could I explain taking her to dinner, the theater, and then ending up in her condo? What if someone saw her in her pajamas kissing me through the window of my car? Oh, Jesus, I'd be screwed.

That night I couldn't sleep. But it wasn't fear that prevented my slumber. It was the erotic thoughts of Erica. She was so alluring, so provocative, and worst of all she apparently wanted me. But why? Why not someone her own age? I knew it was wrong to get involved with her and I had to muster every ounce of strength possible to resist her. But how should I go about doing that? Should I resign as trustee? If I did that, she might seek revenge and concoct a story of how I seduced her. She may even claim we made love. Damn it! How did I get into this mess? Maybe if I talked to Peter, he'd know what to do. Then again, he would have the firm's interest at heart. He might want me to resign. I couldn't bear that. I didn't know what to do. I had to talk to somebody, so I called Joe. Unfortunately, he didn't answer. I finally fell asleep and was awakened the next morning by the telephone.

"Good morning," Erica said.

"Oh. ... Hi, Erica," I said as I looked over at the clock radio and saw it was 9:00 a.m.

"How do you feel? You gotta headache?" she asked.

"I don't know yet, I haven't got up. How are you feeling?"

"I feel great. We had such great fun last night, didn't we? God, I can't believe you took me to the Mansion. I can't wait to tell Monica."

"Listen, Erica, about last night."

"Oh, the microwave alarm just went off. I gotta go. Mass is at ten. Pick me up at 9:45. Bye."

"Erica," I said but the phone went dead. I shook my head and hung it up. I got up, took a shower, and got dressed. It occurred to me that it might be best not to pick Erica up. If I sent a cab to get her with a note explaining the impropriety of our meeting socially, maybe she'd understand. Then again, she might be totally pissed off and do something rash. That seemed the more likely scenario as she seemed somewhat headstrong. I had no choice but to go along with her game.

Despite the perilous predicament, I found myself in, I felt a tinge of excitement as I got in my car and headed for Erica's condo.

It was a cool, breezy spring day. It had rained during the night and the air had that clean smell that I loved. When I pulled down Erica's street numerous people were out walking their dogs, jogging, and working in their yards. There was no way Erica and I could leave without a half-dozen people observing us. I took a deep breath and walked up to Erica's door. I looked at my watch. It was 9:52. I knocked. She opened the door quickly.

"You're late," she said as she came out and closed the door behind her. She was wearing a white crepe suit with a ruffled jacket. She had put on much less makeup and consequently looked much younger than she had the previous evening.

"Let's hurry or we won't get a seat," she said.

"Is it that crowded?" I asked as we walked to the car.

"Yes, ten o'clock Mass is the busiest. We may have to stand."

We jumped in the car and quickly drove off. I didn't know where the church was located so Erica gave me directions. It wasn't five minutes before we pulled into the huge parking lot of All Saints Catholic Church. Erica was right, it was packed. When we got inside, we spotted a couple of seats in one of the back pews and managed to squeeze our way into them. Erica knelt to pray for a minute. As I watched her, I wondered what was going through her mind. Was she calculating her next move or was she really praying? She gave the sign of the cross and sat back.

"This is a beautiful church," I said.

"Isn't it?" she replied. "I'm glad they didn't make it really modern like most of the new churches they are building nowadays.

"Do you go to church regularly?"

"No, not since Mom left."

"Really? What made you want to go today."

She gave me a pensive look. "I don't know. Maybe to thank God for bringing you into my life."

I didn't know how to respond, so I was glad to see the service beginning. As I watched Erica celebrate the Mass so seriously, I wondered if I had misjudged what was going on with her. Maybe it was my own sordid mind that was the problem. Maybe she was innocent after all. When the Mass was over, Erica insisted I meet her priest, Father David. I told her that probably wasn't a good idea, but she insisted.

"Father David, this is my friend, Richard Coleman," Erica said.

"Hi, Mr. Coleman," Father David said. "It's nice to meet you."

I nodded and we shook hands.

"Rich was Daddy's attorney. Daddy asked him to watch out for me if anything happened to him."

"He did, did he?" Father David said and then gave me a quick once over. "Since he got you to church, I would say he's off to a good start."

"Well, I think Erica has expanded my responsibilities a little. He actually appointed me to manage her money," I said. "Church was her idea."

"Are you a Catholic, Mr. Coleman?"

"Yes, but I'm afraid I haven't been too devout."

"Then today is truly a wondrous day. Two lost children have returned home," he said and then excused himself to tend to other duties.

As we were driving back to my apartment, I felt a little sad about sending Erica home. It was a beautiful day and neither of us had anything in particular to do. I looked over at her and she smiled. As we pulled up behind her Porsche, I turned to her and said, "Are you hungry?"

Erica went home to change. I had promised to pick her

up at noon. I went inside and started banging my head against the wall. What was I doing? Jesus Christ was I insane! I convinced myself that a little lunch wouldn't hurt anything. We'd eat. I'd take her home and this bizarre weekend would be history. I changed into some jeans and a blue plaid shirt. Then I drove back to her condo. She let me in and told me to have a seat while she finished doing her hair. I took a seat and waited. When she finally emerged from the bedroom, she was wearing a burnt orange turtleneck sweater and brown stretch velvet jeans. She had pulled her hair back into a ponytail and wrapped it with a big gold band. She came over and stood before me.

"You ready to go?" she said.

I held out my hand and she pulled me up. "What do you feel like?" I asked.

"I don't know. Whatever you want."

"How about pizza? " I said.

"Hmm, I love pizza. There's a Pizza Inn not too far from here."

"Good. Show me the way."

The hostess seated us in a quiet booth in the back of the restaurant. We ordered a medium pizza, half pepperoni for me, and half vegetable for Erica. I noticed several fathers watching the Ranger game in one corner while their kids played video games. It was pretty dark so I felt fairly sure no one would see us.

"Do you think it was smart introducing me to your Priest?" I said.

"Yes. He would have thought it strange if I hadn't introduced you to him. He was a big help to me after my mother left and since Daddy's death. I've gotten to know him pretty well."

I nodded. "So, are you a Ranger fan?"

"Sure, Daddy has season tickets right behind home plate."

"Really?"

"Uh-huh. Daddy and I would probably be at the game right now if-"

"I'm sorry," I said wishing I hadn't brought it up.

"It's okay. We should go some time. You'll love our seats."

The waitress brought our pizza over and set it on the table. The guys watching the game let out a scream as someone hit a home run. Erica looked over at them and smiled.

"So, how about it," she said. "You want to go to a game next week?"

"You know I can't do that Erica," I said giving her a solemn look. "Listen, this weekend's been fun, but we've got to go back to a professional relationship. When we get together in the future it's at the office, okay?"

"Okay," Erica said. "But the weekend's not over yet."

"Huh?" I said.

She smiled, grabbed her purse, and opened it. I watched her intently as she pulled out two tickets.

"What's that?" I asked.

"Daddy's season passes to Six Flags."

It was mid-afternoon when we walked through the front gates of Six Flags Over Texas in Arlington. Don't ask me how Erica talked me into taking her there, but I was learning quickly that Erica always got her way. Soon we were in line for Judge Roy Scream. Luckily, it was a cool spring day because the line was long. I scanned the crowd carefully, praying I wouldn't see anyone I knew. Finally, we got up to the front of the line. The car pulled up and stopped abruptly. I jumped in first and Erica followed. As the safety bars descended into place, she grabbed my hand and squeezed it tightly. I smiled and shook my head. The car took off and we were pulled slowly up to the top of the first crest. As we plunged downward, Erica screamed with delight. I grabbed onto the side of the car to brace myself as we sailed around the first vicious turn. When we plunged again down the second vertical drop, I almost lost my pizza. Erica looked at me and laughed. I guess I must have looked green. Finally, the car came to a halt and I breathed a sigh of relief. We got out and Erica immediately led us to the Parachute Drop. Fortunately, we had to wait in line, so I had time to recover. By sunset, we had ridden most everything that Six Flags had to offer so we stopped at one of the shows.

While we watched a dazzling display of the History of American Music, Erica took my hand and put her head on my shoulder again. Although I should have shunned her display of affection, I didn't. I figured no one would see us and soon the night would be over, and we'd be going our separate ways. At eight o'clock I suggested we go home as I had to go to work on Monday. Erica reluctantly agreed and we got in the car and headed back toward Dallas. While we were passing by Steak and Ale, she begged me to stop for dinner. By this time, I knew there was no saying no to this lady, so I pulled into the parking lot. Once we were seated the waitress stopped to take our drink order. Erica tried to order a margarita, but I made her settle for a Dr. Pepper. During dinner, she wanted to know all about my past. I wasn't usually an open person, but Erica soon had me telling her my most intimate secrets. I don't know why but I couldn't resist her.

By the time we got home, it was nearly eleven o'clock. Erica insisted I come in as she said she was afraid to go into an empty condo so late at night. After checking all the rooms, I started to leave. Erica walked in front of the door blocking my escape.

She smiled and put her arms around my neck. "Don't go yet. Have a seat. You can pour us a drink while I go to the bathroom."

"Erica, come on. You know I have to leave."

"No, you don't," she said sternly. "Just relax. I'll be right back."

She escorted me over to the sofa and waited for me to sit down before she left. I knew I should leave, but I was mesmerized. Erica had me in her control, and she knew it. I waited a few minutes and then got up and went to the bar. I filled up a shot with bourbon and drank it down quickly. I winced from the sting of the alcohol and then poured another. I heard the door open, so I turned around and saw Erica standing in the doorway. She was wearing a black camisole bodysuit under a sheer black robe. I nearly fainted.

"Did you pour me one?" she said as she went to the sofa, sat down, and crossed her legs. I fixed her a drink and brought it to her. I looked down at her, my mind in a fog until she grabbed my hand and made me sit next to her. We talked for twenty or thirty minutes consuming several more cocktails in the process. Finally, she put her arm around me and gave me a kiss. Her lips were so sweet, and she smelled so good I was instantly electrified. I swung myself around, pulled her lips to mine, and squeezed her passionately. As our tongues frolicked joyously, I was struck by a sudden flash of guilt. I stood up abruptly.

"Jesus, Erica. We can't be doing this," I said as I gazed into her disappointed eyes.

Gathering my resolve, I bolted to the front door. My mistake was stopping and turning to get one last look. She had unbuttoned her robe exposing pale pink breasts. I froze at the stunning sight. She slowly began walking toward me confidently, knowing I was powerless to resist her. I looked into her dark calculating eyes and gave up any thought of further resistance.

When I awoke the next morning, Erica was still asleep. I briefly contemplated a hasty retreat from her bed, but the scent of her body was so alluring I couldn't tear myself away. Instead, I snuggled up close to her warm body and held her tightly feeling a kind of sober intoxication that suppressed all rational thought. It was a wonderful state of semi-consciousness that I hoped would never go away.

Unfortunately, it didn't last. By the time Erica started to wake up, I was starting to come to appreciate how badly I had screwed up. What was I thinking going to bed with a seventeen-year-old client who I was supposed to be protecting? As I rolled out of bed, my head pounded from the effects of too much alcohol. I went into the bathroom and tossed cold water on my face to try to clear my head. Suddenly, I felt two warm hands surround my waist.

"Good morning," Erica said.

I sighed and then turned around. She looked so young in the early morning light. I felt sick and it must have shown.

"What's wrong?"

"I guess I had too much to drink last night?"

"You were drinking that bourbon like it was lemonade."

"Was I?"

"Uh-huh."

"Come back to bed and rest. ... That was fun last night, wasn't it?"

"It was, no doubt but, ... we can't be doing this?"

"You keep saying that," Erica said and turned and walked into the bedroom. She grabbed a blue velvet kimono and put it on. I slipped on some underpants. "Why can't we do it?"

"You're underage."

"I'm almost eighteen."

"But not yet."

"Who's gonna know?"

"I'm also your trustee. I've got a legal duty to protect you. I can't be sleeping with you."

"Well, it's a little late to worry about that now, isn't it?" she laughed.

"Oh, God. How did this happen?" I said.

"Don't worry about it. I won't tell anybody you stole my

virginity if you don't."

I frowned. "You were a virgin?"

"Of course, what do you think I'm some kind of slut?"

"No, of course not, but I really don't know much about you."

"You made it so easy. It was just as wonderful as I had always dreamed it would be. Thank you," she said.

"Thank you?"

"For being considerate. You waited until I was ready. I thought you'd go off early."

I laughed. "If you're a virgin, how could you possibly judge my performance."

"I subscribe to Seventeen," she said.

"Oh, I see," I said as I shook my head in amazement over her cool demeanor. Well, I'm glad I pleased you, but I'm serious. We can't mention this to anyone."

"I won't tell a soul. I promise."

"It's not going to be easy keeping something like this secret," I said.

She smiled. "We'll be careful."

"No, you don't understand. We can't do this again," I said sternly.

She laughed and shook her head. "Yes, we can. We're going to have a very long, enjoyable, and profitable relationship together."

"Profitable?"

"Right. Remember what you told me about in Switzerland?"

"I told you a lot of things."

"Remember telling me about your investment club, the Wall Street Wizards. You said you made over a sixty percent return on your money?"

"In theory."

"It wasn't a theory as I recall. It was real, you just didn't actually have the money to make the trades, right?"

"Yeah."

"So I want you to take my $50,000 and make it multiply just like you did in the little game you played."

"I can't take any risks with your money. There are strict rules."

"But I want you to. I want you to use all those tricks you told me about to make me a millionaire again."

I shook my head. "No, it's too risky. You could lose everything," I said.

"It's okay, it's my money. I'll release you from any liability."

"You can't, you're a minor," I said as I began rubbing my temples. My head was throbbing. "Oh, God! I just committed a felony!"

Erica came up from behind me and began rubbing my shoulders. "Relax. I won't press charges."

"You don't have to. The DA could go for an indictment on his own."

"But I love you," Erica said.

I turned around and looked at her. "You love me?"

"Yes, anyway, I thought you were going to get me emancipated so I could stay in Dallas. Won't that make me an adult?"

I looked at her in disbelief. She had everything figured out. "I suppose."

"Then once I'm emancipated, I'll sign whatever you want me to sign just to cover your cute little ass."

She let me go and walked a few feet away, her back to me. "Erica. Come on. You could lose everything if I miscalculate, or we have any bad luck."

"I don't care, I have complete faith in you. You'll do fine and you'll make five percent to boot."

I walked over to her and gently put my hands on her shoulders. She looked up at me. "I don't care about that; I just want what's best for you."

"Then make my money multiply," she said staring into my eyes.

I backed off and turned away from her. "You don't know what you're asking." Then I began to wonder. Maybe I could make her money multiply. I had done it plenty of times before on paper. Why couldn't I do it for real? If I was successful, it would almost make up for my mistake in not sending off the beneficiary change form.

"Yes, I do, you're just afraid to face the real world. It's so easy to play your little game where you can't lose anything. Why don't you use your talents to make us some real money?"

I turned around and glared at her. "I don't care what you say, I can't gamble with your money."

"Yes, you can, and you will," she said coldly. "Our relationship has gone too far for you to quit now."

She was right. I had to do exactly as she wanted. One word from her about our sexual encounter, and I was ruined. I should have been outraged at being blackmailed, but I wasn't. Instead, I felt an incredible high, like I'd been sniffing cocaine. Somehow, I'd lost control of my life but, for some reason, instead of feeling despair, I felt relieved. It was difficult to even pretend I was still in control.

"All right, but I don't want to hear any whining if I lose all your money."

She gave me a faint smile. "You'll do it then?"

"It doesn't appear I have a choice."

Her smile broadened. "No, you don't," she said as she put her arms around me. She pushed me up against the wall and began caressing my tongue with hers. Soon we were making love again. Never in my life had I felt so exhilarated, so alive. We had begun a forbidden relationship which excited and aroused me beyond belief.

It was nearly eleven when Erica made us breakfast. As we ate, I started to worry about the mechanics of keeping our romance a secret. I looked over at Erica and saw that she was staring at me.

"What?" I said.

"I'm sorry, I'm just so happy. I can't believe you're mine."

I shook my head. "Where did you come from anyway?"

"From your wildest dreams."

"I don't think so. None of my dreams have ever come close to this."

She raised her eyebrows and took a bite of her toast.

I sighed. "Listen, you've got to promise me one thing."

She took a sip of orange juice and then licked her lips. "What?"

"You won't tell anyone what we're doing. I mean nobody. Not your friends, your priest, or anybody, okay? I could get in a lot of trouble over this."

"I'm not stupid. I won't tell a soul. You can trust me."

I shook my head. "God, I hope I don't regret this."

She smiled confidently. "You won't, I promise."

5
Emancipation

After Franklin's funeral, I filed the application for Erica to be emancipated. Although it was less than six months until Erica was eighteen, neither of us wanted to delay the day she was an adult. Erica wanted to thwart any possibility of an attempt by Aunt Martha to become her guardian. I wanted to eliminate any potential criminal prosecution should our relationship be discovered. Unfortunately, Aunt Martha didn't sit idly by. She filed an objection and showed up at the hearing with her son to make her opposition known to the court. Before the hearing, I cautioned Erica not to do or say anything to suggest we had anything more than a professional relationship. I could just see her calling me Rich or inadvertently putting her arm around me. I even insisted we drive separate cars.

When Erica and I arrived at the Records Building where the Probate Court was situated, Martha and her son, Arnold, were sitting on a bench in front of the courtroom. There was nothing we could do but say hello.

"So nice to meet you, at last, Mr. Coleman," Aunt Martha said.

Aunt Martha gestured toward Arnold and said, "This is my son, Arnold. I don't know if Erica told you or not, but he's an attorney now. He graduated from Baylor Law School last spring and passed the bar in the fall."

I swallowed hard. Erica had neglected to tell me about

Arnold. Forcing a smile, I said, "She didn't mention it. Congratulations," I said. "Baylor's a good school."

"Thank you," Arnold said.

"Franklin must have really liked you a lot to make you Erica's trustee," Martha said.

"Well, actually I was kind of shocked when he asked me. I didn't know him that well."

"You didn't? Then you must have made quite an impression on him."

"Daddy was a good judge of character," Erica said. "He knew the moment they met that Ri-Mr. Coleman was the right person for the job."

"Really. Well, if that's true, then why hasn't he talked some sense into you. This emancipation thing is not a good idea. You should come live with me for a year or two. You can have Arnold's old room."

"We've been over this Aunt Martha. I'm not moving to Odessa."

"Oh, child. You're so stubborn, just like your mother."

Erica's body stiffened. "Leave my mother out of this," she said.

"Any woman who would–"

"All right, ladies. It's time to go into the courtroom," I said. "It was a pleasure meeting you Mrs. Collins and you too, Arnold."

We all went inside and sat down in the cramped courtroom. I had tried several cases there in the past, so it wasn't unfamiliar territory. At best the room could seat maybe twenty-five spectators, a court reporter, bailiff, and a six-man jury. Two attorneys were arguing a summary judgment motion before the judge. Otherwise, the courtroom was empty. When the judge called our case, Arnold and I stood up. A court reporter hurriedly stationed herself at a table in front of the bench.

"All right, what do we have here?" the judge said.

I explained to the judge the purpose of the hearing, advised him of Erica's financial situation and the availability of the condo for her to reside in. Then Erica took the stand, and Arnold and I questioned her. Arnold explained his mother's concern for Erica's safety and desire to have her live in Odessa where she could watch out for her. He advised the court that Franklin had directed in his will that in the event of his death Martha was to be Erica's legal guardian. When we were done the Judge asked Erica a few questions.

"Miss Fox. Would you tell the Court why you want to be emancipated?"

"Yes, Sir. Well, I've lived in Highland Park for over eleven years and I currently attend Highland Park High School. I've got lots of friends here including adult friends who knew my father and who are just like family. They are always visiting and looking out for me. If I had to go to Odessa, I'd have to change schools which would be very disruptive. I've already been accepted to SMU so just as soon as I got settled in Odessa, I'd have to come back to Dallas to start college. It just doesn't make sense for me to go live with my Aunt. I know she means well, but I'd be much better off just staying in Highland Park in my Dad's condominium."

"How are you doing in school?" the Judge asked.

"Fine, I've got a B+ average."

"Have you ever been in any trouble?"

"Oh, no, Sir."

"No arrests?"

"No."

"Have you ever taken drugs?"

"No way, I'm not stupid."

"Are you sure you want to take on the responsibilities of an adult?"

"Yes, sir."

"You realize if you commit a crime there will be no leniency once you're an adult?"

"Yes, Sir, I understand."

"This doesn't mean you can drink; you know. You still have to wait until you're twenty-one."

"That's not a problem, Your Honor."

"Okay, Miss Fox," the judge said and then began writing something on the docket sheet. He looked up and continued, "Well, after listening to the evidence, I'm inclined to agree with Miss. Fox. It doesn't make much sense to uproot her at this stage in her life when she's so close to graduating from high school and is going to be starting college at SMU very soon. Even though Mr. Fox may have appointed Ms. Collins guardian of the person of Miss Fox, that issue will be moot if the court grants the application for emancipation. Since there is no motion before the court for Ms. Collins to be appointed guardian of the person or the estate, those issues aren't even before the court. Therefore, the court finds there is just cause for the emancipation of Erica Fox, and that it would be in her best interest to be emancipated. Mr. Coleman, do you have an order?"

"Yes, sir. I do."

"Very well, please present it."

I handed the judge the order and gave a copy to Mr. Collins. The judge read it quickly, signed it, and handed it back to me with the file.

"Thank you, gentlemen," he said.

As we were leaving the courtroom Aunt Martha approached Erica and said, "Well, Erica, you got your way as usual. Your father was just too lenient with you. If you were my daughter, things would be different. I'd teach you to have a little respect for authority."

"Listen, my mother told me what you did to her and Daddy. Maybe Daddy was afraid of you, but I'm not. If you think I'm going to let you push me around, you can forget it. Just stay out of my life!"

"Why you little bitch!" Aunt Martha said.

"Okay. Knock it off, both of you," I said.

"Well, the judge has made his decision, so I suppose I can't do anything about it," Martha said. "But I think it's pretty sad when your own flesh and blood treat you like scum. Come on Arnold, I guess Erica's a lost cause."

Aunt Martha stomped off with Arnold close behind. Once outside the courtroom Erica quickly forgot about her altercation with her aunt. She was ecstatic over the judge's ruling and insisted on going out to lunch. We agreed to meet at El Chico on McKinney Avenue.

"Well, how do you feel now that you're an adult?" I asked.

"Wonderful, now nobody can tell me what to do."

"I think you've been pretty much doing what you want for some time, haven't you?"

She smiled. "I suppose, but now it's legal."

"That's right, now you're responsible for all the mischief you get into."

Erica frowned. "I don't get into mischief," she said.

"I know, I'm just kidding."

"So, now that I'm free and you don't have to worry about going to prison, we can finally get down to business."

"What business is that?" I asked.

"Investing my money."

"Oh, that."

"Have you figured out yet how you're going to make me rich?" she asked.

I took a deep breath. "I've got some ideas."

"Like what?"

"Mergers and acquisitions are hot these days. If I can spot an acquisition target before everyone else does, then I can buy in before the stock moves. A lot of times a stock will rise as much as fifty percent or more in a few weeks as soon as a tender offer is made."

"Really?"

"Yeah? And if I really want to live dangerously, I can buy on margin, and then when it peaks, sell it short."

"What's that?"

"After I buy the stock, I can borrow money on it so I can buy more stock. Then when it moves up to a certain target price, I sell it and pay back the loan. That way I make a better return on my money. If it looks like the stock has been overbought and is going to fall, I sell short and make another profit when the stock stabilizes."

"That sounds like a great plan. ... So, do you have a stock in mind?"

"Yes, there's a company in Dallas called Greystone Industries. It's a plastics recycling company. With the plastics industry mushrooming the way it has; Greystone has grown quite rapidly over the last few years. Because of its low overhead and great cash flow, several companies are drooling over it. One of the companies is American Integrated Products. I did some estate planning for one of their executives who told me they were looking at it as a possible acquisition. I've been watching it for about a year now, and I think the time is ripe."

"So, what do we do?"

"We buy four thousand shares at the current trading price of twelve dollars and fifty cents and then buy another twenty-four hundred shares on margin. If the stock moves to eighteen seventy-five or so like I expect, our stock will be worth a hundred and twenty thousand less commissions and interest."

"Oh really? This is so exciting."

"We haven't done anything yet," I said.

"I know, but we're going to, right?"

I knew we shouldn't be speculating with Erica's money, but the truth of the matter was that I was dying to do it. I knew she would never be happy unless I could make her rich, and as each day went by her happiness became more and more important to me. Despite this feeling, I felt compelled to caution her one more time about the risks involved.

"You know a lot can go wrong," I said.

"I don't want to hear about what can go wrong. I trust your instincts. Let's just get it over with. I feel lucky."

"You're crazy, you know."

"And you're not?"

I laughed. "I guess you're right. I am crazy for getting into this situation."

"Oh quit complaining. After we make our trades, we can go back to the condo and I'll remind you how lucky you are."

"I've got to go back to work."

"You are working, I'm your client, remember?"

"Yeah, only too well," I moaned.

After we finished our lunch, we took Erica's car and drove downtown to the Bear Stearns & Co. office where Joe Weston worked. Erica went into Neiman Marcus while I went in to see Joe.

"So, you need another account, huh?" Joe said.

"Yeah, it's a trust account for the Franklin Fox Family Trust."

"I'll go get the forms. Have a seat."

After sitting down, I wondered how I was going to explain to Joe why I was speculating in a trust account. I decided I had no choice but to level with him. It was lucky he was a friend or I probably couldn't get away with it.

"So how much do you have to invest?"

"Fifty grand."

"Okay, I'd recommend maybe forty percent in a bond fund and split the rest between an income and a growth mutual fund."

"No, we're going to do a little speculating. We're hoping to build up the portfolio pretty fast."

Joe frowned. "Can you do that with trust funds?"

"Not usually, but she wants to do it. She's been emancipated, so she's an adult now. I've got her written consent. It's what she wants. She figures if all she has is $50,000 then she might as well be broke."

"God, she sounds like a spoiled brat."

"Well, at times it seems that way, but she's actually a pretty sweet girl."

"You didn't tell her about the Wizards, did you?"

I hesitated. "Well, I mentioned it. Why?"

"Oh shit. She probably thinks you're some kind of financial genius. I can't believe you told her about that."

"I warned her we could lose everything."

"You think she heard the warning? Bullshit. People only hear what they want to hear. You're crazy if you do this."

"You're probably right, but I'm feeling pretty confident."

Joe shook his head. "Okay. Whatever. So, what are you going to buy?"

"Greystone Industries."

"You've been listening to those rumors about a tender offer, huh?" Joe said.

"Yeah, I think something's going to happen really soon. Their profits went up 38% this year, they have barely any debt, and their cash position is getting better every day. Somebody out there's going to pick them up soon. I'm sure of it."

"I hope you're right," Joe said and then started pounding on his calculator. He wrote something down and then looked up. "So that will be about 4,000 shares, right?"

"Yeah, plus I want to do a little margin trading?"

Joe sighed. "You're not serious?"

"Uh-huh, she wants to gamble."

"Rich, come on. This is nonsense."

"Hey, you're going to make some nice commissions, right? Just make the trades, I don't need any lectures."

Joe shook his head. "You're the boss, I sure hope your

timing is right."

"It is, I'm sure of it."

"You have some inside information I should know about?"

"No, of course not. I've studied the company. It's ripe for a takeover, so we're going to make a little money when the game begins."

Joe nodded. "Okay, it's a done deal. I'll get the confirmations in the mail today," Joe said and then sat back in his chair and looked at me. "So, what's your commission for being a trustee?"

"Five percent of the net profit but I've got to give it to the firm."

"I wasn't talking about money."

"Excuse me."

Joe laughed. "Sorry, I shouldn't of-"

Joe's remark startled me. Had he really figured out what was going on that easily? I could be in serious trouble if it was that obvious. All I needed was Aunt Martha or someone at the office to figure out I was screwing Erica. If that happened, it wouldn't be long before I was selling life insurance again.

"Listen. This isn't anything like that, believe me. I just want to make a little money for Erica, so she'll be set for the rest of her life. She asked me to do it for her. I know I'm taking a big risk, but I think it will work out."

"I hope you don't screw up," Joe said.

"You and me both."

After searching through Neiman Marcus for several minutes I found Erica. She was trying on a new dress and admiring herself in the mirror. I watched her for a moment before I made my presence known. She was as beautiful a woman as I had ever known and obviously at this minute very happy. I just prayed to God my investment strategy worked. I knew if it didn't, things could get nasty.

"You look spectacular," I said.

She turned and smiled. "Thank you. So, did you do it?"

"Uh-huh."

"Wait a minute. I'll be right back," she said and went back into the dressing room. When she returned she wasn't smiling. "You know I was thinking. Maybe trading on margin is a little too risky. What if the stock dives?"

I couldn't believe what I was hearing. My adrenalin began to pump as anger consumed me. "What? I warned you."

Erica started laughing. "Just kidding. I love to get you riled up. You're so cute when you get mad."

I didn't think it was funny. "I don't understand you. Aren't you worried? You could lose everything. Have you heard a word I've said about the risks involved here?"

"It doesn't matter. I've already lost everything, but now I've found you so I'm richer now than I've ever been in my life. No pun intended."

I shook my head. "Are you serious or are you teasing me again?"

"I'm serious. When we get back to my condo, I'll show you just how serious I am."

Just listening to Erica got me aroused. I could scarcely wait to get her home. My life had lost all semblance of reality. My mind was consumed with lust for Erica, and there was little time for rational thought. Although I had fifty things going on back at the office, I gave them scarcely a thought. It was like I was given a new identity and the past had been erased from my memory.

Erica unlocked the door and we rushed inside. We kissed briefly, and then Erica pulled her sweater off over her head, her cheeks red with passion. She was wearing a black bra with a red ribbon in the middle. I watched her intently as she pulled off her pants exposing her bikini panties. After I had taken off my shirt, we embraced and kissed each other madly. We struggled down the hallway to the bedroom, leaving a trail of clothing behind. After our lovemaking we fell asleep. When I woke up it was after six o'clock. As I was putting on some pants and a T-shirt, Erica turned over and yawned.

"You getting up?" she asked.

I looked at her and replied, "Yes. I've missed a whole day of work."

"You worked all morning. So, you took the afternoon off, big deal."

"You know, you can't have me every minute of the day. I've got to make a living."

Erica sat up and sat Indian-style on the bed. She folded her arms across her breasts. "I know, but hopefully that'll change," she said.

"I don't think so. I'm not the type to sit home all day."

"Why not? We'll set you up a little office and you can trade stocks all day."

"No way, I would be bored to death. Anyway, I like practicing law. It's what I do. I wouldn't be happy doing anything else."

"Wouldn't you rather be home with me?" she asked.

"I would, but you'd soon tire of it. Besides, you're going to be busy with college here pretty soon. You won't have time for me."

"I'll always have time for you," Erica said and then got up and strolled into the bathroom. I followed her. She began brushing her hair.

"I don't know. With homework, housework, and shopping it might get a little hectic for you."

"It doesn't matter. I'll make time for you."

"You promise?" I persisted.

She turned around and smiled. "Yes."

"What about children. Do you want children?" I asked.

"Of course, what's life without kids? You've got to have

someone to inherit all your stuff when you die, right?"

"I would hope so."

"But not anytime soon, maybe when I'm twenty-five or thirty I'll have a baby. There's plenty of time for kids later," Erica said as she put her arms around my neck. We kissed and then I turned to go get dressed.

"Don't go yet," she said. "Let's play some more."

I laughed. "I'm not as young as you. Once a day is my limit."

Erica smiled. "That's what I get for falling in love with an old man."

"You should have thought of that before you seduced me," I said.

"You think I seduced you?"

"I know you did."

Erica smiled. "And it was so easy."

"I know. I'm a sucker for schoolgirls."

"So, do you regret it?"

"Absolutely not. The fear of self-destruction intensifies the pleasure."

"You worry too much. Nothing's going to happen. We were meant for each other."

"Then why weren't we born in the same decade?"

Erica shook her head. "If this is so wrong then why did you let it happen?"

"I couldn't help myself. I fell in love."

6
Impatient Vigil

Erica became keenly interested in the stock market once we had purchased the Greystone Industries stock. Every morning she got up early and checked the Wall Street Journal. During the day I'd often catch her listening to the stock report on KRLD. It was actually quite amusing for a while until she grew impatient with the stock's lackluster performance. After sixty days Greystone Industries had advanced barely a dollar per share and Erica was ready to abandon ship. I can't say that I wasn't a little worried as I had expected something to break almost immediately but I still felt I had made the right move. Erica didn't share my confidence and let me have it one night.

"Did you see what Greystone did today?" she asked.

"No, I didn't get a chance to call Joe today."

"Well, it was down three-eighths."

"Shit," I said. "I don't understand it. It makes no sense at all. There must be something going on that we don't know about."

"I don't think anything is going to happen. It's been over two months. Maybe you should find something else."

"Mergers and acquisitions don't happen overnight. It's difficult to time them perfectly without inside information. I know it's going to happen. It's just a matter of time. We've just got to be patient."

"Right, and in the meantime, we're using up all my

money. By the time the damn stock moves I'll be broke."

"I warned you this was no piece of cake. It could be worse; the stock could have nose-dived. This is a risky game we're playing."

"I know, but I thought you knew what you were doing."

"Oh, thanks a lot," I said. "Listen, if you don't like what I'm doing that's fine with me. I'll sell Greystone and let Joe pick your investments from now on. I'm sure he can get you an eight or nine percent return on your money. Of course, you won't have any money this time next year."

"Okay, I'm sorry. I just thought-"

"Quit thinking. That's your problem. You asked me to handle your money for you so let me do it. Watching your stock is like watching the grass grow, it's no fun and can be damn frustrating if you're expecting excitement. You didn't watch the stock market before you bought Greystone, did you?"

"No."

"So, don't watch it now. You said you had confidence in me, so show it."

"Okay, okay," Erica said. "I'm sorry. I'm just scared."

I went over to Erica and put my arms around her. "I know you're scared, but it's just money. I'm going to look after you no matter what happens. Don't worry."

The next day I decided it was time to do some investigation into why nothing was happening with Greystone. I called Joe and asked him to ask around and see if he could find something out. He did and called me that afternoon.

"I may have your answer for you," Joe said.

"What is it?"

"It looks like Greystone has some environmental problems. Rumor has it the EPA is investigating Greystone's Beaumont plant for illegal toxic waste disposal. This has dampened enthusiasm for a takeover. Nobody's going to touch them until the EPA concludes its investigation."

"Shit. How long will that take?"

"Another sixty to ninety days."

"Damn it! I can't believe this. Now, what am I going to do?"

'I don't know. Maybe you should sell. You'll only take maybe a ten percent loss if you unload it right now."

"Yeah, and Erica will have a stroke. I think I'll do some checking into the EPA investigation before I make a decision. Can you send me whatever reports you've got?"

"Sure, how are you going to investigate it?"

"I don't know," I said. "Maybe I'll call the local newspaper in Beaumont and see what they know about it. There must have been some stories about it when the investigation was instigated."

"Okay, if I can help let me know."

When I contacted the Beaumont Register, they sent me copies of two stories about the EPA investigation of Greystone. In one of the articles, there was a name of the contractor who was hired to do the inspection and testing of the Beaumont facility. I contacted them but they refused to give me any information. Not satisfied with what I had learned so far, I decided to go to Beaumont and check out the facility myself.

When I arrived I went straight to the Beaumont Plant. I waited until the day shift was leaving and then followed several of the employees to a local bar where I struck up a conversation with a quality control supervisor named Bob. We talked about politics, football, and his job. He told me he had worked for Greystone for nearly five years and that he was expecting a promotion. I told him I was an attorney in town for a probate hearing the next morning. After we had downed a few Coors the conversation wandered to the topic of excessive government regulation and its effect on production. Eventually, this led to the EPA investigation and it was then I learned that the Texas Water Commission had already given

Greystone a clean bill of health and that the EPA would likely do the same when it completed its investigation in several weeks.

Armed with this information I decided to hold onto the Greystone stock and wait for the pall of the EPA investigation to go away. It was nearly six weeks before the EPA issued its report and another month before the stock began to move. By this time, Erica had celebrated her eighteenth birthday and we were becoming more relaxed in our relationship. Erica had not been a patient investor these several months, but I told her patience was an essential ingredient to successful investing. I had been at the courthouse proving up some wills and was on my way home when the music stopped, and the mid-day news came on KVIL radio.

"In a news conference today, American Integrated Products announced a tender offer to shareholders of Greystone Industries. AIP has sent out an offer to all of Greystone's shareholders at $16.00 a share. That's nearly three dollars over yesterday's close at $13.25 There has been no response to the offer from Greystone's board of directors, but analysts predict the offer will be rejected. Several other companies have expressed interest in acquiring Greystone and will most likely join the bidding. Greystone stock was up today 1 1/4 on the news of the tender offer."

I was ecstatic as my prediction had finally come to pass. Greystone's stock would soon be soaring. I was so proud and excited I had to call Erica and tell her the news. I pulled into a gas station with a payphone, called her, and told her what had happened.

"That is so cool. I'm so happy," she said. "Why don't you come home and we can celebrate?"

"I can't, honey. I've got three appointments this afternoon."

"Come on. Cancel them."

"You know I can't do that, but I'll try to leave at five,

okay?"

"Okay. ... I'll be waiting for you. I'm so excited."

During the next ten days, two additional companies made tender offers driving the Greystone Stock to $18.25. My gut feeling was that it was time to sell. While we were eating dinner one night, I decided to discuss it with Erica."

"So, can you believe it?" I asked. "Greystone's at eighteen and a quarter today."

"I know, I saw it in the paper. How high do you think it's going to go?"

"Who knows, but I think it's time to get out."

Erica frowned. "Why?"

"We've achieved our objective. There's no reason to stay in it."

"But why not ride it to the top?"

"If we knew where the top was and when we were going to get there that would be fine," I said, "but we don't. It's time to take our profit and run."

"Okay, you're the financial genius. Whatever you say. So, have you located another company that meets your acquisition profile?" she asked.

"No, and I'm wondering if we should cool it for a while. We'll have over a hundred grand in the bank when we cash in. That's a nice chunk of change. Maybe we shouldn't push our luck."

"We're just getting started. Now don't go losing your nerve on me. There's no reason to stop now when you're doing so well," she said.

"I really think we ought to just be satisfied with my salary and the hundred grand. We don't need a million dollars."

"My Daddy said I was going to be a millionaire when he died so I got my heart set on it. I won't be disappointed. I have complete confidence that you're going to come through for me."

"You didn't have much confidence a few weeks ago when the Greystone stock was dead in the water."

Erica sighed. "Well, I'm sorry about that. I shouldn't have second-guessed you. I just don't understand the market as you do. Will you forgive me?"

I smiled. "Maybe."

As I watched Erica eating her dinner, I wondered why I loved her so. Yes, she was young and beautiful but I knew that would only suffice for so long. She was spoiled and selfish without a doubt. She was so immature sometimes I couldn't stand it. But I did love her, there was no doubt about that. She was so confident, so fearless and she knew exactly what she wanted in life. I really liked that. And she worshiped me, I didn't know why exactly, but it felt good. She believed I could do anything; to her I was invincible. Her belief in me gave me strength and confidence that I had never experienced before, but most of all I was as happy as I'd ever been. With Erica in my life, every day was a new adventure that I joyfully anticipated.

The next day, I called Joe and suggested we go to lunch. He agreed and at 12:30 the following day we met at a little restaurant in the Adolphus Hotel. The waitress grabbed two menus and escorted us to a table. After we ordered we started talking about old times.

"You shocked the shit out of everybody when you went to law school. You had such incredible instincts for trading it seemed like a sin not to use them," Joe said.

"I figured if I didn't like practicing law I could always come back anytime and get a job here with you or with another firm. I had nothing to lose but a little time by going to law school."

"Time and money. You could have made at least fifty thousand a year the three years you were in law school plus you must have run up a hell of a student loan."

"About a hundred grand."

"So, it cost you a quarter of million dollars to become a lawyer," Joe said.

"Huh. I hadn't thought about it, but I guess so."

"That was quite a gamble."

"I considered it an investment and luckily it worked out okay," I said.

"Yeah, your luck's always been pretty good. I thought for sure you had screwed up on Greystone. I was surprised you didn't dump it when we found out about the EPA investigation."

"I almost did.".

"So, you going to sell it now or ride it out a little longer?" Joe asked. "It's already up one and three-quarters today."

"Sell, it's reached my target. It's time to move on to something new."

"What if it goes to twenty-five like some are predicting?"

"It doesn't matter, it's done what I wanted it to do. I don't want to push my luck."

"Okay, let's see, your little lady will end up with a little less than a hundred-grand after you pay off your margin. Not bad, you doubled your money in a couple of months."

"That was the plan," I replied.

"So is your little lady happy?"

"Delirious."

"You're still a long way from a million though."

"True, but we just have to take one step at a time. I've been thinking about investing in some oil futures."

"Really?"

"Yeah, I think the situation in the Middle East is going to get bad. There's bound to be a disruption in oil production which will drive prices up. What do you think?"

"I don't know," Joe said. "What if Iran's new leaders flood the market with oil to raise capital?"

"No, I think the new government's going to be very unstable. There are still a lot of the Shah's people in control of key government positions. It's a good bet they'll be preoccupied with survival and solidifying their control. I'm convinced production will drop off sharply."

"How can you be so sure?" Joe asked.

"I've been watching the news reports since Khomeini has returned from exile. All he's worried about is getting revenge and purging the country of anyone who opposes him. I just know Iran's economy is going to go to pot at least for the next year or so."

"So how much do you want to invest?"

"All of it."

"All of it. Haven't you ever heard of diversification? Don't you have a duty as a trustee to diversify?"

"No, I drafted the trust document to give me complete discretion in handling the trust's property without the necessity of diversification. Besides, I'm getting Erica's written consent to all these transactions."

"I hope you know what you're doing. We handle a lot of trust funds here, and none of them ever touch commodities," Joe said.

"Yeah, if I were just investing for an ordinary person, I wouldn't do it either, but remember Erica is a gambler. She wants to make it big fast, and who am I to stop her?"

"You're her trustee for godsakes, it's your duty to control her."

"You don't understand," I said.

"Oh, right. Unless she has a million bucks she might as well have nothing, right?"

"Exactly."

"Do you honestly believe she's mature enough at her age to know how to invest her money? That's why her father made you the trustee."

"She's probably not the most mature eighteen-year-old

I've ever known, but there are a lot of people over thirty I know who aren't very mature either. She's a smart girl, and she believes in me. In fact, she's got more confidence in me than I do. That's pretty sad, huh?"

"You know something, Rich?"

"What?"

"You're a bigger gambler than she is."

I didn't answer him. I knew he was right. I had bet my job, my career, and maybe even my life on a teenage girl whom I hadn't known but for a few months. I wanted to explain to Joe what had happened, but I didn't know if it was a good idea to get him involved.

"This isn't like you," Joe said. "You're a lawyer for godsakes. It's not like you to break the rules. There must be something you're not telling me."

I decided to play dumb to see how much he had figured out. "What do you mean?"

"You wouldn't take the kind of risk you're taking unless there was a pretty compelling reason. You're not that stupid."

"So why am I taking such a risk?" I asked.

"You're screwing her, aren't you?"

I laughed. "How do you figure?"

"Because you're too smart for this, only your dick could get you in this kind of trouble."

"All right. You sure you want to hear my confession? You have a fiduciary duty to Erica too. You're her stockbroker. If I tell you what's going on and you don't do anything to stop it you could be in trouble too."

"It's too late. I've already let you get by with so much shit I'd lose my license anyway if anybody found out."

"All right, you want to hear it. Here it is. ... I have been sleeping with her."

"Oh God, I knew it," Joe said as he shook his head.

"That's not the worst of it. I started sleeping with her when she was a minor."

"Oh, my God," he moaned. "You didn't, Jesus Christ! I can't believe you could be that stupid."

"Believe it."

"Do you think Erica will tell anyone?" Joe asked.

"No, as long as she gets her way. Erica's never said it outright, but I get the distinct impression that it's either her game or no game. It's really weird, I love her, and I'm sure she loves me, but I can't quite bring myself to trust her a hundred percent."

"This is dangerous, Rich. What if she gets tired of you? How can you live with her, knowing she could turn on you at any moment?" Joe said.

I laughed. "She's made it worthwhile so far."

"I couldn't live like that. How can you sleep at night? You've got to make her that damn million dollars and then maybe she'll release you."

"I'm not sure I want to be released."

Joe looked at me and shook his head again. "You're hopeless, Rich. You've become a damn masochist."

I didn't respond right away. Joe was right, we both knew it. Finally, I said, "Are you going to make my trades for me, or do I have to get another stockbroker?"

"Oh, I'll make your damn trades for you, but I can't promise I'll be there when your luck runs out. I don't know if I'll have the stomach for it."

7
Shattered Dreams

During the next six months, Erica and I were obsessed with the situation in Iran. We watched every news report, read every article, and even went to meetings of the Iranian Student Organization at SMU. We watched with keen interest when Ayatollah Khomeini came back from exile and was given unlimited power because he was believed to represent the infallible Twelfth Imam in the line of successors to the Prophet Muhammad. After his landslide victory in a national referendum, Khomeini proclaimed Iran an Islamic republic. The Iranian people united behind him in hopes of obtaining greater freedom, a fairer distribution of wealth, and a government that conformed with the teachings of Islam.

Unfortunately, the broad coalition that had been responsible for the overthrow of the Shah began to collapse soon after Khomeini became the head of state. In the struggle for power that followed, the peasants and urban lower classes, under the leadership of the clergy, became the dominant force in Iran. The nationalists and their leaders including Abolhassan Bani-Sadr, who had been elected president by a large majority of the Iranians were ousted from office, and militant Islamic revolutionaries took over the country. Hundreds of Iranians were executed for political or religious reasons.

It was November 4, 1979, Erica and I were watching a movie on TV when the program was interrupted by a special

NBC bulletin.

"This is Roger Wilkins of the NBC news staff. We're sorry to interrupt your regular programming, but we have a special report live from Washington, D.C. where correspondent, Jody Roth, has news of a late-breaking story in Iran. Jody, are you there?"

"Yes, Walter. We've just been advised that Iranian militants seized the United States Embassy in Tehran and took sixty-six Americans as hostages. Details of the takeover are sketchy but apparently, the seizure of the American Embassy was in retaliation to the Shah of Iran being admitted to the U.S. for medical treatment."

If it weren't for the sixty-six Americans that had been taken hostage, Erica and I would have had a party. In the last six months, oil prices had gone from seventeen dollars a barrel to twenty-three. With this latest turn of events, we were convinced prices would reach our target of thirty-five dollars within a few weeks. Prices never quite got that high but they did reach thirty-four dollars which was good enough for me so I called Joe and told him to cash us out. After paying off Erica's margin account, taking out commissions and interest we deposited the tidy sum of $319,221 into her cash reserve account.

That kind of money would have satisfied most people, but not Erica. She was still dead set on becoming a millionaire. Although I was pretty proud of myself for parlaying $50,000 into more than $300,000 the worry and stress associated with such aggressive investing and the fear that my relationship with Erica would be discovered was weighing heavy on my mind. Although I pleaded with her to stop this obsession with money and enjoy what she had, she insisted that I plan my next move in bringing her dream to fruition.

It was the first anniversary of our meeting, and we had planned a quiet dinner in a suite at the Fairmount Hotel. Erica was to check into the hotel at 6:30 p.m., and I was to meet her in the room at seven. She insisted I wear a tuxedo for our private little party as she said it was a very special day. On the way there I bought her a dozen red roses and a little anniversary present. When I got to the room, I knocked on the door. Erica quickly opened it. She was wearing a long white satin gown with a lace top. I wondered if she had a priest stashed in the closet.

"These are beautiful. Thank you," she said and then pulled me into the room and closed the door. We kissed briefly and then I pulled out a small package from my side coat pocket and handed it to her.

"What's this?"

"Just a little something to complement your beauty."

She smiled and her eyes began to glow as she quickly unwrapped it. She held up the small black velvet box and then gave me a quick glance before opening it.

"Oh, my God!" she said as she held up the diamond necklace to the light. It had cost me $5,000 and I hadn't used any of Erica's money. I had received a referral fee on a personal injury case, and I couldn't think of a better way to spend it. Erica made me put it on her, and then she gave me a memorable kiss. We turned on some soft music, lit some candles, and rang for room service. After we had been served dinner, we took our time eating, laughing, and talking about all the brash things we had done during our relationship. Then we brainstormed on how we were going to extricate ourselves from this fantasy world in which we lived. We longed for the day that we could walk down the street hand and hand, go to the movies, dine in fancy restaurants, and enjoy life without fear of our world collapsing around us.

After dinner, we turned off the lights and danced by candlelight to the soft jazz playing on the radio. After a while, Erica stopped in mid-song and gave me a pensive look that made me uneasy.

"Honey," she said, which was unusual because she

didn't often call me that. "Take me down to the ballroom. I want to dance to live music and real people. I've got to show off my diamond necklace otherwise what's the use of having it."

"You know we can't do that," I said. "What if someone we know sees us?"

"Nobody we know is going to be here tonight. Most of the people here are businessmen from out of town. Come on, I want to dance in a real ballroom. ... Please! I'll make it worth your while."

How could I resist the pleas of the woman I loved? She begged me to take her to the ballroom. I tried to be strong, but she wore me down until I capitulated. "Oh, all right, but let me go down alone first and make sure there isn't anyone there I know."

Erica put her arms around me and gave me an ecstatic kiss. "Thank you."

After she let me go, I left and went downstairs. The ballroom was crowded with frolicking guests. I walked around the perimeter of the floor looking at everyone and making sure they were all strangers. Then I scanned the dance floor but didn't see a familiar face. When I was convinced it was safe, I started to leave to go bring Erica down but realized we'd have difficulty finding a table when I got back. So before I left, I found a waiter and paid him fifty dollars to take care of that problem while I was gone. I got Erica and we took the elevators down to the second-floor ballroom. We must have been a handsome couple or an odd couple, I don't know which, for everyone seemed to stare at us as we went by. When we got to the ballroom, there was a table ready for us. We took our seats and ordered drinks. When the music stopped and the band started a new song, Erica pulled on my arm signaling she was ready to dance.

We got up and took the floor along with a hundred other dancers. Erica was so happy she floated across the floor. She was so smooth and elegant I was mesmerized by her performance. Luckily my mother had forced me to take dancing lessons as a teenager, so I managed to keep up. As we danced, I noticed many eyes on Erica. She was like a bride at her wedding ball. When the dance came to an end we went back to our table.

"That was so much fun. Thank you, honey, for letting me come down here," Erica said.

"Where did you learn to dance so well?"

"Mother insisted I take ballet and tap dancing when I was a child, and then as a teenager, I took ballroom dancing. She wanted me to be a ballerina, can you believe that?"

"A ballerina, huh? Isn't that every mother's dream?"

"I suppose. Anyway, she had to settle for a cheerleader. I'm not the ballerina type."

"You were a good cheerleader too."

"How do you know?"

"I didn't tell you this, but just after we got involved, I went to one of your pep rallies for the basketball team just before they went into the playoffs."

Erica sat up straight with a half-smile on her face. "You didn't?"

"I swear to God, I did. ... I had to see you perform. I know I should have told you, but I was feeling pretty guilty about our relationship. I knew it would probably be your last performance and if I didn't go, I'd never be able to see you perform again. Anyway, you were incredible."

"I can't believe you did that," Erica said. "What if someone had seen you?"

"That's why I didn't tell you. You would have been looking for me and probably come running over to me."

"You're right. I'm glad you didn't tell me," Erica said and then sighed and stared off into space."

"What's wrong," I asked.

"Oh, I was just wishing my mother had been there too."

"Your mother?"

"Yes, I think about her sometimes, you know, particularly when I see other kids with their mothers."

"Like Mother's Day coming up," I said.

"Right, that will be a tough day."

"I know. I'm sorry."

"You know, someday I'd like to look for Mama. I want you to meet her. She's a wonderful woman."

"How can you say that? She left you," I protested.

"She must have had a good reason. She loved me; I know she did."

"Well, maybe when things settle down, we'll hire a private investigator and find her," I said.

"Could we?"

"Why not? There's no reason for you two to be apart now, right?"

"No. Not a reason in the world."

"Come on, the music is starting again," I said. "We're not going to be able to go dancing again for a while so let's not waste any of it."

"You won't have to ask me twice," Erica said.

As we were walking to the dance floor, I thought I saw someone staring at us. I stopped and looked at the man for a second, but he turned his head, so I didn't get a good look.

"What's wrong," Erica said giving me a puzzled look.

"Oh, nothing I guess. I'm just a little paranoid."

As we began to dance to the slow music I looked over to the table where the man had been, but he was gone. After a moment of anxiety, I blew it off as my imagination and turned my attention back to Erica. She was so vibrant and stunningly beautiful I felt so proud and profoundly lucky to have her in my arms. She smiled radiantly at me. I could feel the warmth of her love. If only we could legitimize our relationship, we could emerge from our isolation and have a normal life. I prayed for such a miracle. When the music stopped, and we reluctantly returned to our table.

"What do you think would happen if we announced we were engaged?"

"Who said I'd marry you?" Erica said with a grin.

"Will you?" I retorted.

"You have to get down on your knees."

"Right here?"

Erica laughed. "Uh-huh."

"Well, it probably wouldn't be a good idea to attract attention, do you think?" I said with a grin.

"Maybe not, but you realize you're shattering one of my most cherished fantasies."

"Shall I call your shrink?" I asked.

"You better, this could have a lasting impact on my mental well-being."

"Seriously, what do you think would happen?"

"Aunt Martha would have a stroke, and she'd call my cousin and have you in court in twenty minutes, maybe even arrested."

"You think so?" I asked. "Even if you talked to her and told her how much you loved me?"

"Who said I loved you?"

"Come on, I'm serious."

"She doesn't give a shit about me. She'd be more interested in proving she'd been right all along about me being alone in the big city. She'd say you seduced me and brainwashed me so I would be your sex slave, which may have been what happened now that I think of it. After all, I'm so young and naive I can't tell the wolves from the sheep."

I laughed. "Where did I get you?"

"I was a gift from my father, remember? The day you met me was the luckiest day of your life."

"And the most perilous," I said.

"If there were no risk, there'd be no excitement. Besides, if we get through all of this, you'll appreciate me much more."

"Perhaps, but at some point, we need to come out of the shadows. Hey, what if I quit my job, and we moved to the Cayman Islands? We could get married and live in a little beach house."

"We don't have enough money yet. Besides, I want a big wedding. You're not going to destroy that dream, are you?"

"If we stay here, we may lose everything?" I noted.

"You worry too much," Erica replied.

"Somebody has to worry. Making money isn't as easy as you seem to think."

"Speaking of money, what's your next investment move?"

"Is becoming a millionaire all you think about?" I asked.

"No, I think about other things too . . . once in a while."

I laughed and then leaned over and whispered, "I didn't tell you this at the time, but about a week after I cashed you out of oil, I bought gold."

Erica gave me a nervous look. "Gold? Gold's going up, isn't it?"

"Going berserk is more like it. I bought it at $507 and last I heard it was at $835 an ounce."

Erica smiled. "Oh. You are so good. I can't believe this. Oh, honey, you're a genius. I love you."

"Hey, a minute ago you couldn't make that commitment," I said.

"I was joking. You know I was joking. I've always had confidence in you."

"Uh-huh."

"So, how rich are we?"

"I figure we're getting close to six hundred thousand."

"All right. We're going to make it. I know we are."

"I must admit, I'm good," I said.

Erica looked at me and sighed, "You are, I knew it from

the first day we met. You just needed somebody to make you believe in yourself."

"The little capital infusion you provided didn't hurt either."

"So, what now?"

"I don't know. There's a new invention I heard about called the compact disk. I was thinking of getting into that."

"Come on, let's go back upstairs. I think you deserve a little reward."

"I like your thinking."

By June Erica's trust reached the magical figure of $1,027,007.48. I was so relieved to have reached our goal I could have screamed. Lurking in the back of my mind, however, was the horrible thought that even this achievement would not satisfy Erica. But when I informed her of our achievement she finally seemed content and didn't press me for more miracles. We continued to live happily together in our private little world for some time, but we still longed for the end to the secrecy of our relationship. It was July, and we were in Barbados celebrating our new status as millionaires when our luck abruptly changed.

We were staying at the Ginger Bay Beach Club. It was a warm day, and we were sunning ourselves on the beach. There was a breeze coming off the ocean which made it quite pleasant. I was reading a novel, The Establishment, by Howard Fast when I saw Peter approaching. My heart sank like a depth charge off a battleship.

"Well, you didn't tell me you were bringing a friend to Barbados," Peter said.

Erica looked up and upon seeing Peter turned as white as the sand on which she was lying.

"You didn't tell me you were coming here either," I replied.

Peter looked at Erica, nodded, and said, "Hi, Erica."

Erica struggled to her feet, dusted off the sand, and

replied, 'Hi, Peter."

Peter took a deep breath. Erica and I didn't make a sound.

"So, how long has this little relationship been going on?" he asked.

I thought about lying but knew it wouldn't work. Peter was no dummy and if he had come all the way from Dallas to see us, he must know the truth. "From the beginning," I said meekly.

"You mean right after you two met."

"Well, after my trip to Switzerland."

"It was my fault," Erica said. "I shouldn't have called him. I should have called Aunt Martha."

"But I thought you couldn't get a hold of her," I said.

"I didn't try."

"Oh, God," I said and then buried my face in my hands.

"So, do you two love each other?"

"Yes," Erica eagerly replied. "More than ever."

I nodded and watched for Peter's reaction.

"The firm can't be involved in this," Peter said. "Do you realize how you've compromised us?"

"I know. How did you find out anyway?"

"A few months ago, you two were a little careless. I believe it was a little ballroom dancing at the Fairmount. My brother-in-law saw you two and mentioned it to me. I had a private investigator follow you for a while. We're just lucky it was my brother-in-law who saw you and not someone else."

"So, what now?" I asked.

"I think you're going to resign from the firm just as soon as you get back. You've always wanted to go into private practice, right?"

I didn't respond.

"You can't stand the pressure of a growing law firm," Peter said. "You're working too hard, you want to have a life, don't you?"

"I guess you're right," I said. "Life is too short to spend behind a desk eighty hours a week."

"Good, your resignation will be accepted with our deepest regrets. Oh, and you two are history, right?"

"No! Erica screamed. "That's not going to happen."

"You don't have any choice, Erica. Rich will be disbarred if this comes out. He may even go to jail."

"That's ridiculous," Erica said.

"Not necessarily," I noted.

Erica began to cry. "You both are paranoid. What did we do wrong? We didn't hurt anybody. What does it matter if Rich and I love each other? I consented to everything that happened. This whole thing is stupid."

"It's complicated," Peter said. "It's a question of fiduciary duty."

"Huh?"

"As your trustee, Rich has a fiduciary duty towards you. It's one of the highest and most stringent duties imposed by the law. When he allowed your personal relationship to happen, he breached that duty. He took advantage of your youth and vulnerability for his own advantage. It's kind of like a policeman on the take."

"But that's not what happened. We fell in love. He's the best thing that ever happened to me. If anyone took advantage of anybody, it was me. I wanted him, not as a trustee but as a lover. It was my fantasy, and I made sure it happened."

"Maybe so, but Rich should have resisted. Part of his job is to protect you from yourself."

Erica sobbed. "This isn't fair. You can't destroy what we have. I won't let you."

"I'm not going to do anything, okay," Peter said. "It's up to Rich. He's got to decide what to do now. I won't blow the whistle on him just as long as you both assure me the firm won't be dragged into this mess."

"Thank you," I said. "I'm sorry I compromised the firm. Being a trustee was a personal matter. It had nothing to do with Rogers, Phillips, and Coleman. I'll make sure you're kept out of it."

Peter got up, brushed the sand from his swimsuit, and said, "Good luck. I hope it was worth it."

8
The Search

We stayed in Barbados another week, not wanting to come home and face the inevitable turmoil of the breakup of Rogers, Phillips, and Coleman. It would be bad enough having to leave the firm, but I was afraid news of it might give Aunt Martha reason to poke around in my affairs. I was sure she would be interested in the cause of the firm's breakup since she had been looking for a reason to have me removed as trustee. It was early in the morning on the day we had decided to go back to Dallas. We had just been seated for breakfast in a cozy little restaurant by the seashore.

Erica said, "I'm so sorry you lost your job. I never intended this to happen."

"You've already told me that twenty times this week. Forget about it. It's probably for the best."

"But you were doing so well. I shouldn't have called you from Switzerland."

"Well actually, I shouldn't have gone. The proper thing would have been to call your aunt, but the truth is I think I wanted to go. I didn't recognize it at the time, but when you called, I was excited about the prospect of spending some time with you."

"You see, we were destined to be together," Erica said with a gentle smile.

"I think you're right. So, whatever happens now is

going to happen and there's probably little we can do to change it. We'll just have to accept it and somehow deal with it. We have no other choice."

"I'm just scared of losing you," Erica said. "Let's get married before we get back. That way nobody can take you away from me."

"Are you serious? You sure you want to marry a washed-up lawyer?"

"You'll get another job if you want one," Erica said. "You really don't need to work anyway. We've got plenty of money now."

"There's bound to be a Catholic Church somewhere in Bridgetown," I said. "Maybe we can round up a priest before our plane leaves."

"Good idea, I'll go change into my white dress."

"I'll put on my tux."

We took each other's hand, left the restaurant, and hailed a cab. It wasn't too hard to find a priest to marry us. The most difficult part was getting a marriage license so fast. Luckily by spreading around a few hundred-dollar bills to the right people it was all arranged by eleven o'clock. We were both very excited as we stood before the altar of St. John's Catholic Church on a hot Saturday, the third day of April 1980.

Luckily, I had thought of buying the ring on the way to the church. It was one karat with a ring of eight 1/8th karat diamonds surrounding it. Although a little shaky, I put the ring on Erica's finger. When I was done, she smiled radiantly.

"Then by the power bestowed upon me by God and the Republic of Barbados, I pronounce you husband and wife," the priest said. "What God does joineth together let no man put asunder. You may kiss the bride."

We kissed lovingly while the three witnesses we'd rounded up clapped enthusiastically. After thanking the priest and the witnesses we went back to the hotel, changed, and packed our things. We caught a cab to Grantley Adams

International Airport and waited for our plane. It was late when we arrived back in Dallas. Although we were tired, we were still excited about our marriage. When we got to the door of Erica's condominium, I insisted that she let me carry her over the threshold. She giggled as I picked her up and kicked the door open.

I carried her into the bedroom and put her on the bed. Then I turned on the light.

Erica screamed. The room was in shambles. Drawers were opened and books and papers scattered all over the floor. I went into the other rooms and they were in an identical state of disarray.

"Who could have done this?" Erica asked.

"It must have been a thief. I guess we better call the police. ... Check and see if anything's missing."

I went to the phone and dialed the police. The dispatcher said they would have someone there directly. While we were waiting, I noticed the drawer to my desk was empty. Someone had taken all my financial records. I couldn't figure what anybody would want with worthless sheets of paper. After a few minutes, there was a knock at the door. Erica opened it and two uniformed police officers were standing there.

"Come in. Someone ransacked our condo," Erica said.

"Are you Erica Fox?" the shorter policeman said.

"Yes."

'We've been looking for you," he said. "There was a missing person's report filed by your aunt."

"Why would she do that?" Erica said.

"She said she came to visit you and you were gone. She didn't know where you could be, so she filed a missing person report. We got the manager to let us in so we could make sure you weren't inside sick or something. I guess she must have done this after we left."

"So you didn't search our condo?" I asked.

"No, sir. This isn't our work. Is there anything missing?"

"Just a few records," I replied.

"And who are you, sir?"

I told him.

"Are you two related?"

"Erica's my wife."

The officer looked at Erica. "Mrs. Collins didn't mention that you were married."

"God damn her!" Erica screamed. "She had no right to meddle in my affairs."

"Did you tell her you were going out of town?"

"No, it was none of her damn business," Erica replied.

"I'm sorry ma'am but we were just doing our job," the officer said. "We thought you might be in some kind of trouble."

Erica stormed off toward the bedroom. I wanted to follow her, but I felt I needed to get rid of the officers. The last thing I needed was them snooping around.

"It's all right, officers," I said as I eased them to the door. "Thanks for stopping by. We're sorry we disturbed you."

"Do you want to file a complaint?" the officer asked.

"No, it appears to be a family matter. Thanks."

"No problem. Call us if you need us," the officer said and then left with his partner.

Hearing Erica crying in the bedroom, I quickly went to her.

"Are you okay?"

"That bitch! I could kill her. Why doesn't she just stay out of my life?"

"She's still bitter over what your grandfather did to her after all these years. I guess hurting you is her way of getting revenge."

"What are we going to do?"

"She's got my records," I said. "That means she knows about us, and she knows about the million dollars. We've got to find her before she tells Arnold about it. Maybe we can talk some sense into her."

"I could strangle her with my bare hands. That stupid bitch!"

"Calm down. We've got to analyze the situation rationally and figure out what to do. I just wish I knew where she was staying. Maybe Arnold knows. You could call him and see if he knows how to contact her."

"All right," Erica said. "But I need a good reason why I want to find her. Arnold's going to be really surprised to hear from me."

"Just tell him she stopped by and you're feeling really bad that you missed her. Tell him you want to call her before she leaves town so you two can get together."

"What if he already knows that she searched our condo? Hell, he may have been with her or told her to do it."

"I don't think so. He's a lawyer. He wouldn't let your aunt do anything that might get her in trouble."

"I don't know," she said, seeming to ponder the situation briefly. "Okay, I'll call him."

"Good."

Erica picked up the phone and called Arnold at his home in Odessa. The phone rang and rang but nobody answered. Erica angrily hung up the telephone.

"Well, I guess we're not going to find Aunt Martha tonight," I said. "I need to go to my office anyway to check if Peter disturbed anything. Will you be all right alone for a while?"

"Of course, go ahead and go. I'm going to try and get some sleep. I'm exhausted."

"Okay, you sure you're okay?" I said.

"Yes. Go."

When I got to my car it wouldn't start. After flooding it a few times I finally got it started. My luck didn't improve when I got to my office building. I slid my access card through the card reader, but nothing happened. I tried again but the door didn't budge.

"Shit," I said as I realized Peter had locked me out of the building. "That little bastard."

Frustrated, I looked around trying to decide what to do next. Then I saw another tenant enter the building. I smiled at him and said, "Damn, I left my access card at home. Do you mind?"

"No," he said. "Come on in."

"Thanks."

Luckily the elevator code was still good, but I wasn't so sure about the lock on the front door. When I got to the office, I tried my key, but it didn't work.

"Damn it," I said and took a deep breath. As I was contemplating what to do next, I heard voices. I put my head to the door and heard a male and a female voice talking. I figured it was a couple of law clerks that had been hired for the school year. I waited. Finally, the woman came out leaving the door unlocked so she could get back in. When she was out of sight I quickly entered and carefully made my way to my office. Slowly I pushed the door open as my pulse quickened. I turned on the light and my heart sank. The room was empty.

At that instant it finally hit me. I had destroyed my career. There was nothing I could do now; it was all over. Even if Peter kept quiet, sooner or later everyone would find out what I had done. I turned off the lights, closed the door, and sank to the floor. Tears welled in my eyes as I sat in the darkness contemplating my dire circumstances.

After a while, I got an urge for a drink. I got up and went into Peter's office to his private bar. I opened the cabinet and pulled out a bottle of Jack Daniel. ... I brought it back to my office, sat back down, and started drinking straight from the bottle. The rest of the evening was a blank.

The next morning, I woke up in the hospital. My head was pounding, and my vision was blurred. A nurse came over to me.

"What happened?" I asked.

"Somebody mugged you last night," she said.

"They did?"

"Uh-huh, you've got a pretty nasty concussion."

"Where am I?"

"Baylor Medical Center."

"You're kidding? . . . So, will I be okay?"

"I'll get the doctor, and he can tell you," the nurse said, and then left the room.

I remembered Erica had been home alone. I started to get up to leave but the pain was too intense, so I dropped back into the bed. The doctor entered my room. He had a chart in his hand and was wearing glasses halfway down his nose.

He smiled. "I wouldn't go just yet, Mr. Coleman. You've suffered a serious head injury. You're going to have to stay here a few days."

"I need to call my wife. She's home alone. It was our first night back since we got married. She must be worried sick."

"You just came back from your honeymoon?" the doctor asked.

"Yes, we got married in Barbados."

"Well, congratulations. Who's the lucky woman?"

"Erica. ... Erica Fox."

"Erica Fox?" he said.

"Yes, well it's Erica Coleman now."

The doctor took off his glasses and looked me in the eye. "Did your wife recently lose her father?"

"Yes, in a skiing accident."

The doctor shook his head and took a deep breath. "Mr. Coleman, I've got some bad news for you."

"Huh?"

"Your wife's been arrested."

"What?"

"It's all over the news. They say she killed someone ... her aunt, I think. ... Martha Collins."

"No. There must be some mistake. That can't be. God, please. ... No."

9
Making Bail

Knowing Erica was cooped up in some cell in the Dallas County Jail made me ill. I knew jails weren't safe. The doctors promised me they would let me go home in a couple of days after they had run some tests. I pleaded with them to let me go see Erica immediately, but they refused. They said some of my test results were abnormal, and they needed to watch me a while. While I was impatiently waiting for the noon news to get the latest on Erica's case, a police detective came to visit me.

"Mr. Coleman, I'm Detective Vincent Perkins of the Dallas Police Department. I need to have a few words with you."

"Yes, what can I do for you?"

"I'm investigating the murder of Martha Collins. As you know your wife has been charged with her murder."

"She couldn't have done it. She's incapable of murder," I said.

"Well, she was arrested fleeing from the crime scene."

"She was? I can't believe that. There must be some explanation."

"I hope so for her sake," Perkins said. "Her prints are all over the room where they found the body."

"Did anyone see her do it?"

"No."

"Then I don't believe it."

"When did you see her last?" Perkins asked.

"Oh God, it was eight or nine o'clock after we got back from the airport."

"The airport?" he said.

I told him about Barbados.

"Were you living with Erica before you got married?"

"Yes, I stayed at her condo with her."

"You're an attorney, right?"

"Yeah."

"How old a man are you?"

"Thirty-one."

"Erica's what? Sixteen?"

"She's eighteen."

Perkins thought a moment then he asked, "How long have you two been together?"

I hesitated sensing where his questions were leading. "Over a year, but she was emancipated when she was seventeen."

"Oh, you got it fixed nice and legal you could have her all to yourself."

"Excuse me! Her father died and left her an orphan. She wanted to go out on her own rather than live with her aunt. We fell in love. What else can I tell you?"

Perkins shook his head. "I take it they didn't get along-Erica and her aunt."

"There wasn't any real hostility between them, just a old family feud that began before Erica was even born. Erica wasn't a participant in the feud, she just wanted to live her own life."

"Did she know Mrs. Collins was in town?"

I explained what happened when we got back to the condo.

"Apparently your wife found out where her aunt was staying."

"I guess so, but I don't know how."

"Was your wife upset about her aunt searching your condo?"

"We were both upset about finding the place in shambles, obviously. We didn't know for sure she was the one who did it. It was just a suspicion. We figured she searched the house for clues as to where Erica had gone. Erica didn't call her and tell her she was going on vacation. It was all just a big mistake. Nobody was mad at anybody."

"Your wife, does she usually make social calls at eleven o'clock at night and then jog home?" Perkins asked.

"No, I told you, there must be some explanation. If I could just talk to her, I could probably straighten this out."

"Well, I hope you're able to do that, because it doesn't make a lot of sense right now."

"I'll talk to her, and then I'll call you."

"Sure. Now about your mugging. Did you see who hit you when you were going into that bar?"

"Hell no." I laughed. "I don't even remember going to the bar. They caught me by surprise, I guess. I really don't have any recollection of what happened."

"What time was it?"

"I don't know, I told you I don't remember anything. The last time I looked at my watch it was about eight-thirty."

"They didn't find you in the alley until after midnight."

"Really?"

"Yeah, so I guess you were just lying there three or four hours?"

"I guess so, I don't remember any of it."

Detective Perkins took a deep breath and thought a moment.

"Okay, that's all for now. You're not planning any more trips out of the city, are you?"

"No, why?"

"I'm sure I'll have more questions for you later. I just don't want to have any trouble finding you if I need you."

"You won't," I said.

Hearing that Erica had been at the crime scene disturbed me. I felt guilty. If I hadn't left her, this wouldn't have happened. I was being selfish, just worrying about my ass and not thinking about what was going through poor Erica's mind. I knew she was upset but I just ignored that and left her there alone. How could I have been so thoughtless?

Since I was a captive in the hospital, and I couldn't let Erica sit in the jail any longer than necessary, I called a criminal attorney acquaintance of mine, Robert Webster, to see what he could do to get her out. He had been a guest speaker at a Dallas Bar Association luncheon and had impressed me. I told him the situation, and he promised to call the jail and get back with me. As I was hanging up Joe Weston walked in. He cringed when he saw my face up close.

"You look terrible. Does it hurt?"

"Not now but it's pretty sore when the medication wears off. Luckily, all I have to do is push this little button when I feel the pain coming back and the nurse brings me more medication."

"That's good. ... So how in the hell did you get mugged?"

"How did you know I got mugged?"

"I've been trying to get a hold of you ever since Peter called me."

"When did he call you?"

"When he got back from Barbados. I knew you'd get caught sooner or later."

"Why would he call you?"

"He wanted a complete rundown on your stock transactions. I guess he wanted to see how much trouble you'd got the firm in."

"What did you tell him?'

"I told him I couldn't give him any information since he

wasn't the trustee. Of course, he didn't like that response too much."

"I bet."

"So, you didn't answer my question. How did you manage to get mugged?"

"I don't know. I don't even remember going to the bar."

Joe scratched his head. "I'm surprised someone would mug you in that part of town. It's not a bad neighborhood."

"I know. You wouldn't think so. I wish I could remember what happened."

"What's this about Erica? I couldn't believe it when I heard she had been arrested. Is she all right?"

"I hope so. My attorney's checking into getting her out on bail right now. As a matter of fact I'm going to be needing a little cash from her trust account to cover the bail premium."

"How much?"

"I don't know yet. The judge hasn't set the bail yet. Hopefully, it will be less than a hundred-grand. That would make the bail premium $10,000."

"That wouldn't be a problem." he said.

As we were talking, I looked at the clock and saw it was 11:58. Since I wanted to see how the press was handling the story, I had Joe turn on the TV. After a few commercials, the news came on.

"Good afternoon, this is Peter Brantley with the noon news.

"Police this morning arrested a young woman, Erica Fox, for the alleged murder of her Aunt, Martha Collins. Police were called to the Starlight Motel on West Northwest Highway last night when the manager discovered Mrs. Collins dead in her room. Police report that Mrs. Collins was apparently hit over the head and then smothered with a pillow. The motel manager told police she saw Miss Fox enter the victim's apartment at about 9:45 that evening. The body was found shortly after midnight.

"In other news, China canceled talks today on improving relations with Russia in light of the recent Russian Invasion of Afghanistan-"

Joe shut off the TV and shook his head. "I wonder how Erica knew where her Aunt was staying?"

"She must have got a call from her and then went over to the motel. Had I just stayed home this wouldn't have happened."

"Well, hindsight is better than foresight. ... What I'm worried about is all the attention you two are going to be getting in the next few weeks. Your relationship with Erica is going to get dissected in the press and in the courthouse."

I signed. "I know. I'm screwed, aren't I?"

"I warned you this was going to happen."

"I know."

The phone next to my bed rang. It was Robert Weaver."

"I've checked at the Sheriff's office and your wife's been charged with murder. No bail has been set but we can get a bail hearing later this afternoon, if you'd like."

"Yes, of course."

"The bail won't be cheap," Webster said.

"Do you know a bondsman?"

"Yes, but unless you've got collateral it's going to have to be cash."

"Oh, well it doesn't matter. Whatever it is, I'll pay it."

"We could be talking six figures."

"Really?"

"Yeah, this is a murder case, and the DA has a lot of evidence against your wife. I'd prepare for the worst."

"Listen, Erica has a lot of money. She'll post whatever bond is set, okay? I've got her stockbroker here with me right now. Just get her out of jail."

"All right. I'll need some information," Webster said.

After filling-in Mr. Webster on Erica's past and

finalizing financial matters with his law firm I hung up. Joe, who had become bored and picked up a magazine, looked up.

"So, what's the word," he said.

"We'll know later today how much the bond is. I'll call you when I know how much I'm going to be needing."

Joe and I talked awhile longer and then he left. When he was gone, I began praying that Erica would soon be out of jail. As I gazed out the window, I noticed a norther had come through. The wind was whipping up paper and debris along Haskell Avenue and it was starting to sleet. It occurred to me that Detective Perkins had not mentioned anything about me being Erica's trustee. I wondered if they had found the records that had been stolen from Erica's condo. Maybe they hadn't had time to review them or maybe that's why Erica went to see her aunt. She wanted those records. I wondered if she could have killed Martha. It didn't seem possible, yet Erica was angrier than I'd ever seen her before. No, I told myself, she couldn't have done it. No, no way. As I was thinking the phone rang. It was Webster.

"The judge granted your wife bail."

"Oh. Thank God. How much?"

"The judge set it at one million dollars," Webster said.

"What? That's ridiculous!"

"I know, I'm sorry."

"But why so high? I can't understand it. She's got a clean record; she's going to SMU. It just doesn't make any sense."

"I told the judge she wasn't a flight risk, but the judge was concerned about her age and the fact she had no relatives in Dallas."

"What about me?"

"I didn't think it was wise to dwell too much on the relationship between you and Erica. It could have easily backfired on us."

"Hmm. I guess you're right."

"So anyway, I guess Erica will just have to stay in jail pending her trial."

"No, I'll post the bail. Get her out of there immediately and bring her here. Have your bondsman call me, I'll arrange whatever collateral he needs on the bonds, okay?"

"Erica has a million dollars?" Webster asked.

"Yes, she does."

10
Tearful Reunion

Erica rushed into my hospital room, ran over, and put her arms around me. We kissed passionately. Robert Webster stood in the doorway half smiling.

"I missed you terribly!" Erica said with tears running down her eyes. "It was horrible in that cell. I've never been so scared in all my life. It was cold and everybody in there was so creepy. I get the shivers just thinking about it."

"I know, honey. Are you all right? I was so worried about you."

"I'm fine now, what about you? How did you manage to get mugged?"

"I'll tell you all about it in a minute," I said as I gently pushed Erica away so I could see Robert. "Did you have any problems?"

"No, since you put up the bond it was a piece of cake," Webster said.

"Good. Thanks for bringing Erica here. I really appreciate it."

"No problem."

"I guess I need to take her to your office in a few days so you can start working on her case."

"Definitely, call my office next week and make an appointment. We'll need to discuss strategy and possible defenses."

Erica began kissing me in earnest again. I pulled away

a minute and said. "Right, we'll call you."

Webster smiled, raised his hand, and said, "Okay, I'll leave you two alone. Take care."

"Goodbye Mr. Webster," Erica said. "Thank you."

Webster left and shut the door as he went out. We kissed some more and then Erica snuggled up next to me in my bed. I was so relieved to have her next to me I nearly started to cry.

"God I'm glad I got you back," I said.

"You missed me, huh?"

"Oh man, you just don't know how worried I was."

"I guess it wasn't such a smart idea going to see Aunt Martha," Erica said.

"I guess not. What happened anyway?"

"You don't remember?"

"No, the last thing I remember clearly was going into Peter's office and curling up with a bottle of Jack Daniel. The doctor says it's not unusual to have a little memory loss after a blow to the head. Post-traumatic amnesia I think he called it. He said it could last a week, a month, a year or it could be permanent."

"Permanent?" Erica asked.

"Possibly," I said.

"Hmm. That's interesting."

"So, what happened," I pressed.

"Well, after you left, she called me. I guess the police told her we were home. I was livid and I really let her have it.

"What gave you the right to break into our apartment," I asked.

"Well, I was worried about you, honey," Aunt Martha said. "I'd tried to call you for several days and there was no answer. I just got so worried."

"I never checked in with you before. What made you think I would know?"

"Well, since your Daddy died, I just thought for sure you'd tell me if you were going to be out of town. I mean somebody's got to keep tabs on you. What if you had been kidnaped?"

"That's a bunch of crap and you know it! I'm an adult. You were there, you heard the judge. I don't have to answer to you, and you don't have a right to invade my privacy."

"Well, I can see now why you didn't want me in your apartment. I knew you needed someone to look out for you," Aunt Martha said.

"What are you talking about?" I asked.

"You know what I'm talking about. That sleazy lawyer has moved in with you, hasn't he?"

"He's not sleazy. He's a wonderful man and it's none of your business."

"Hah! It damn sure is my business now. I'm your aunt and I'm not going to let him take advantage of you. I'm going to talk to Arnold just as soon as I can find him. We'll put a stop to this pronto."

I began to cry. "You have no right to meddle in my affairs, besides Richard and I got married."

"Oh my God. When did this happen?"

"That same day you broke into our apartment."

"Well, don't you worry. It won't stand up. We'll get an annulment."

"I don't want an annulment. I love Rich."

"You think you love him. He's just taking advantage of your youth and immaturity. Can't you see that?"

"No, that's not it at all. ... Listen, maybe I should come over and we can talk about this face to face. I don't think you understand the situation. I really need to explain it to you," I said.

"I understand it perfectly," Martha said.

"Aunt Martha, come on. Where are you staying? I'll be right over."

"It's no use child, you're not going to change my mind. I've left messages everywhere for Arnold. I'm sure I'll hear from him soon. He'll know what to do."

"You can't talk to Arnold. Tell me where you are? I want to come over."

Erica rubbed her forehead, "I was so frustrated. She just wouldn't tell me where she was. Finally, after pleading with her, she told me she was at the Starlight Motel near Love Field. I told her I was coming right over and hung up the phone. I knew what would happen if she talked to Arnold and he saw your records. I found my car keys and went out to the car to drive over to the motel. Unfortunately, the battery was dead."

"Yeah, mine gave me trouble too," I said.

"I had to get over there before she called Arnold, so I called a cab. When I arrived at the motel, I realized I didn't know what room she was in so I went to the motel office and asked the manager. She wasn't too cooperative, but I finally convinced her I was a relative, so she gave me the room number. When I got to the room, I noticed the door was ajar. I knocked but there was no answer, so I pushed the door open and went inside. Martha was lying on the floor. There was a pillow next to her and a broken lamp lying on its side across the room.

"Not realizing that Aunt Martha was dead I went over to her and shook her. Her body was cold and stiff. I was so upset I nearly screamed, but I knew I couldn't. I felt for a pulse but there was nothing. She was pale and her eyes were wide open. I started to cry. Then I remembered the records. I searched the room looking for them, but they weren't there either. It occurred to me that she might have put them in her car, so I dug through her purse and found the keys. Then I went outside and searched the car, but they weren't there either. I was so upset I just collapsed on the asphalt next to it. Then I heard a noise. Several teenage boys were coming out of a room where they had been having a party. I didn't want them to see me, so I ran down the street. It was dark and cold, and I've never been so scared in my life.

"After a while, I just started walking. I didn't want to go back to the motel office to call a cab for fear the police might have been called. I figured I'd find a payphone somewhere and call you. Several cars drove by very slowly sending chills down my spine. I've never felt so alone. Finally, I came to a Seven-Eleven. It was then I realized I had left my purse in Aunt Martha's room. I tried to borrow a dime from the guy working in the store, but he didn't speak English. About that time, two girls drove up and went inside. When they came out, I asked them if I could borrow a dime. I told them someone stole my purse and I needed to make a phone call. They were very nice and gave me one. Then I called the condo, but you didn't answer. All I got was an answering machine. I looked around for the girls to borrow another dime, but they were gone. Then the lights went out inside the store. I couldn't believe he was closing up. What was I going to do?"

"Finally, I just sat down next to the telephone and bawled. The clerk must have heard me and called the police. Before I knew it, two squad cars were pulling into the parking lot. I got up and tried to act like nothing was wrong, but they made me sit in the back seat of one of the cars while they talked on the radio. After several minutes, one of the officers said they had been instructed to bring me downtown. I protested but they said I had no choice."

"Oh, honey, I'm so sorry," I said as I took her hands and squeezed them gently.

She took a deep breath. Tears were running down her cheeks. I leaned over and pulled out a tissue and handed it to her. She wiped her eyes and then continued.

"When we got to the station, they put me in an empty room. There were just a table and two chairs. That was it. I sat there forever it seemed. Finally, Detective Perkins came in and started asking me questions. He told me I had left my purse in Aunt Martha's room. I didn't know what to say. Should I tell the truth, should I come up with some kind of story to try to explain what happened? I just didn't know what to do, so I just demanded they let me see you."

"I bet they didn't like that much," I said.

"No joke. They became rude and abusive. They just assumed I was guilty, which really made me mad. They insisted I confess. They said it would go easier for me if I just cooperated with them. I kept telling them I wasn't talking, but they were relentless. Finally, I told them I wanted a lawyer and I kept repeating that after each question. ... That seemed to get the message across that I wasn't going to confess.

"I was so relieved when they finally gave me a dime to call you, then you weren't home. They thought that was so funny and started laughing. That's when I slapped Perkins across the face."

"Oh shit," I said, half smiling.

"Perkins grabbed my arm angrily then dragged me over to another officer to be booked. It was horrible after that. Two ugly female cops came and took me to a room where they fingerprinted me, took my picture, stripped me, and sprayed me with some smelly shit. Then they gave me a ghastly-looking orange jumpsuit and made me put it on. Before long I found myself alone in a cell. It was freezing inside, and I could feel the eyes of the other girls watching me. I couldn't sleep, it was just too scary. It's a good thing you bailed me out, I couldn't have survived in there much longer."

"I wonder why they decided to charge you with the murder. They really didn't have that much evidence," I said.

"I don't know. A couple hours after they put me in a cell, a jailer came by and informed me the DA had decided to drop the assault complaint and charge me with murder instead."

I shook my head at Erica's story and said, "God, Erica. I'm so sorry you had to go through all of that. ... I can't believe our luck. We had everything under control until this shit had to happen. ... damn it!"

"What are we going to do?" Erica asked.

"I don't know, honey. Since you were at the scene of the crime, you're going to be presumed guilty. The only way to save you is to find the actual killer. That's our only hope."

"Who would want to kill Aunt Martha? I mean nobody would have any reason to kill her except-"

"Except us?" I said, "Is that what you were going to say?"

"I guess, but I didn't do it, and you were unconscious when it happened."

"So, who else would have wanted Aunt Martha dead?" I asked.

"Maybe her death was just a coincidence? Maybe somebody robbed her, and when she resisted, they killed her," Erica replied.

"Maybe, but I kind of doubt that's what happened."

"Then who would have wanted to kill her?" Erica said.

"I have no idea. ... I guess we'll have to learn a lot more about your aunt to find out the answer to that question."

"I guess."

For a few moments, we sat speechless, mesmerized by the sound of sleet hitting the hospital window. Erica cuddled up next to me and took a deep breath. "Maybe we should get the hell out here," she said. "We could go back to Barbados or disappear somewhere in South America."

Erica's suggestion shocked me. I wondered if she really had killed Aunt Martha and knew the truth would eventually come out. Why would she want to run unless she were guilty? I ran my hand through her long silky black hair and then kissed her on the forehead. She reacted by snuggling up closer and giving me a squeeze. I was glad my head injury hadn't affected my memory of Erica. I couldn't imagine life without her. Even if she were guilty, I would have to protect her. I couldn't let her go to prison.

"But honey, you had to put up a million-dollar bond remember. You run; you lose it."

"I know, but it's just money," Erica said. "Even if I get off, guess who's the number two suspect?"

Erica's sudden lack of concern for her million dollars startled me. Maybe her little stay in jail had given her a more mature sense of priorities. I hesitated to see if she realized what she was saying. She looked at me. Did she really think I could kill someone? Surely not, but she was right. I would be a suspect.

"That's true. Do you think I did it?"

"No, of course not, but I'm sure the police would wonder if maybe you weren't really unconscious for those three hours before they found you. Maybe you took a cab over to Aunt Martha's to retrieve your records, killed her, and then returned and pretended to be unconscious."

"But I wouldn't even think of doing such a thing, honey," I said, a little hurt Erica would suggest such a thing.

"You wouldn't?" Erica laughed.

"No," I replied. "And there's one problem with that scenario too."

"What's that?"

"How would I have known where Aunt Martha was staying?"

"Well, that's a good point, but I'm sure the police could figure a way to tie up that little loose end."

"Well, running is out of the question. The cops will have someone watching both of us closely. They may have our condo bugged too so be careful what you say when we get home."

"They can do that?" Erica asked.

"Sure, if they have probable cause to think a crime has

or will be committed, they can get a judge to give them permission to tap our phones, bug our house, our cars, or whatever."

"That's terrible. I thought the Constitution protected us from stuff like that."

"Not completely."

Erica yawned. "I'm tired, but I don't want to go home. Do you think the nurse will mind if I sleep here with you tonight?"

"She'll probably frown on that, but I bet she'll bring you in a cot if you ask her."

"I haven't slept in thirty-six hours."

Erica closed her eyes, and I pushed the button for the nurse. When she came in, I whispered that Erica needed a cot. She smiled and went to fetch one. When the nurse had it made up, Erica reluctantly left my bed and went to sleep on the cot. As she slept, I prayed that somehow, we'd get through this mess and enjoy a long life together as husband and wife. After losing one wife, the thought of losing another one was unbearable.

11
Arnold's First Move

Two days later the doctors discharged me as the remainder of my tests came up negative. Erica and I left Baylor Hospital and went back to the Condo. The weather had improved dramatically from the previous two days and was a balmy sixty degrees. As we drove home, I breathed in the cool, clear air and for a few brief moments felt optimistic. When we got to the condo, however, we were faced again with the reality of our predicament. Not only was the condo still in shambles from Martha's search, but it was obvious the police had come and searched it as well.

"What a mess! You'd think they'd clean up a bit after they finished," Erica said.

"Well, they had a warrant. In their mind, it gave them the right not only to search but to destroy."

"Oh, no," Erica said as she picked up a glass picture frame with a photo of her and her father. "They broke Daddy's picture. Those bastards!"

"I wonder if they found anything that could hurt your case?"

"What could they possibly have found?"

"I don't know. They're probably looking for a motive. There isn't any obvious reason why you would want to kill your aunt, so I'm sure they see that as a weakness in their case."

"What kind of things would help them establish a

motive?"

"Something that would shed light on your relationship with your aunt. Letters, phone messages, photographs-you know."

Erica put down her father's picture and started walking toward the study. "I'll look and see if anything like that is gone."

"Okay."

Erica left and I started straightening the place up. When she returned, I smiled and asked, "So, is anything missing?"

"Yeah, everything's gone. They even took my diary."

"Diary?"

Erica laughed, "Don't worry, I haven't written anything in it in years."

"You scared the shit out of me. I could just imagine them having a day-by-day account of what's happened over the last year."

"No, but when Aunt Martha was trying to get Daddy to give her half of Grandfather's estate there were several confrontations between them. All their bickering bothered me, so I found if I wrote about it in my diary it relieved some of the tension."

"Oh Lord, what kind of words did you have to say about your Aunt Martha?"

"It's probably pretty bad. Obviously, I was on Daddy's side. I remember he used to call her the 'West Texas Bitch.' I didn't know what a bitch was, so I called her the 'West Texas Witch.' There's probably a picture in there of her riding on a broom over Odessa."

I started laughing and pretty soon Erica was doing likewise.

"Wait until Webster hears about this. He's going to croak."

Erica frowned. "Do you think I'm screwed?"

"No, you were just a kid when you wrote that stuff. It's not important."

The diary was a serious problem, but I didn't want Erica to be worrying about it, so I had played down its significance. She was already so distraught over what was happening to her I was concerned about her mental health. She was strong, but a person can only take so much.

"We'll find out who killed your aunt, don't worry."

"You better. Or you'll be visiting me in prison."

With that sobering thought, we began diligently cleaning up the condo. As we were working the doorbell rang. We looked at each other, wondering who in the hell would be visiting us. I shook my head, walked to the door, and opened it. It was Constable Mark Mayfield. The firm used him often to serve civil litigation papers on the people our clients were suing.

"Mark. ... What are you doing here?" I asked.

"I'm really sorry, Rich, but this paper showed up in my box today. I thought about losing it for a few weeks, but I guess that wouldn't help much. I'd eventually have to serve it on you."

"What is it?"

"It's an Original Petition for the Removal of Trustee filed by Arnold Collins against you."

"Oh shit. Let me see it."

Mark handed me the paper and then left. I looked up at Erica, shook my head, and began reading aloud, "Count One, Conversion. On or about January 27, 1979, Richard Randolph Coleman was appointed trustee of the Franklin Fox Life Insurance Trust. On February 11, 1979, Franklin Fox died in a skiing accident in Zermatt, Switzerland whereupon Mr. Coleman took over as executor of his estate and trustee of the trust. In the process of the administration of the trust, Mr. Coleman fraudulently converted the proceeds of one Metropolitan Life Insurance Company policy for one million dollars."

"What! This is total bullshit," Erica said.

"I know."

"Where did he get this garbage?" Erica said. "The insurance policy lapsed, didn't it?"

I looked at Erica feeling hurt that she had asked that question. "Yes, it did. I showed you the letter where they declined the death claim."

"Right, I'm sorry."

It baffled me as to why he thought I had taken a million dollars. I figured he must have seen some of my brokerage statements showing large oil and gold transactions. He must have assumed I had actually received the million-dollar policy proceeds and concealed it from Erica.

"Damn, he's got me," I said. "Once I answer this suit, he's going to make me produce all my records and it won't matter that the conversion claim is bogus. He'll have plenty of other legitimate complaints to focus on."

Erica put her arms around me and squeezed me tightly. She said, "Oh God, Rich. What are we going to do? Our life is falling apart."

I pulled back a little and looked her in the eyes. I had to be calm as she was so frail and vulnerable at that moment. "I don't know. I'll just have to defend myself as best I can. As long as you didn't get hurt and the jury sees that we love each other, maybe they'll be lenient."

"You want a jury trial?"

"You're damn right. I'd get slaughtered in front of a judge over something like this. A jury, on the other hand, might not see it as such a big deal since everything worked out for the best."

"Oh, God. Why did this have to happen," Erica said. "I know you're against it. But seriously, maybe it would be best if we left the country? Isn't there someplace we can go where they could never find us and we'd be safe."

Erica's second mention of flight got me thinking. Maybe she was right, the situation was only going to get worse. If we lingered, we might lose our last opportunity to escape. The odds of us getting out of this mess unscathed were pretty remote. But I was still skeptical.

"We'd have to figure out a way to lose the cops," I said. "Then maybe we could go to the Cayman Islands or Argentina, I suppose."

"Okay. Let's go," Erica said.

"It wouldn't be easy. We could easily get caught and if we did, you'd not only lose your bond, but I'd be in jail for helping you escape."

The idea of going to jail was frightening. I couldn't believe that things had deteriorated to such an extent that incarceration was a definite possibility. If Erica and I tried to escape and failed our lives would be ruined. At least if we stayed and fought, there was a distinct possibility that we might somehow prevail.

Erica took my hands and held them tightly. "We'll plan it very carefully, so we won't get caught," Erica said sounding almost like she was excited by the prospect of fleeing the country.

"I don't know. I think we better just fight. Worst case I get removed as trustee, someone else manages your money for you until you get to age thirty then it's all yours."

"If I'm not in prison," Erica reminded me.

"We've got to assume we'll be able to get you off. Our judicial system isn't perfect, but it is designed to protect the innocent more than it is to convict the guilty."

"Yeah, that's easy for you to say. You're not the one under indictment," Erica said.

"I know, I'm sorry, Honey. I wish there were an easy way out, but there isn't."

"So, who would manage my money if you didn't?"

"I don't remember, and my copy of the trust was with

the papers that were stolen."

"So what's Count Two?" Erica asked.

"Count Two - Breach of Fiduciary Duty. - While acting as trustee for Miss Fox, Mr. Coleman intentionally invested in highly speculative stocks and commodities putting the trust corpus at great risk and peril. Count Three - From the very day Mr. Coleman took over as trustee he attempted to seduce the beneficiary of the trust, Erica Fox, into a sexual relationship to gain the use and benefit of her trust fund and concealing the fact that he had stolen money from it."

"That's total bullshit," Erica said. "I was always in control. You did what I asked you to do. Hell, you made me a million dollars. What could be wrong with that. ...You can't let him get away with this."

"It doesn't matter. He's got me nailed. What I did was wrong whether you consented to it or not, no matter how much money I made for you. I told you that at the time, remember? There are rules that have to be followed, and I ignored them."

"I know, but-"

"I guess I'm going to have to hire another attorney," I said.

"Can't Mr. Webster handle both cases?" Erica asked.

"No, that wouldn't be a good idea. Besides, I don't want him to be distracted from your defense. I'll find someone else to defend me."

"I'm sorry," Erica said. "I didn't mean to get you in this mess. If I'm the beneficiary of the trust and I'm happy with you, that should be enough."

"Unfortunately, it doesn't work that way."

"What are we going to do?" Erica said, tears running down her eyes. "I couldn't bear to live without you."

I wiped away a tear that was running down her cheek. "I don't know yet, sweetheart, but we'll think of something. Let's turn on the news and see if there's anything on about your case."

"Okay," Erica said and then walked into the living room and sat on the sofa.

Erica was depressed and I didn't like seeing her so down. I sat next to her and put my arm around her. She was stiff and unresponsive, so I let her go, got up, and turned on the TV. It was quarter to six and a documentary on religious cults was almost over.

"The most recent U.S. religious cult to rock the nation was of course The People's Temple, a California-based religious cult operating in Jonestown, Guyana. The world was shocked less than two years ago when Congressman Leo Ryan and four other Americans were shot as they tried to board their plane home. But that was just the beginning as 911 men, women and children died soon after, including the cult leader, Jim Jones, in a shocking orgy of suicide and murder. Jones, a preacher who believed he was God, had moved his cult from California to the jungles of Guyana offering them new hope. Yet there were also stories drifting back to California of torture and brainwashing. It all ended on November 18, 1978, when large tubs of cyanide-laced Kool-Aid were prepared and the cult members drank from them, dying minutes later.

"So ends the bizarre story of religious cults in America. Experts do not agree on what causes people to drop out of society and join these fanatical groups, but they do agree on one thing-we haven't seen the last of them. Good day."

"Can you believe that 911 people committing suicide?" I asked.

"Yeah, I can believe it," Erica said. "I know exactly how they feel. I wonder what it's like to take cyanide?"

A cold chill shot through me. I looked over at Erica, shocked by the implications of her question. She ignored my worried glance and just kept staring at the TV set. I noticed her face was pale and her body limp. I was afraid she had given up before the battle had even begun. How was she going to survive this ordeal if she was already acting defeated?

"Erica. Come on. Don't even think about something grotesque like that."

Erica glanced over at me, raised her eyebrows, and then looked back at the TV. I couldn't imagine anyone taking their own life. Erica's sudden lackluster attitude bothered me. Was she contemplating killing herself? Suddenly I felt cold, so cold I began to shake.

"What's wrong?" Erica asked.

"There's a little chill in here," I said trying to hold back the tears that were welling in my eyes.

"I'll get you a blanket," Erica said as her maternal instincts kicked in. She got up and went into the bedroom. While she was gone the news came on.

"The Mt. St. Helen eruption has claimed the lives of at least twenty people. The massive blast blew away more than a thousand feet of the mountain top sending smoke and debris over 150 square miles. The blast could be heard 135 miles away and was 500 times as powerful as the atomic bomb dropped on Hiroshima in 1945. Rescue efforts are underway to bring out hundreds of local residents who were caught off guard by the eruption. Witnesses say that all trees and vegetation within fifteen miles of the summit have been destroyed."

Erica walked back into the room, handed me a blanket, and sat down. Our attention was drawn back to the television where Arnold's lawsuit against me was the subject of the next report. At the conclusion of the story, the reporter indicated that Channel 4 was trying to obtain a statement from me.

"Rich, you've got to talk to them. Tell them it's all a lie."

As I was reeling from the vicious news report the doorbell rang. I got up and went to the door and saw several news vans unpacking. As I watched them, I wondered if I should respond or would it be best not to try the lawsuit in the media. I knew it would be dangerous to talk to the press because they might ask questions that I couldn't answer, or I could say the wrong thing and hurt my case. I didn't know what to do so I decided to play it by ear.

"Are you Richard Coleman?" a reporter asked.

"Yes, what can I do for you?"

"Mr. Coleman," several reporters screamed.

"One at a time, please," I said and then nodded at one of the reporters to continue.

"Are you aware of the suit brought against you today by Arnold Collins?"

"Yes."

"Do you have any comments," the reporter asked.

"Yes, the allegations are totally false and so ridiculous that Erica and I had a good laugh."

"What about the life insurance policy? Did it really lapse?"

I smiled. "Yes, you can check with Metropolitan Life. They didn't pay me a million dollars, I guarantee you."

"What about the alleged seduction of Ms. Fox?"

"There's been no seduction. While we were working together to settle her father's affairs, we fell in love. We were married several days ago in Barbados."

"Is Erica inside there with you?" another reporter asked.

"Yes."

"Will she come out and talk to us?"

"No, her attorney has advised her not to talk to the press, so she won't be able to come out," I said.

"Sir, if all these allegations are false, why do think Mr. Collins would bring this suit against you?"

"Well, I haven't had a lot of time to analyze it, but one possibility comes to mind. Erica's charged with killing his mother. He knows the trust that I administer is funding her defense. He figures if he can get me ousted or get the trust tangled up in a legal battle it will subvert Erica's defense effort and make a conviction more likely."

"What about the charge of speculating with Erica's money?" a reporter asked.

"I think I've said enough. Before I say anything further, I need to consult with a lawyer. Thank you," I said and went back inside wondering how I'd done. Erica was smiling which made me feel a lot better.

"How did I do?"

"Very good. I'm proud of you. I bet Arnold wishes he had checked out his facts a little better. They must think he's an idiot. Do you really think he's trying to torpedo my defense?"

"Yeah, that's the point of this whole thing, I would imagine."

"That bastard, I hope he rots in hell!"

"Don't be too hard on him. Someone just murdered his mother. He has a right to be angry. I just wish I could figure out to whom he should be directing his anger. Who would profit from Aunt Martha's death besides you and me?" As we were talking the phone rang. It was Suzie.

"Hey, I just saw your little impromptu news conference."

"Did you? Can you believe the allegations Collins put in that petition?"

"Actually, it was pretty creative speculation. I still don't understand where you got a million dollars for Erica's bond unless that policy did pay off."

"No, it didn't pay off. You saw the claim rejection letter."

"I know, but I thought maybe you paid off a secretary over at the insurance company to write it for you."

Susie's comment stung but she had never been one to hold back what she was thinking. I was used to her brutal honesty and actually appreciated it. "You know I wouldn't do something like that. I'm surprised that even crossed your mind."

"Well, it never crossed my mind that you would marry Erica. Where is your head anyway, up your ass?" Suzie said.

"I know it looks bad, but we just fell in love. You can't deny the heart."

"In this case, you should have," Suzie said. "What were you thinking?"

"Okay, I made a mistake, but nobody got hurt. Erica and I are married and quite happy together."

"So how did you put up the million-dollar bond?"

"Prudent investing," I said.

"Really? Well, you'll have to explain to me what that means."

"I will," I said. "But it's too complicated to go into over the phone now."

"So what happened between you and Peter? I was never so shocked in all my life as I was when he locked up your office and forbid anyone to go inside. You didn't call me, write me or anything. What's the deal, Rich, huh?"

"I'm sorry, Suzie. Everything has been collapsing around us. I haven't had a chance to call you, although you were on my list of people to contact soon. Are you okay?"

"No, I lost my job."

"Oh God, I'm so sorry. I can't believe Peter let you go. I guess he was afraid you'd remain loyal to me even after I left. ... Listen, if you're game I could use a good secretary right now. I've got this lawsuit, Erica's defense, and I need to call my clients and see if they're going to stay with the firm or come with me."

"You're starting your own law practice?" Suzie said.

"I guess, I still have to make a living, right?"

"I suppose. You want me to be your secretary, huh?"

"Yes, I really do."

"Gee, I'll have to give up my unemployment benefits."

I laughed. "You'd be bored sitting at home watching soap operas and sipping cheap wine, don't you think?"

"I don't know. I'm starting to enjoy being a drunken couch potato."

"I don't want to put you out," I said.

"Oh, all right. Since you're desperate, I'll take the job."

"Good, I'll see you tomorrow at one at Erica's condo. Your first job will be to find me a temporary office. You wouldn't happen to know where all my furniture ended up, do you?"

"Yeah, it's in storage up in Addison somewhere. I could call Peter and see if he'll let you retrieve it."

"He better or I'll sue his ass for conversion."

"All right, I gotta go. Say hello to your teenage bride for me."

"Come on, Suzie. Give me a break, would you?"

"Okay, that was my last jab for the day, see you tomorrow."

12
Incriminating Evidence

The next day we had a meeting with Robert Webster. His office was in a plush suite on the thirty-seventh floor of One Main Place in downtown Dallas. We checked in with the receptionist and then took a seat. I thumbed through several magazines nervously. There was a large fish tank with beautiful saltwater fish swimming around lazily. It was quite mesmerizing. Finally, Robert showed up and took us back to his office. We told him the whole story.

"The police found my diary," Erica said and took a deep breath. "I'm afraid it's full of entries where I said a lot of unflattering things about my aunt. I know that must sound terrible, but you've got to understand that my father and she had been feuding for years. She had always been a joke around the house."

"So, you really called her the 'West Texas Witch,' huh?" Webster said.

"Yes, I'm afraid I did."

Webster shook his head. "Oh Jesus, this isn't good."

"I thought you'd think it was kind of funny," I said.

"Yeah, ordinarily, but the DA will blow it way out of proportion. The diary itself shows a long history of animosity between Erica and her Aunt. It could be used as evidence to show a motive for the murder. Did they find anything else in your condo that could hurt us?"

"Not that I know of," Erica said.

"Well then, let me talk a little about possible defenses and mitigating circumstances that we can raise as issues in the case. Like Rich, I'm sure, has told you, Erica, the state has the burden of proof. To convict you of murder they must prove beyond a reasonable doubt that you intentionally killed your aunt. This is a tough burden because they have to prove intent. If you killed your aunt but didn't intend to do it, then it's not murder but perhaps manslaughter or negligent homicide. Do you understand, Erica?"

"Yes, sir."

"Then we have what is called mitigation defenses-if you killed your aunt, but there was a reason or excuse for it. Perhaps you were provoked and killed her in a fit of anger, or you feared for your life and felt like you had to kill her to prevent being killed yourself. Then, of course, there's temporary insanity, where you, because of some mental defect or condition, lost control of your mental capacity and killed your aunt."

"You mean I could have killed her and not been guilty of anything?"

"Yes, did you hear of the case up in Oklahoma where a mentally abused wife killed her husband with an ax hitting him over and over again, yet was found innocent by reason of temporary insanity?"

"Really?" Erica said. "That's incredible. How could that be?"

"Well, she had taken so much abuse from her husband, I guess she just broke. The jury believed she didn't know what she was doing and was totally out of control when she started hitting him with the ax."

"I suppose she had to spend the rest of her life in a mental hospital, right?"

"No, I think she was released after just a few months. She was perfectly sane before the incident and probably within hours after it."

Erica listened intently as Webster went on and on, explaining all the various defenses and different degrees of murder. It was a long tedious session, and I was glad when it began to draw to a close, particularly since I was supposed to meet with Suzie at one.

Webster continued, "So you'll have to report in with the court once a month until your trial. In the next few weeks, you'll have to enter a plea and then the Court will set a trial date."

'When do you think that will be?" Erica asked.

"Probably in 90 to 180 days," Webster replied.

"We don't have much time then," I said.

"No," Webster said and turned to Erica. "Okay, that's about it for now. We've covered a lot of territory today. It's been a productive session. What I think has become clear, at least to me, is that if the DA can piece together everything you've told me, then there is a distinct danger of conviction. The case would be based primarily on circumstantial evidence, but sometimes that's enough."

"What's circumstantial evidence?" Erica asked.

"Well, you've admitted you were at the scene of the crime near the time of death, you had been in an argument with the decedent, and you had the physical ability to kill your aunt. That doesn't mean you did it, but a jury could make that inference," Webster said.

"Oh," Erica replied giving me an anxious glance.

"The fact that there was a history of animosity between you and your aunt, and she had threatened to expose Rich and subject him to civil and possible criminal prosecution, doesn't help. The DA will say you killed your aunt to protect Rich."

Erica lowered her head. "I see."

"On the other hand, no one saw you kill your aunt, so it's quite possible someone else did it," Webster said. "If you testified, you might convince the jury that you're innocent."

"And the DA doesn't know about the argument you had with your aunt or that she had threatened to tell Arnold about our relationship," I said.

"Well, we don't know that," Webster said. "Mrs. Collins might have called and told Arnold about it after she and Erica hung up but before she was murdered. Judging from the civil suit he filed I think that's probably what happened."

"I don't know," I said. "The suit looked pretty much like a shot in the dark. There was almost nothing in the pleadings that resembled reality. I don't think he knows much, and I'm sure he doesn't have my records."

"If that's the case, then they may have a motive problem. Since Erica doesn't have to testify as the defendant, and you don't have to testify against your wife, they'll be hard-pressed to come up with a good reason why Erica would have killed her aunt except for a child's diary."

"If they can't prove I had a motive to kill Aunt Martha do I get off?" Erica asked.

"Not necessarily, but not too many juries will convict on circumstantial evidence without a good motive. Since no one saw the murder take place, it's not going to be easy for them to sustain their burden of proof. It's possible your aunt's death was a random act of violence by a person who didn't even know her."

"So, does that mean I don't have to worry?"

Webster laughed. "No, not at all. The DA is still ahead in the race but it's not over. It's going to be up to us to find some concrete evidence to disprove the logical conclusion from that evidence that you were the killer. Specifically, we've got to find other persons who had the opportunity and motive to kill your aunt. I've assigned a private investigator to look into your aunt's life and her relationship with her son, Arnold. Perhaps we'll find something there or at least a lead. In the meantime, be thinking about other people who might have reason to want to see your aunt dead."

"Okay, we will," I said. "Thanks, Robert."

"You're welcome. Good luck on your civil case."

"Thanks."

We both felt better after seeing Robert. He seemed very confident and upbeat. On our way home Erica and I stopped for lunch at the Highland Park Cafeteria. It was Peter's favorite hangout, and I was hoping to see him. Since I had been discharged from the hospital, I had been trying to reach him, but he hadn't returned my calls. It was very irritating since I was still a stockholder in the professional corporation and had a right to know what was going on. Besides, Peter and I had become quite close over the past few years, and it was upsetting to me that he wouldn't at least talk to me.

We ate a leisurely lunch, hoping we'd spot Peter, but he didn't show up. Finally, we gave up and went on back to the condo. It was ten minutes to one when we walked up to the front door and found Suzie there waiting for us. We all went inside, and Suzie and I started working on the kitchen table. Erica left us alone and went into the bedroom to do her homework. She had wanted to drop out of school when our lives began to unravel, but I wouldn't let her do that. I didn't want her to have too much time to think about all our problems.

"So, you got any leads on a temporary office?"

"There's a legal office suite over in Preston Center. I checked with them and they've got a two-room suite. It'll cost six hundred dollars per month, and they'll provide a copier, library, conference room, receptionist . . . the whole nine yards."

"Good, when can we move in?"

"Anytime, they said."

"Have you been able to talk to anybody about getting my office furniture and records back?"

"I talked to Margie, Peter's secretary, this morning and

she said you were welcome to pick up your desk and furniture, but that the firm was keeping all the records."

"That's okay. I'll just have the clients who stay with me go pick them up. It's unethical for the firm to refuse to give a client his records. Did Peter say why he hasn't returned my calls?"

"No, but Margie suggested that the firm didn't want to have anything to do with you because of all your legal problems. She said you should have your attorney call them to work out the details of your withdrawal from the firm."

"That's just sweet. Nobody wants to touch me."

"I'm here, aren't I or am I dreaming?" Suzie said.

"Yes, you are, Suzie. You and Joe are the only ones who have stood by me."

"Good, then it's probably a good time to talk about my salary."

I laughed. "How about I pay you what you were getting on unemployment."

"Right, and I'll come to work twice a month to pick up my check," Suzie replied.

I laughed again and shook my head. "You're the only person I know who could make a person laugh while they're passing a kidney stone. ... It's so good to have you back."

"Yeah, well I kind of missed you a tad too."

"Anyway, maybe I should just call a news conference and tell the press how Franklin was Peter's client and how he encouraged me to accept an appointment as trustee to keep his client happy. Not to mention that he insisted my trustee's fee be paid to the firm."

"Didn't he notice your fees were pretty high?" Suzie said.

"He may have, but who's going to complain about excess revenue?"

"Then if he gives you any shit, you can drag the firm right into the middle of this mess," Suzie said.

"Better yet, I bet I can talk him into giving me the Trustee's fees back so the firm can have totally clean hands."

"How much would that be?"

"Nearly $50,000," I said.

"Oh! I smell a bonus."

"Well, if Erica gets off, I'll damn sure give you a bonus."

"You mean when not if, right?" Suzie said.

"Right, that's the spirit."

13
Collins v. Coleman

After putting up Erica's bond, paying Webster, and now having to hire an attorney to defend me, I was getting concerned about money. Funding two major trials and defending myself against an expected assault by the State Bar would cost a fortune. Although I had good credit, I doubted many lending institutions would seriously consider giving me a loan under the present circumstances. Recovering the $50,000 in Trustee's fees from Peter and obtaining a cash settlement for my stock in the corporation became my most pressing projects. The only problem I had was time. If I hired another lawyer to negotiate a settlement with the firm, that would cost more money and could take weeks or months. I couldn't afford that kind of delay.

That night I was so stressed out I had trouble sleeping. The next morning, I was so exhausted I didn't feel like getting up, but I knew I needed to camp out in the office garage and corner Peter. If I could just talk to him maybe I could convince him to skip the bullshit and just get on with a quick settlement of our affairs. It was seven forty-five when I parked my car and walked into the parking garage. Peter had an assigned parking space, so I hid in the shadows and waited. At seven fifty-five he drove up. He got out of his car and when he saw me, he started to walk away.

"After all we've been through, you don't have the

decency to talk to me for five minutes?"

He stopped, turned around, and said, "Decency? You talk about decency when you're sleeping with Erica."

"Erica got exactly what she wanted."

"She was off-limits, and you knew that. You didn't care about the law firm; all you cared about was your dick."

"It wasn't like that. Sure, there was lust, but it went far deeper than that. Erica and I are happy together. You may have heard, we got married."

"I heard all right," Peter said. "Pretty clever to marry the one witness that could put you behind bars."

"She wouldn't testify against me anyway, she loves me."

"Sure, she does," Peter said.

"Forget about Erica. Why did you move me out of the firm like I was a leper? You couldn't wait for me to get back and let me move out with a little dignity?"

"Your reckless conduct has jeopardized this firm. I had to show the other associates that we wouldn't tolerate this type of breach of trust."

"Then you won't mind giving me back the $50,000 in fees the firm took in as compensation for my acting as trustee," I said.

Peter's face turned red with anger.

I said, "And I want $125,000 for my stock in the corporation or when I visit my civil litigation attorney this afternoon, I'm going to suggest he file a cross-action against the firm for contribution since it actually received the trustee's fees. Won't the press love that?"

"You son of a bitch! You can't blackmail me," Peter said.

"Blackmail, who said anything about blackmail? We're just negotiating the firm's redemption of my stock. If you don't want to take my offer, we'll go to court. You always told me when you sue someone go for the jugular, right?"

"All right, have your attorney call me this afternoon, and we'll work out the details of the settlement. Then do me a favor and stay the hell out of my life!"

"No problem," I said. "I'm glad our friendship meant so much to you."

Peter shook his head and then left the parking garage. I had accomplished my goal but for some reason didn't feel triumphant. Peter had been a good friend, and I couldn't believe how he had turned on me so quickly. I know I did some stupid things, but he never even tried to give me the benefit of the doubt. All he could think about was the precious image of the firm and how to distance me from it as soon as there was a hint of trouble.

After my confrontation with Peter, I went home and took a nap. I slept better with that task behind me, but I still felt horrible when I woke up at noon. At two I went to the North Dallas Bank Building to the offices of Harper & Polk to discuss the Collins suit with Michael Harper. I had been co-counsel with Michael a few times and knew he was a first-class litigator. He was cocky and had a way of irritating opposing counsel that I loved. Usually, when we worked together, he'd get the other side pissed off, and then I'd go in and suggest they might want to settle, or Michael would put them through hell. By then they could appreciate what they were in for, so they often became much more amenable to a settlement.

"So, did you bring me the paper?" Michael asked.

"Yes," I said and then pulled out the citation from my inside coat pocket and handed it to him.

"Okay, let me see," he said as he scanned the pleading. "What about this life insurance policy? Do you have proof it lapsed?"

"Yes, and I brought you a copy of the declination letter."

"Good, okay. What about speculating with the trust assets?"

"Guilty."

I explained to Michael how well I'd done. He was impressed.

"So does the fact I made money help any?" I said.

"Well, yeah," he said. "You're guilty of making improper investments, failing to diversify, and a half dozen other prudent investing rules, but because you were successful there aren't any damages."

"Good."

"Okay, what about Erica," Michael asked. "What were you doing fooling around with her?"

I explained how we met and fell in love.

"The fact that you got married helps."

"What effect do you think the murder trial will have on this case?"

"I have no idea. This is the most bizarre situation I've ever seen. I liked your little impromptu news conference, though. That was quick thinking. What you said made a lot of sense. What we might want to do is file a plea in abatement. We'll ask the Court to suspend this case until the murder trial is over so that Erica's case won't be prejudiced."

"That's a good idea, I bet the judge would go for that," I said.

"I think so and then you can concentrate on getting Erica off the hook without having to worry about losing control of the trust."

"That sounds like a great strategy to me. Go ahead and move on it."

"Okay, I'll file it tomorrow," Michael said. "The judge will probably hear it in a week or ten days."

"Excellent," I said.

"So, what are you going to do now that you've left the firm?"

"Obviously, no law firm in Dallas would touch me right now so I'm going out on my own."

"Hell, I bet Merrill Lynch would hire you," Michael said.

I laughed. "I doubt it. I broke a few of their rules too. Anyway, I hadn't planned a change in occupations."

"Listen, if I gave you $50,000 would you invest it for me?"

"Right, that's exactly what Erica asked me to do, and look where that got me."

Michael nodded. "True. Just a thought."

"Well, I better go and let you get that answer filed," I said as I stood up. "Thanks for your help."

Although I had been in Michael's office a dozen times and spent countless hours with him and his staff, today I had felt like a stranger. For the first time, I understood how it felt to be on the other side of the desk. The humiliation, the nagging fear, the uncertainty-all had been difficult to bear. If somehow, I survived this ordeal, I certainly would have more empathy for my clients.

Feeling extremely fatigued, I opened the front door of my Mercedes and dropped into the driver's seat. At some point during the afternoon, I'd developed a headache and my head was throbbing. I began feeling sorry for myself. Why is this happening? How did I let myself fall into Erica's little trap? I closed my eyes and took a deep breath while I massaged the back of my neck. It didn't help.

On the drive home, my melancholy began to fade in anticipation of being with Erica. No matter what she had put me through or what pain there was yet to endure, it was all worth it as long she was mine. Somehow, we'd get all this behind us. We had to. There was no other alternative. At least, that's what I had thought.

When I got home, Erica was sitting on the sofa obviously upset. My good spirits took a nosedive. Her eyes were red and swollen and she had a box of tissues in her lap. When she saw me stood up and embraced me. After a second I pushed her back a little so I could see her face.

"What happened?" I asked.

She walked a few steps away. "Robert called me to let me know he had been over to the DA's office to look at the evidence they've gathered so far."

"Uh-huh."

"Well, he said they had lab reports that showed cotton fibers and down under my fingernails and on my nylons. The police think I held a pillow over Martha's face and suffocated her. Oh, Rich! I'm going to be convicted. What am I going to do?"

"What does Robert think?" I asked.

"He said he wasn't concerned about the reports," she said. "He tried to downplay their significance, but I could tell he was upset."

"Damn! ... How in the hell did you get those fibers under your fingernails?"

"I know exactly how it happened. When I got to Aunt Martha's apartment, I didn't know that she was dead, so when I saw her lying there on the floor I went over to her. There was a pillow next to her with a big rip in it. The down and fibers inside the pillow were everywhere. I picked it up and tossed it out of the way and then I shook her hoping she would wake up. It's no wonder they found the fibers under my fingernails."

"That makes perfect sense to me. I'm sure the jury will believe you."

"No, they won't," she moaned. "They're still going to think I did it."

I went to her and wrapped my arms around her. "No, they won't, honey. I'm sure they will believe you."

She pulled away. "But what if they don't. ... Oh, God. ... I'm screwed!"

"No, you're not, don't even talk like that. It's a perfectly good explanation."

She looked up at me, tears running down her cheeks.

"Why did this have to happen? ... Why doesn't everyone just leave us alone? We were so happy? It's not fair!"

I took Erica back in my arms. She cried for several minutes. I wiped away her tears and began massaging her shoulders hoping to make her feel better. When she had calmed down, we went into the kitchen and I sat down at the table while she removed a roast from the oven. She set it on the counter and began cutting it up. The table had been carefully set and several candles were burning. Then I noticed my glass filled with a red liquid.

"What's this?" I said as I held up the glass.

Erica turned and took a casual look at the glass and said, "Kool-Aid."

A chill darted through me. Erica had never served Kool-Aid before. "What?"

She turned away from me. "Kool-Aid, it was on sale. You like Kool-Aid, don't you?"

I glared at her. She turned around, gave me a disturbing look, and then replied, "Don't worry, I haven't found anyone who sells cyanide yet."

Gooseflesh broke out on my arms. I stood up and threw my napkin on the table. "Jesus Christ! Erica, what is wrong with you. You've got to pull yourself out of this depression. You're not going to be convicted."

She looked at me earnestly. "But if I am convicted will you . . . will you drink with me?"

"Erica, for godsakes, cut it out!" I gasped and took the glasses of Kool-Aid and dumped them into the sink.

"Don't you understand?" she said evenly. "I'd rather die than live without you . . . don't you feel the same way?"

I looked at her not knowing how to respond. Finally, I said, "Of course, but suicide's not the answer. I'm not ready to die . . . and I don't want to lose you. Besides, we would both end up in hell if we killed ourselves. Is that what you want?"

Erica shrugged as she picked up a knife and turned it,

watching the light glisten off the steel blade. "Do you really think there is a heaven and a hell ... I don't think so. When we die, it's just over. We don't go anywhere; we just fade into oblivion."

I was appalled at what I was hearing. Erica had always professed to be a good Catholic. I rushed over to her and jerked her around so I could look her in the eyes and scold her. "You've never told me you felt that way. Your depression is poisoning your mind. God is out there, and he'll help us get through this. I know he will."

She looked up at me with an empty stare. "Won't it be a wonderful display of our love to die in each other's arms?"

"No! Not at all. People will just think we're crazy. "

She put her arms around me and nestled her head on my shoulder. "Of course, I'd much rather have a long life together but if that's not our fate then, at least, we can die together."

Tears began to well in my eyes. "Oh, Jesus, honey. You're losing it. I'm going to get you help. ... Don't worry. I'll find you a good psychiatrist. Everything will be all right. I promise you."

Erica looked up at me with an eerie smile. "It's no use, honey. There's nothing you can do ... you know I always get my way."

14
Temporary Insanity

Robert Webster had suggested a psychiatrist name Herman Beckman as an expert witness. I was glad we were going to see him as Erica was obviously in need of professional help. We arrived at the doctor's office at about 10:30. The receptionist gave us coffee and we waited. After twenty minutes we were taken into a small room with a couch, a table, and a couple of chairs where we waited until the doctor came in. He was a short, robust man and was smoking a pipe. We shook hands.

"Good morning," he said smiling at Erica.

Erica nodded warily. "Hello, doctor."

He took a seat behind an oak desk and looked down at his notes. We sat inside chairs across from him. "So, Mr. Webster referred you, I see."

"Yes," I replied.

"That means I get to go to court and razzle-dazzle the jury, right?"

"Well, maybe. I hope that won't be necessary though. What we really need is for you to help Erica get through all of this."

Dr. Beckman looked at Erica sympathetically. "Well, these criminal trials are never easy but most everybody manages to get through them somehow."

Dr. Beckman's cavalier dismissal of my concerns upset

me. Erica really did need help, but he didn't seem to appreciate how far her mental state had deteriorated.

"I hope so, I'm really worried about her," I said hoping he would press for more information. I was afraid to be too direct for fear of upsetting Erica. It was a delicate situation.

"Why don't you let me talk to Erica alone?" Dr. Beckman suggested.

"No," Erica protested. "I want Rich with me when we talk."

"That wouldn't be a good idea. I'm going to ask you questions about your relationship with Rich, so it may be difficult if he is sitting here."

"Rich and I have no secrets."

"I'm sorry, but I'm afraid I must insist. There cannot be any distractions if I'm going to help you."

"He's right, honey. I can't be in here."

I was ambivalent about staying with Erica during the session. If I was there, I could be sure the doctor understood what was going on with Erica and came up with an appropriate treatment. On the other hand, with me present, Erica might be reluctant to be totally candid with the doctor for fear of hurting my feelings or appearing weak in front of me.

"Yes, you can, I want you with me," Erica said.

"The doctor may be right, sweetheart. I'll go sit in the waiting room. I need to make some phone calls anyway."

Erica glared at me as I left her alone with Dr. Beckman. I felt like I was abandoning her but there was no choice. If the treatment were to be successful, she had to be honest with him. When I got back to the waiting room, I picked up the phone and called Suzie who was back at the new office getting settled in.

"You won't believe this," Suzie said.

"What?"

"Martha was designated alternate trustee and if she can't do it, Arnold is the trustee."

"I was afraid of that," I said. "Okay, look at the beneficiary provisions. Who gets the trust corpus if Erica is dead?"

"Guess what? It's the same, Martha and then Arnold," Suzie said.

"So if Erica goes to prison for life, and I've been removed as trustee then Arnold gets control of the money as trustee. When Erica dies, it's all his."

"But he couldn't spend it while she's alive," Suzie said.

"Well, with a million dollars at stake, how long do you think it would be before Erica would get iced by one of her cellmates?" I said.

"You think Arnold would do that?"

"I don't know. I've only met him once, but the temptation would be strong, particularly if he thinks Erica killed his mother."

"Yeah, a million dollars definitely would be tempting," Susie replied.

"I have another idea," I said. "What if Arnold knows she didn't do it. Suppose Arnold killed his mother and then made it look like Erica did it?"

"Well, it's hard to believe anyone could kill their mother, but Martha had a black belt in irritating people," Susie said. "I don't imagine Arnold's childhood was too pleasant."

"That's a safe bet."

"So how do we go about proving Arnold actually did it?" Suzie asked.

"Maybe I'll call Detective Perkins and suggest it to him. He would have the resources to check it out."

"That makes sense, but do you think he'll give a shit?" Suzie asked.

"If he's a good cop he will."

"I've never met him, but if he's like a lot of cops, he'll quit working once he's got a suspect locked up."

"I don't know him very well myself. He doesn't like me

much, I know that. He thinks I took advantage of Erica. But, for now, we'll have to give him the benefit of the doubt and assume he's after the truth as we are."

"Whatever you say, boss."

"Well, I'll see you later. I don't know how long Erica will be in there with the doctor but hopefully not more than another forty minutes. When she's done, we'll swing by and see how the place is shaping up."

"Well, if you like the aftermath of a hurricane, you'll love this place," Suzie said.

I called Detective Perkins to see if he was still working on suspects or, as Susie suspected if he had shut down the investigation since they had charged Erica. I hoped she was wrong.

"I have some information that might interest you," I said.

"What's that?" Perkins said.

"You know Arnold Collins, Mrs. Collins' son?"

"Yes."

"Well, you obviously must know about his efforts to remove me as trustee, right?"

"I watch TV just like everybody else."

"Well, I was reviewing the trust document and noticed that if I'm out of the picture then Arnold takes over as Trustee."

"I figured as much," Perkins said.

"That's not all. If Erica dies, he gets everything."

"Really?"

"Yeah, he had a strong motive to kill his mother."

"There are a lot of sons out there who would inherit money if their mothers died, but not too many would kill them to get it. I'm afraid that motive isn't strong enough."

"But aren't you even going to look into it?" I said.

"Oh, I've already looked into it and came up with a big fat zero. All of Mrs. Collin's friends say Arnold was a model son who worshiped his mother. Besides, on the night of the murder, he was in Waco at the annual Alumni Ball."

"He was?" I asked.

"Yes, he was. ... Listen, Mr. Coleman, I'm sure you'd love to have Mr. Collins locked up so your lawsuit would go away, but he's a very unlikely suspect. In fact, you're more of a suspect than he is."

"What?" I said.

"Yeah, I've surveyed the neighborhood around the bar where you were allegedly mugged. It's really strange but a lot of people passed by that area and didn't see you lying in the alley," he said.

"Well, as a detective I'm sure you know that most people are so preoccupied with what they are doing they're not very observant."

"True, but it's just strange that nobody saw you there," Perkins said.

"I don't know what to tell you. I have no memory of what happened. Anyway, if you think I went over to Martha's motel and killed her, I'd sure like to know how I found out where she was staying."

"I haven't figured that out yet, but when I do, you'll be the first to know," Perkins said.

"I'm not worried about it, Detective. I'm just glad you're still looking for the killer. You must have your doubts about Erica's guilt," I said.

"No, that's not it at all. I just want to be able to destroy any of Webster's suggestions that someone other than Erica killed Mrs. Collins. I hate to tell you this, but we've got your little lady pretty much nailed on this one."

"Don't count on it. I know Erica very well. She wouldn't have done this. The murderer is still out there somewhere. If I were you, I'd be out there looking at every possibility, because you're going to be pretty embarrassed if I find the killer while you're back at your office picking your nose."

"Listen, Mr. Coleman, I don't need any advice from the likes of you. Just stay out of my face. And be careful playing junior detective, this isn't the movies. If you break the law, I'll slam your ass in jail!"

I hung up the phone, frustrated that Detective Perkins hated me so. It was not only unsettling, but his attitude was going to make it more difficult for me to help Erica prove her innocence. I wasn't used to having enemies, and I didn't like it.

When Erica finally emerged from Dr. Beckman's office, she looked much better than when I had left her. When she said goodbye, I even overheard her laugh, which was something I hadn't heard for a while. On the way home I asked her about the session.

"So, how did it go?"

"Good. I really like Dr. Beckman."

"What did he tell you?"

"He thinks that, if things really get desperate, I might be able to win on a plea of not guilty by reason of temporary insanity."

"What?"

"He says that with the long history of hostility between my father, mother, and Aunt Martha, so much anxiety, fear, and anger had built up in me over the years that when she threatened to take you away from me, I just lost it. He says I became so frustrated with Aunt Martha's refusal to be reasonable I just lost all rational control over myself. Consequently, I was incapable of knowing right from wrong or the consequences of what I was doing."

"So, you really think you killed her?"

"No, I don't think I killed her, but everyone else does. Until you or the police find the real killer, I've got to assume the worst and be prepared to deal with it."

"What about your depression? Did you talk about that?"

"No. Not specifically. We mainly talked about our defense strategy."

"Hmm. I was hoping he'd give you a prescription or something. They've got some good drugs to help fight depression."

"Don't worry. It's not that bad. I'm feeling much better already."

"Did you tell him you were contemplating suicide?"

"No. That's none of his business."

My stomach tightened with the news Dr. Beckman wasn't going to treat Erica for her depression. His only concern was his testimony at trial. I thought of suggesting Erica go to another psychiatrist to deal strictly with her mental health, but I knew she'd never agree to it.

"So, Beckman really thinks a temporary insanity defense will work?"

"Yes, he says it's a classic case. He's very optimistic."

"I don't know, Erica. You'd be admitting you killed your aunt. It's too big a gamble. I'm afraid the jury wouldn't buy it, and then you'd be sunk."

"Dr. Beckman thinks it will work, and I think he's right."

"I can't say I agree with him."

Erica gave me a scathing look. Her cheeks became flushed. "What the hell do you want me to say?! Do you have some better idea you want to share with me? I wanted to get the hell out of the country a long time ago, but you wouldn't do it. Now I'm about to get convicted of murder and there's nothing I can do. God damn you!" she said starting to cry. "Why didn't you take me away."

I tried to put my arms around her and hold her, but she pushed me away. She turned her back to me and continued to sob. I took a deep breath, not knowing what to say.

"I'm so sorry, honey. You're right. We should have left the country. God, I'm so sorry. How stupid I've been."

Erica didn't answer immediately. She took a deep

breath and wiped the tears from her eyes with her sleeve. She turned around slowly and gave me a faint unearthly smile.

"It's all right. ... I forgive you. ... The poison won't be so bad. At least we'll be together for eternity."

15
Plea in Abatement

When Michael Harper filed my answer in the civil suit brought by Arnold Collins it created considerable media interest. So far, I had been lucky that the press hadn't found out where my new office was located, but they knew where Erica lived, and they were waiting for me when I got home. As I parked my car, I was surrounded by news reporters.

"Mr. Coleman, is it true in less than a year you parlayed $50,000 into a million dollars for your wife?"

"Where did you hear that?"

"The answer you filed today in Court," the reporter replied.

"Oh. ... Well, you can read as well as I can."

"Mr. Coleman, could you tell us how you were able to do it?"

"Well, it's a little complicated to go into right now, but it was primarily by the strategic purchases of stocks, oil, and gold," I replied.

"What about charges of insider trading?" another reporter asked.

"No, I had the same information everybody else had."

"Mr. Coleman, what does Mrs. Coleman think about the suit to have you removed as her trustee?"

I smiled. "She likes things just the way they are. Okay, that's all I have to say, thank you."

As I pushed my way through the mob of reporters, I felt

good. The press at least seemed to be focused on the success I had in investing Erica's money rather than the violation of prudent investing rules. I could only hope the Court would do the same. Erica was laughing when I finally got into the house.

"Rich, come here," Erica yelled. "They're talking about you on the radio."

I walked quickly to the radio and sat next to Erica.

"This is Ron Chapman, you're on KVIL."

"Hey Ron, this is Wanda."

"Hi, Wanda."

"You know, Ron, my parents left me a nice trust fund which I certainly thank them for, but they made Republic Bank my trustee. Last year the bank lost six percent on my money and they don't even send someone over to tuck me in at night. Tell Mr. Coleman if he loses his job to give me a call, okay?"

Ron said, "If he's listening, I'm sure he heard your offer. I suspect there are a few other rich lonely ladies out there who could use a good live-in investment advisor, am I wrong?"

"Hello, Ron Chapman, you're on KVIL."

"Hi, Ron. This is Paul."

"Hi, Paul."

"You know Ron. If Richard Coleman gets fired, he may be the only person on the planet who can appreciate how Billy Martin has felt these last few years."

Ron laughed. "Well, that's a good point."

"I always knew Justice was blind," Paul said, "but I didn't know she was dumb too."

Ron laughed. "Is Lady Justice a blonde? I wonder. Okay, I know this is fun, but we better play some music. Here we go, Kenny Rogers and Kim Carnes, 'Don't Fall in Love with a Dreamer.'"

Erica shut off the radio, turned around, and sat facing me in my lap. She must have just taken a shower because she smelled like a field of wild bluebonnets. She smiled and slowly inched her mouth to mine. When our lips touched, I closed my eyes and savored the sweet kiss. Erica broke from my embrace and started to unbutton her blouse. I pulled off my shirt. Tensions from weeks of frustration and worry quickly exploded into a fiery sexual encounter that was as painful as it was exhilarating. When it was over, we succumbed to our exhaustion and fell asleep.

When I woke up, I carefully extricated myself from Erica's grasp. Sharp pains emanating from my back and shoulders reminded me of the bestial sex in which we had just engaged. What had gotten into Erica? Her mood swings were becoming more and more pronounced. It was obvious fear and worry over our predicament had twisted her in knots and she was ready to explode. I considered calling Dr. Beckman for advice on how to deal with the situation, but I figured it was only temporary. After Erica was exonerated, all would be well. As I eased out of bed, Erica woke up.

"What time is it?" she said.

"Eight-thirty, I think."

"I'm hungry,"

"You want me to order some pizza?" I asked.

"Yeah, go ahead."

As I started to pick up the phone, I noticed one of the front window curtains was open.

"Oh, God. We didn't close the front blinds, Erica."

"What? . . . Oops."

"You don't think the press watched us make love, do you?"

"God, I hope not. I think they left after you came in."

"Well, if they didn't, the next time we go to Tom Thumb we may see ourselves naked on the front page of the National Inquirer."

"That'd be kind of cool," Erica replied.

"Erica!"

"What? she giggled.

"You'd probably pose for Playboy if they asked you, wouldn't you?"

"Of course."

Ten days later the judge granted our Plea in Abatement, and the civil case was suspended until the outcome of Erica's murder trial. I was very thankful because I didn't want to have to rely on establishing reasonable doubt or, God forbid, a temporary insanity defense. Somehow, I had to find the real killer so Erica would be exonerated. For several days I racked my brain trying to think of anyone who might have a reason to kill Aunt Martha. Then a thought hit me. Peter had acted very strangely after our confrontation on the beach. Although his behavior had bothered me at the time, I never thought to analyze why he had acted the way he did. As I thought back, I realized when Aunt Martha searched our condo and discovered my involvement with Erica the first thing she would have done was contact Peter.

Peter knew that if Martha contacted her son, Arnold, it would be all over. Arnold would not only sue me but the firm as well. Peter couldn't let that happen, so I figured he must have gone to Martha's motel and pleaded with her to be reasonable and not do anything rash. When she refused, he killed her. Martha had probably told him she'd taken the trust records from the condo so after he killed her, he took them with him. That would explain why Arnold's lawsuit was so far off the mark. He was speculating as to what had happened. Peter was probably elated when Erica showed up shortly after he had killed Martha. Her most fortunate appearance allowed him to make his getaway undetected and pin the murder on Erica.

It all made sense, but how could I prove it? If Peter had thought the whole thing through, he would have been careful not to leave any evidence. How could I prove he was the killer? He might still have my records. If we found out he had them, it would be pretty strong evidence of his guilt. The only problem was I had no clue as to where to look.

The next day I suggested my theory to Suzie, hoping she might have some ideas.

"So where do you think Peter would keep something like that?"

"Maybe in his closet. That's where he puts most of his important papers since he's the only one who has a key to it," Suzie said.

"His closet is identical to the one I had," I said. "It can be opened quite easily with a credit card. I figured that out one day when I misplaced my key."

"What are you suggesting?"

"Well, somebody needs to check out that closet," I said.

"That's breaking and entering," Suzie replied.

"Well, what if you went back for a visit to the firm? You could sneak into Peter's office and check out the closet."

"I don't think so. I don't want to end up in the county jail, thank you," Suzie said.

"So that means I've got to do it," I said.

"I guess so or hire a private investigator," Suzie replied.

"If the records are in his closet, then we can alert the police and let them ask him to explain how he got them."

"Are you really going to break in?"

"I guess I don't have any choice, Erica's life is at stake."

Getting into the office would be easy. I had done it before without a hitch. I'd just wait for one of the firm's law clerk slaves to go to the bathroom and then slip inside. I didn't tell Erica what I was doing for fear she'd want to come along. If I got caught it would be bad enough, but if Erica got caught with me, they'd revoke her bond and put her behind bars. After telling Erica I had to meet a prospective client at his club, I drove to my old office building. Someone was just coming out as I walked up so I smiled at them and entered the building. As I had planned, the security guard was away from his station when I went by. Once an hour he went out to the parking garage to make sure everything was okay. That's when I came inside. When I got upstairs, the door was locked as expected so I waited. After forty minutes, the door finally opened, and a clerk left the offices and went to the elevator. I ran over quickly and tried the door, but it was locked.

"Damn it," I said.

Quickly, I returned to my hiding place and waited another twenty minutes until I heard two voices laughing. Two of the clerks had apparently become bored and decided to have a sex break. They stumbled out of the offices in each other's arms, kissing.

"Hey, wait, Rod," the girl said. 'Be sure the door's unlocked so we can get back in."

Rod stopped the door before it closed and pushed in the locking mechanism. "Okay, now where's that couch you were talking about?"

"In the ladies' room. Come on."

The two lovers made their way slowly down the hall to the ladies' room and then disappeared inside. When I got into the suite, I went straight to Peter's office. I knew it was going to be dark, so I had brought a flashlight. I checked out his office and rummaged through the papers on his desk to see if there was anything there of interest. Not finding anything unusual, I went to the closet. It was locked, so I got out a credit card and before long the closet was opened.

I shone the flashlight around the closet. There was nothing there. As I turned around, I heard a noise outside Peter's office. I shut off my flashlight and crouched behind Peter's desk. My heart began to pound as fear overwhelmed me. What would I do if I got caught? I remembered Detective Perkin's admonition about breaking the law while I was playing amateur detective. Oh God, don't let me get caught.

The door flung open, and a security guard entered the room with his revolver pointing straight ahead. I lowered my head, closed my eyes, and took a deep breath. "Hold your fire," I said and then stood up. Another security guard turned on the light.

"What are you doing here?"

"Ah. ... just looking for some files I left here."

"Aren't you Richard Coleman?" the other guard said.

"Yes, put those guns down. Jesus! I'm unarmed," I said.

"You're not supposed to be in here," the first guard said.

"Who told you that?"

"Mr. Phillips was quite clear about the fact that you were not to be allowed in the offices."

If the guard called Peter or the police, I was screwed. Detective Perkins would be over in a minute. I had to convince them to let me go. I prayed for inspiration.

"He has no right to do that. I'm still a member of the firm. We haven't finalized the buyout yet."

"I'm sorry, Mr. Coleman. I'm going to have to call the police."

Fifteen minutes later, Detective Perkins smiled broadly as he entered Peter's office and saw me sitting meekly in a side chair. He talked a moment with the security guard, and then he came over to me.

"Well, you don't listen very well, do you, Mr. Coleman?"

"I heard what you said, but I don't have much choice but to keep looking since you have no intention of finding Martha Collins' killer."

"What did you expect to find here?"

"The thought occurred to me that Martha must have contacted Peter before Erica and I got back from Barbados. He knew Martha had the power to destroy the firm and he knew she had the proof necessary to do it in her possession.

I think he killed her and took the records. I came here to see if I could find anything."

"Did you?"

"No."

"Tough luck, Mr. Coleman. Now I'm going to have the pleasure of throwing your ass in jail for breaking and entering. Get up! Turn around."

Perkins slapped a pair of cuffs on me and told one of the uniformed officers he had brought with him to take me down to his squad car. I couldn't believe what was happening. What would Erica do when she found out I was in jail? The officer led me downstairs and put me in the back seat of Perkins's car. Never in my most melancholic nightmares had I ever seen me in jail. It seemed like I was dreaming and that sooner or later I would have to wake up. When Perkins returned to his car, I knew I was wide awake.

"You comfy back there, Coleman?" he laughed. "Let's get you downtown so you can experience some good ole Dallas Police Department hospitality."

After Perkins paraded me around the precinct gloating over his catch, he personally escorted me to a holding cell while they processed my paperwork. I asked him to let me make a phone call, but he refused until the paperwork was done. He wasn't sure how long that would take. Two hours later I got to call Webster. He got there within the hour and we met with a thick glass between us. We picked up the old, tarnished phones and began talking. I explained what had happened.

"If you walked in, it's not breaking and entering."

"I'm a signatory and a guarantor of the lease too. According to the terms of the lease, I can be up there any damn time I want."

"I don't think they have a prayer of convicting you. You might even have a claim against them for false arrest. How do you want to play it?"

"Just get me out of here. Erica must be frantic by now. Tell them I won't sue if they let me out of here immediately."

The guards took me back to my cell, and I waited. I wondered what Erica was thinking, how she would be taking my disappearance. She was already so unstable I couldn't imagine what she would be like when I finally returned. Without parents and friends, I was her only companion, and when she was alone, she seemed to hover on the brink of a mental breakdown. I paced back and forth praying that Webster would be successful.

16
The Alibi

It had been nearly two hours since Webster and I had talked. By now Erica knew I was in jail. At least she also knew that Webster was working diligently to get me released. What was taking so long? I dreaded the thought of spending the night in jail. Then I heard the metallic clang from a steel door resonate through the hall followed by footsteps. A guard was coming my way.

"Okay, Coleman," he said. "You got lucky. The charges against you have been dropped. You're free to leave."

"Thank God."

Erica was on the front porch when I pulled up. As I got out of my car, she ran over to me and we embraced. Her eyes were red and swollen. She smiled at me and we kissed.

"I've been so worried about you. What happened?" she said.

We went inside and sat on the sofa. I explained what had transpired. She took my hand and pulled me to her.

"Your poor boy. You must have been so scared."

"I was more concerned about you. They wouldn't let me call you. I knew you would be frantic. I missed you so."

"Perkins is a bastard. I'd like to smack him again but this time with something metallic."

"I just wish I would have been there when Webster threatened to sue him. That would have been sweet."

"You should sue. They made you sit there eleven

hours before they let you make a phone call. I can't believe what pathetic bastards they are."

"Forget Perkins. We've got more important things to worry about, like finding a killer. Time is getting short. Every minute of every hour from now on must be focused on developing plausible theories and developing leads. I just wish I knew what Peter did with my records."

"I don't know," Erica said. "Maybe he burned them. That's what I would have done."

"You're right. He probably burned them rather than risk getting caught with them. Damn it."

While I was thinking of another angle to determine if Peter was the killer, I decided to do some more checking on Arnold. Detective Perkins had said he was in Waco on the night of the murder. Waco was only a couple of hours south of Dallas, so the fact that someone had seen him there the night of the murder was not a conclusive alibi. Somehow, I had to learn more about what Arnold was doing in Waco. I remembered that Robert Webster had said he was putting a private investigator on Arnold, so I figured I'd call the investigator to see what he had learned. When I got through, he informed me he had a complete report already typed out and ready to submit to Webster. Within an hour I had the report in hand, so Erica and I went over it together.

"Let's see, Arnold Sebastian Collins. Nickname, Arnie. His mother and father were divorced when he was thirteen," Erica said. "His father never paid child support nor visited him. He attended Odessa-Permian High School and graduated in 1972. He graduated from UT El Paso in 1976 and from Baylor Law School in Austin in 1979."

"He hasn't been practicing law too long," I said. "Does it say where he works?"

"Uh . . . let me see, he works for Simpson & Jones out of Odessa. He specializes in family and criminal law."

"What does he do besides work?"

"His hobbies are flying and sky diving?" Erica said. "A daredevil, huh?"

"I guess."

"Does he have his own plane?" I asked.

"I don't know, it doesn't say."

"I wonder if he flew to Waco," I said. "If he did it would only be a thirty-minute flight from Waco to Love Field. Love Field's not ten minutes from the motel Aunt Martha was staying in."

"That's true. Maybe you're onto something."

"I hope so, I don't like Arnie much. Although I only met him that one time in court, he gives me bad vibes," I said.

"Guess what? He's a member of the John Birch Society," Erica advised.

"Oh really, that's certainly interesting. I wonder why he became a right-wing fanatic?"

"Who knows, maybe because Aunt Martha was so domineering."

"You suppose?"

"Yeah, we've been studying about that in psychology class," Erica said. "Negative parents can cause tremendous psychological damage to their children. They often have such low self-esteem that they suffer from depression and paranoia."

"I wonder if he was a fan of the Fuhrer. It wouldn't surprise me. If so, killing his mother might not be out of the question. As I recalled, squealing on parents and then watching them shot by a firing squad was very fashionable in Nazi Germany."

"Was it?"

"Didn't you read the Rise and Fall of the Third Reich?" I asked.

"Are you kidding? I couldn't even lift it," Erica laughed.

"I think we should have Mr. Clark do a little more checking into Arnie's itinerary on the day of the murder."

"It certainly wouldn't hurt."

The excitement and hope I felt after reviewing Arnold's background report were incredible. For the first time in weeks, I felt we were closer to solving the puzzle as to who had actually killed Martha Collins. I called Clark Investigations immediately.

"Thanks for sending that report right over. Listen, we need some more information on Arnold Collins," I said.

"Okay, what do you need?"

"His flying is of particular interest. Find out if he owns a plane and whether he flew it to Waco on the night of the murder. If not, then check and see if he rented any planes or bought a ticket on any flights to or from Dallas the night of the murder."

"Sure, what are you looking for?"

"We think he might have flown to Dallas on the night in question, murdered his mother, and then flew back to Waco. If there's a ticket or a flight plan it might prove he was in Dallas on the night of the murder."

"Okay, I'll get right on it," Clark said.

"Oh, also check and see exactly where he was from six to midnight on the night of the murder," I said.

"He was at the Alumni Dance. He was there from approximately seven to midnight."

"How do you know?" I asked.

"I didn't talk to anyone who was with him the entire evening, but we did speak to a couple witnesses who saw him around seven and one who saw him leave at 11:45. We're still working on the time in between."

"When you find out, let me know. He may have gone to the dance, made sure people saw him, and then left. He could have come to Dallas and still made it back to the dance before it was over."

"Okay, I'll check it out."

As I was pondering the conversation with Ronald

Clark, the phone rang. It was Peter.

"My security people just told me they caught you snooping around my office. How did you manage to get out of jail?"

"My attorney convinced them I had a perfect right to be there."

"A perfect right, my ass. What in the hell gives you the right to sneak into my office and search through my things?"

"Calm down. I'm sorry, but I'm getting desperate. I thought maybe you killed Martha Collins."

"What? You're losing it, my friend."

"You had a good motive to kill Martha."

"What possible motive would I have?" he asked.

"To save the firm, what else? Martha called you, didn't she?"

There was quiet on the other end of the phone.

"She called you, didn't she?" I repeated.

"Well, what did you expect her to do when she finds out you're sleeping with her niece?"

"So what did you tell her?"

"Nothing. I told her to take it up with you. The firm had nothing to do with your personal appointment as a trustee."

"I don't believe that's what you said, and I don't think for a minute that would have satisfied her."

Peter coughed. "I don't care what you think. That's what happened."

"You went to her place, didn't you?" I said.

"No way, you think I'm crazy?" Peter replied.

"You killed her, didn't you?"

"Now you've gone completely off the deep end. This conversation is over." He hung up.

Maybe I'd gotten a little too dramatic with Peter, but I wanted to see how he'd react to being accused of murder. Unfortunately, not being face to face made it difficult to assess his reaction. He was upset but was it just from being accused or from fear of imminent discovery? What would I do if I were the killer and I thought someone was on to me? In this case, I would want to destroy the evidence that could link me to the crime.

I found Erica and asked, "Want to go for a ride?"

"Where?"

"I want to follow Peter and see where he goes. I got him pretty upset and I think he might go to where he has the trust's financial records hidden."

"I told you Peter didn't do it," Erica said. "This is a waste of time."

"How do you know he didn't do it? You should have heard how upset he was. Come on, let's go."

"Okay, but you're wasting our time."

"Hey, it will be fun either way. If it turns out to be a bust, I'll buy you dinner any place you want to go, okay?"

Erica smiled, "Any place?"

"Yeah, come on."

On the way over to Peter's office, Erica snuggled up next to me and put her head on my shoulder. I grabbed her hand and held it while I drove with my left hand. A light mist was falling and the reflection on the street made the night quite spectacular. When we arrived at the office building, I pulled up across the street where we had a clear view of the exit to the parking garage. We waited about ten minutes before Peter pulled out in his grey Cadillac. When he was half a block away, I eased out and started following him.

He headed north on McKinney Avenue to Knox and turned left past the Highland Park Cafeteria and then right again. It was his regular route to his home in Highland Park. I was beginning to get discouraged as he neared his street, but he didn't turn down it. Instead, he continued all the way to Northwest Highway and turned right. I got a little closer, not wanting to lose him. When he got to Greenville Avenue, he turned left and went several blocks, and then turned into the

Silver Slipper Saloon.

"He's going to a damn strip joint," I said.

"I told you this was a waste of time," Erica replied.

"I know, but I really thought he'd lead us to something. Damn it!"

Erica kissed me on the cheek. "I know you're doing your best, honey. I've never had someone care about me the way you do. It feels wonderful to be loved. I guarantee you no one will ever keep us apart. We'll always be together."

"I know, but I want to be alive and together. We need a break here."

As I spoke Peter came out of the club with another man. It was dark so I couldn't make out who it was. Erica was still on my shoulder with her eyes closed.

"Who's that?" I said

Erica sat up and looked out at the two men standing by Peter's Cadillac. "I don't know. It's too dark. Maybe if you turn on your high beams, we can make out his face."

I started up the engine, turned on the bright lights, and eased the car towards the two men. They turned and looked towards us shielding their face from the bright lights."

"Oh my God," Erica said. "It's Arnold!"

We drove right past them and continued up Greenville Ave to the Railhead, where we stopped for dinner. We were both in shock as we were seated at a booth. Was Aunt Martha's death the result of some kind of conspiracy? What was going on anyway? Erica and I just stared at each other, not knowing what to say. The waiter stopped by and we both ordered a cocktail. Finally, I said, "Boy, that boggles the mind, doesn't it?"

"It sure is strange," Erica said. "I just can't believe those two would be working together."

"I thought I was starting to figure this thing out but now I'm back to square one."

"Don't read too much into this, honey. We have no

idea what Peter and Arnold were talking about. It might not be about the murder at all. Maybe they were discussing Aunt Martha's estate or something."

"Arnold's a lawyer, I'm sure he's handling it himself, and Peter doesn't usually conduct business at a strip joint," I said.

"I don't think we're ever going to figure this thing out, honey. You're not a detective and you're not even a criminal lawyer. If you had the resources of the police, I'm sure you could find the killer, but you don't. Just let Webster handle my defense now. You've done all you can. I really think Webster will be able to successfully defend me."

"You think I should give up?"

"No, not totally but I think our primary focus should be on preparing me in case I have to plead temporary insanity."

"The thought of that makes me sick," I said.

"I really think I can pull it off."

"When are you scheduled to meet with Webster next?"

"On Wednesday. We're going to go through the elements of our defense step by step. Then Dr. Beckman is going to give me some psychological tests."

"Temporary insanity is rarely successful from what I understand."

"Dr. Beckman told me at our last meeting that Webster has successfully used this defense several times in the past. I think we should trust him."

"Whatever you say, honey," I said. "I'm just glad you're finally feeling optimistic about all this."

Erica's complete mental turnaround was a great relief to me, but I couldn't help but wonder if it would last. During the time we had been together she had shown a propensity for quick and radical mood swings. I attributed this to her youth and the fact that she was a woman. So, I was cautiously optimistic that her turnaround would last. I hoped Dr. Beckman had really done her some good.

"Dr. Beckman says I've got to have a positive attitude if I'm going to pull this thing off."

I nodded and said, "He's right."

Erica leaned over the table and took my hands. She smiled and squeezed them gently. "So, don't worry, okay?"

I shook my head and laughed. "Don't worry. ... Yeah, right."

17
Dress Rehearsal

Erica's suggestion that I quit looking for the real killer disturbed me. Was she telling me in a roundabout way that she was guilty? Maybe that was why she was so sure that Peter wasn't the killer and why she didn't seem to care that Peter and Arnold were having covert meetings at the Silver Slipper. Perhaps she knew that I would never find the real killer, because I couldn't bring myself to realize that it was her.

Before I gave up and acquiesced to the plea of temporary insanity, however, I vowed to follow-up with Ron Clark and see if he had found out anything about Arnold's activities on the night of the murder. It had been several days since I had talked to him, so I gave him a call.

"It seems Mr. Collins got to Waco via American Eagle," Clark advised. "He stayed in the La Quinta Motor Hotel on I-35 near the Baylor Campus. I wasn't able to find anyone else who saw him that evening. I'm sorry."

"What about plane tickets or a charter?" I said.

"There were no charters that night, but there was a flight from Waco to Dallas at 7:48 arriving in Dallas at 8:28. There was no return flight, however," Clark said.

"So it's possible he could have been at the Starlight Motel at 9 or 9:15 p.m.," I said.

"Maybe, but the airline records don't show he was on the plane."

"Really?" I said. "Maybe he used a different name.

Why don't you take a picture of him, find the stewardess who was on that flight and see if she saw him?"

"Okay, but it might take a while to find the stewardess," Clark said. "Plus, it's not likely she would remember one face when she sees so many."

"I know, but it's possible she might remember. A trial date hasn't been set. We've got some time so go ahead and check it out."

On Wednesday I took Erica to Webster's office to work on her case. Before he made me leave the session, he filled us in on the status of the case.

"The judge has set a trial date for August 16, 1980," Webster said. "It's a special setting so we'll definitely go to trial on that date. If we're going to plead temporary insanity, we have to give the judge thirty days' notice. That means we have a little over a week to make a definite decision. Of course, we can withdraw that defense up until the day of trial if some new evidence turns up, but once you've told the judge you're going to rely on a temporary insanity defense, he's going to assume your client is the killer."

"Damn it. Can't we get more time?" I said.

"No, the judge is anxious to get this case tried. He made it clear there would be no continuances."

"God, I hate this. I just know Arnold or Peter did it," I said.

"There's a lot of evidence against Erica but it's possible we could establish reasonable doubt. It's just hard to do it without someone else to point the finger at."

"I know. I just feel like I'm so close, you know?"

"Listen, I've had Clark trying to come up with something for two months. The police have thoroughly investigated the case from day one and haven't found anything to suggest someone else might be the murderer. You, yourself have been busting your ass for weeks trying to find evidence that someone else killed Mrs. Collins. Despite all this effort we're still no closer to finding the real killer than we were on the day we all started looking."

"You're right," I said.

"Since the judge has set the case for trial, we best decide on a strategy very soon if we're going to have any chance at getting Erica acquitted."

"You're Erica's lawyer. If your advice is to go with temporary insanity, then I guess that's what it will be as much as I hate the thought of it."

"Well, it's a crap shoot. I've explained the pros and cons of each defense to Erica. It's her decision. I'm prepared to proceed either way. It's just that we can abandon the insanity defense at any time if we find the real killer or evidence that someone else did it. But once the deadline passes to assert the insanity defense then that defense is lost forever."

"I think Robert is right, we don't have a choice under the circumstances," Erica agreed.

"All right then, temporary insanity it is. I'll get out of here so you all can get to work. Thanks, Rob."

"It's all right. Let's see, it's about nine-thirty. Why don't you pick Erica up at noon? That's about all the time I've got today to work on her case."

"Fine, I'll be back at noon," I said and then gave Erica a goodbye kiss.

When I got back to the office, Suzie was working on a mailing to all my old clients advising them of our separation from Rogers, Phillips, and Coleman and giving them our new address. After picking up my messages, I went into the library to do some research on the defense of temporary insanity. I read all the leading cases on the subject and learned that in Texas to be successful with a temporary insanity defense it would be necessary to show that as a result of a mental defect or disease, Erica did not know her conduct was wrong, or she was incapable of conforming her conduct to the law.

Webster would have to convince the jury that when Erica was confronted by Aunt Martha that she reacted without conscious thought or understanding. After satisfying myself that I knew what we were up against, I decided to get Suzie's opinion.

"But you'll have to admit Erica's the killer."

"I know."

"Erica is the most stable person I know," Suzie said. "There is no way she was temporarily insane. If she killed Aunt Martha, she knew exactly what she was doing. . . . Not that I think she did it, of course."

"I understand," I said. "But the jury will not know Erica the way we do. They may believe she was temporarily insane although that is kind of a stretch. Perhaps I should hire an acting coach for her."

"That's a great idea," Suzie replied. "Just don't let the DA find out about it or he'll have a field day in front of the jury."

"I was just kidding."

"I knew that. What about Arnold? Is there any more news about the Alumni Ball?"

"Nothing startling, although we did figure out that he could have been in Dallas at nine that evening. There was a flight that would have got him in at 8:28."

"Maybe you should show the motel manager a picture of Arnold and see if she recalls seeing him that night," Suzie suggested.

"Good idea. I wonder if we could get a list of the names and addresses of the people who stayed at the Starlight Motel that night. One of them might have seen him."

"I'm sure the police did that," Suzie said.

"They probably got the list but I doubt they showed the guests Arnold's picture. I'm sure the only picture they saw was Erica's," I said.

"Rob can get the list from the DA, can't he?"

"Yeah, they should give it to him," I said. "The problem

is getting the picture to all those people. They are scattered all over the damn country, no doubt."

"There goes our phone bill," Suzie said.

"That's the least of our worries. You call everyone on the list and tell them what we need them to do. Then Fed Ex them a photograph of Arnold. I wonder where we can get a photograph of Arnold?"

"Erica's probably got one."

"Oh, that's right," I said. "I think I remember seeing one at the condo, now that you mention it."

"You can call Rob's secretary and see if she can get the list of guests for us. I'll get copies of the photograph made tomorrow, and you can send them off just as soon you get the list."

"Okay, anything else?"

"Not right now, but if you have any more ideas let me know."

At noon I went back and picked up Erica. I was anxious to see how the session had gone, as it was supposed to be kind of a dress rehearsal for Erica's testimony in Court. Dr. Beckman was going to explain to Erica how she should testify, and then Rob was going to pretend he was taking her direct examination in court. When I got to Rob's office, they were still working so I read a magazine. At twelve-thirty Erica emerged from the conference room. She wasn't smiling.

"Hi, honey. Have you been waiting long?" Erica asked.

"Oh, a little while. Twenty or thirty minutes."

"I'm sorry, but Dr. Beckman was giving me his comments on my testimony. I've got a lot of work to do to get ready for trial."

Dr. Beckman walked over and extended his hand.

"Hi, Dr. Beckman," I said as I shook it. "How did it go?"

"Erica did pretty well," Dr. Beckman said. "We still have a lot of work to do but we're making progress."

"Good. So what happens now?"

"Oh, Erica has to go see Dr. Melvin Bentley. He's the state's psychiatrist. He'll want to interview her and do some testing on his own."

"Do you think he'll agree with you?" I asked.

"No, he'll determine that she was quite sane when she killed Mrs. Collins, but that's expected."

"So what makes you think the jury will believe you and not him?" I asked.

"You've selected a good defense attorney. I've seen him rip Dr. Bentley to pieces. The key to all of this is how Erica does on cross. If she does exactly what we say she'll be fine, but if she lets the DA get to her, then there's no telling what will happen."

"Well, thanks for your help, doctor," I said. "I guess we'll be seeing you later."

"Yes, I'll see both of you in a week or so."

On the way home Erica was very quiet. I was worried about her as she usually was quite talkative. I figured the preparation she had received must have been pretty enlightening. Perhaps she was worried now that she knew what to expect.

"Are you all right?" I asked.

"I've got a headache," she said.

"You do? Are you getting sick?"

"No, I guess it's just stress. Mr. Webster's questioning was pretty intense."

"Well, the DA's will be worse. Rob just wants you to be prepared."

"I know. I'm sure I'm going to screw up."

"You can't screw up; the consequences are too severe."

"I'm going to, I can feel it."

"Then you should plead innocent and take your chances? I'd feel a lot better if you did that."

"I can't," Erica said.

"Why not?"

"I just can't," Erica repeated as tears began streaming down her cheeks.

"Oh God," I said handing her my handkerchief. "Don't cry. I know the situation looks pretty bleak, honey, but we're bound to get a break here sooner or later."

She wiped her eyes and then breathed in deeply. "I found out where I can get the cyanide," she said evenly.

"Oh, come on. You're not going to start on that again, are you?"

"I've got to know, Rich. If they convict me, will you die with me?" she said.

"Erica, come on. Cut it out."

"I've got to know. You've got to make a decision. I need to know now."

"You'd really rather die than go to prison?" I asked.

"Yes, absolutely. I can't live without you. It really bothers me that you don't feel the same way about me."

"I do feel the same way," I said. "I love you more than anything on Earth, more than I could ever express in words."

"Prove it then."

"But I don't want to die," I said.

"I don't either, but without you there is no life for me. Could you live without me now that we've been together?"

I sighed desperately. "Okay. Okay. If that's what you want. If we can't live together, we'll die together."

Erica scooted over next to me in the car, took my right hand and said, "I'm so relieved, for a while there I wasn't sure you loved me. Now I'm prepared to die for you."

18
Shopping For Cyanide

Shopping has never been something I enjoyed, but when Erica told me we needed to go shopping for cyanide I nearly fainted. It's true, I had somehow consented to end my life if Erica was convicted, but it still didn't seem real. I had agreed to an idea, a concept, but could I really take my life? Erica, however, was adamant about getting our poison so we'd be ready to take a romantic exit from this earth if the jury's verdict was unfavorable.

It was now a week before Erica's trial, and we were at the public library trying to figure out where cyanide could be purchased. When Erica suggested we go to the library to start our search, I was skeptical that there would be anything there on the topic. Much to my surprise, the library had a wealth of information about this very popular instrument of death. We learned that Cyanide was widely used for industrial purposes in the manufacture of the anti-cancer drug, Laetrile, insecticides, fumigants, rodenticides, electroplating solution, and metal polish. It occurred to us that we could most likely find what we needed at the local nursery, drug, or hardware store. Before we left to make our purchase, I read to Erica how cyanide worked on the human body. I hoped this information would scare her into canceling our pact.

"Cyanide interferes with enzymes controlling the oxidative process, preventing the body's red blood cells from absorbing oxygen. Swallowing or smelling a toxic dose of cyanide as a gas or a salt can cause immediate unconsciousness, convulsions, and death within one to fifteen minutes. If an amount near the lethal dose is absorbed through the skin, inhaled, or swallowed, the symptoms noted will be rapid respiration, a gasping for breath, dizziness, flushing, headache, nausea, vomiting, rapid pulse, and a drop in blood pressure causing fainting. A bittersweet almond scent often is associated with cyanide poisoning."

"We should take a strong dose so it will take just one minute. I shouldn't want to suffer for fifteen," Erica said.

"Why don't we skip it altogether?"

"Rich, come on. We have an agreement," she said.

"I know. Just a thought."

"Let's go to Wolf's Nursery and see if they have an insecticide that will work."

"Okay," I said.

"If they don't, then we can try Handy Dan. Maybe they have some metal polish that will do the trick."

"Metal polish? I don't think so," I said. "You know I'm feeling kind of sick already, my heart's beating pretty fast, I feel hot, and I think I'm going to throw up."

"This isn't funny," Erica said.

"You're telling me. I've got a splitting headache."

"Okay, forget it! I'll get the cyanide. I just thought we could do this together. I know it's not pleasant, but I just wanted it to be our last act of love."

Or insanity. "Why don't we just close the garage door, turn on the engine and drift off into oblivion?"

"We can't," Erica said. "If I'm convicted, they'll haul me off to jail, and we won't ever be together again."

"How about a quick gunshot to the head?"

"We'd never get a gun in the courtroom," she said giving me an exasperated look.

"How do you plan to get Kool-Aid into the courtroom?"

Erica laughed. "We're not using Kool-Aid, obviously.

We'll put the poison in aspirin gel caps. If the jury convicts me, we'll put the pills in our mouths and start chewing. Within a minute, we'll both be dead."

"You got it all figured out, don't you?"

"Pretty much, but I need to write a suicide note," she said.

"A suicide note?"

"Yes, we have to tell the world why we died. Otherwise, they'll just think I was guilty and too ashamed to face my punishment. I want them to know I was innocent."

"Oh God, I'm sick," I said.

"You're not going to chicken out on me, are you?"

I took a deep breath. "No, don't worry."

It was a lie. I hadn't really resigned myself to dying even if Erica was convicted. In my heart I felt like somehow, she would escape conviction. She already had me wondering about her mental state in general. How anyone could plan their death so coolly like it was a Sunday picnic had baffled me. Was this her way of making the stakes so high she couldn't fail? Would the thought of imminent death make her performance before the jury so passionate, so convincing that they would have to believe her? Who was I to second guess someone facing life in prison?

If nothing else our little trip to the library gave me even greater motivation to keep looking for Aunt Martha's killer. While Erica was shopping for cyanide, I went back to the office to see if the names and addresses of the guests at the Starlight Motel had come in. Suzie was on the telephone when I walked in. After a minute she hung up.

"So, did the DA come through with our list yet?" I said.

"Yes, as a matter of fact, I was just talking to someone who stayed at the motel that night," Suzie said. "I made a Xerox copy of Arnold's picture and I'm going to Fed Ex it to them tonight."

"Good. How many names do you have?"

"One hundred and four," Suzie said.

"Oh my God," I said. "It will take you forever to contact all those people."

"You're right. I was hoping I might get Erica to help out."

"Not today, she's out shopping."

"For what?" Suzie asked curiously.

"Don't ask."

"Well, I could use some help," Suzie said as she looked out the window. "Guess what? Joe Weston is here."

We both smiled. "Hmm. Help has arrived," I noted.

The door opened, and Joe Weston appeared. He gave us a suspicious look, I guess because of the look on our faces.

"What's so funny?" he said.

"Nothing, we're just glad to see you," I said. Suzie went back to what she was doing and I took Joe into my office.

"Well, I just came over to see your new place and to see how things are going."

I told him about our little project and our need for help. He agreed to stay and pitch in. Then he told me the real reason he had come by.

"I've had a few visitors since we last talked."

"Who?'

"Arnold Collins for starters."

"What did he want?"

"The details of all your stock transactions. He had a subpoena duces tecum. He picked up a copy of all our records on the trust and your personal account as well."

"Oh shit. Now he's going to know everything."

"Well, you didn't think you could keep it a secret, did you?"

"No, but—"

"Then I got a visit from the SEC."

"The SEC?"

"Yeah, some guy named Porter Young. He got a copy of your records too."

"What the hell!" I said angrily. "What did he want with them?"

"He was investigating a rumor of some insider trading on the Greystone deal."

"What? That's total crap. I can't believe this."

"He also was curious as to why I stood by and watched you break every fiduciary rule in the book with Erica's account."

"You're kidding?"

"I wish I were. The firm has put me on suspension until the investigation is concluded."

"Oh God, Joe. I'm so sorry. I never thought any of this would affect you."

"Bullshit! You knew I could get in trouble if your relationship was discovered. I told you I had a duty to report your outrageous conduct to the proper authorities. ... Why did you do this to me?"

Joe was right. I hadn't taken seriously the possibility that he might get in trouble for what I was doing. In my mind, I was doing him a favor by giving him my business but actually, I went to him because I knew he was the only broker in town who wouldn't blow the whistle on me. What I had done was unforgivable.

"You're right." I agreed. "I guess I was just too entangled in Erica's web to think about what I was doing to you. Don't worry. Just let me take all the heat. I'll tell them you didn't know anything about Erica and me. I'll tell them that I lied to you and kept you in the dark."

"Yeah, I'm sure that's going to fly," Joe said dejectedly.

"So what are you going to do?"

"Help you track down the killer, I guess. I seem to have plenty of free time on my hands."

I smiled. "You're a good friend. I'm so sorry I screwed

up your life."

"Just give me part of the list," he said. "Maybe if we can get Erica off the hook, you'll have time to figure out how to save my job."

For the rest of the day Suzie, Joe, and I called people all over the country who had been at the Starlight Motel that evening. Most were friendly and promised to look at the photo and call us immediately, but a few refused, not wanting to get involved. By six o'clock we had over half of the people called and had prepared overnight mail packages to be sent to them. The following day we finished up our task and then waited. As expected, most of the callers had no recollection of seeing Arnold that night. By the end of the second day, over eighty percent of those contacted had called and denied ever seeing Arnold. Then we got a call from New Orleans from Melvin Potter.

"I may have seen this guy before," Potter said. "I'm not sure where, but it was probably at the motel."

"Do you remember anything about the circumstances of your meeting?" I asked.

"No, not really. The face just seems so familiar."

"What were you doing in town?" I asked.

"I was at the builder's convention," Potter said.

"On the night of April 3, 1980, do you remember what you were doing?"

"My partner and I had gone to a club after dinner. We got back to the motel around nine-fifteen or so."

"Could you have seen the man in the photograph when you returned?"

"Yes, but I'm just not sure," Potter said. "I know I saw him that evening somewhere. I just can't remember the exact circumstances."

"Well, why don't you think about it some more, and if something comes to mind give us a call, okay?"

"Sure, it might come to me. You never know."

It was gratifying to finally get a lead on the one hand, but frustrating that Mr. Potter couldn't be surer of his sighting of Arnold Collins. At least now there was a little hope. All we needed was to find another person who had seen Arnold and then things would get interesting. Fortunately, it wasn't long until a second call came in.

"This is Henry Strathmore. I got your photo and just wanted to tell you I'm pretty sure I saw this gentleman on the night of April 3, 1980, at the Starlight Motel."

"You are?" I said.

"Yes."

"Are you positive?"

"Well, pretty much," Strathmore said. "You see not only did I see this man, but I had a short conversation with him."

"Did you know him?"

"No, I just met him that night for the first time."

"What did you talk about?" I asked.

"College football," Strathmore replied.

"How did that come up?"

"I was wearing a Texas Tech sweatshirt and he asked me if I went there. I told him I got my B.A. from there."

"What happened after you talked?"

"Nothing. He said he had just brought his friend back to the motel and was about to head home."

"Did he say where home was?" I asked.

"No, I don't recall that he did," Strathmore replied.

"Do you remember what time of day this was?"

"It was in the late afternoon or early evening. I'm not exactly sure of the time."

"What was he was wearing?"

"He had on khaki pants and a flannel shirt; I believe."

"He was alone?" I asked.

"When I saw him, he was."

"Well, thank you, Mr. Strathmore. I guess you know someone was killed that night and the man you identified is a suspect. You may get a call from a detective Perkins or the defense counsel, Robert Webster, about our conversation."

"Okay."

"They may need you as a witness. Should you think of anything else that might be helpful, give me a call."

Now I was convinced that Arnold had been in Dallas at or near the time of the murder. It occurred to me that I should call Detective Perkins and advise him about this new development. I doubted he would care but I felt compelled to tell him anyway. I picked up the phone.

"I've got some interesting information on Arnold Collins's whereabouts on the night of the murder," I advised.

"I thought Erica was pleading temporary insanity?" Perkins replied.

"She is, but I still don't believe she did it."

"Well obviously her attorney does."

"I don't care, but I'm sure someone else did it, and I intend to prove it. As I recall the purpose of this trial is to get to the truth."

"Whatever, so what do you have?"

"Two men who saw Arnold Collins at the motel on the day of the murder."

"Really?"

"Yes, I've got their names and telephone numbers for you."

"So, you still think Mr. Collins killed his own mother."

"The thought still lingers."

"Well, I'll look into it, but frankly I wouldn't get your hopes up."

"Just check it out. That's all I ask."

Detective Perkins's enthusiasm for finding the truth continued to amaze me. It was clear the last thing he was going to do was look for evidence that might help Erica. I called and told Robert Webster what I had found. He wasn't enthusiastic about this new evidence either but reluctantly agreed to meet for lunch the next day to discuss it and evaluate any other evidence that I thought might create doubt in the juror's minds.

I was frustrated. I questioned whether Webster was as good an attorney as I had thought. He seemed to have abandoned the search for the truth. It was all up to me now, but no matter how hard we worked, I couldn't quite get enough to crack the case. On the way home I was feeling pretty depressed, and it only got worse when I got there and joined Erica in the kitchen.

"What are you doing?" I said.

"I found what we needed, and I've got the pills already."

"Great," I moaned.

"I wrote our suicide note," she said.

"Already?"

"Yes, I want to get all of this done so I can just forget about it."

"It almost seems like you're enjoying this," I said.

"Yeah, right. I want to die."

"Well, sometimes I wonder."

"We've got to be realistic. I might be convicted. If I am, now we're ready. Hopefully, we won't need the pills."

"So we don't have to talk anymore about our pact?"

"No. We can concentrate on winning at trial now," she said.

"Good, what's for dinner?"

"Don't you want to read our suicide note?"

"No, I don't."

"But I want to be sure you like it."

"I don't give a shit what it says," I spat.

Erica glared at me and said, "I don't know why I'm doing this for you."

"Doing what?" I replied glaring back at her. It was no use; I could see that. "Okay, read the damn note."

Erica didn't move for a moment, just stared at me. Finally, she took a deep breath and began reading from a sheet of paper she had picked up off the table.

"To those who care:

"Richard and I were brought together by fate. Neither sought out the other or even dreamed that we'd fall in love. But it happened, and no matter how wrong it looked, it felt right, and we were happy. We knew from the beginning no one would understand what had happened, and if we were discovered, our lives would be destroyed by those who were jealous of what we had. The fact that this letter is being read, proves us right.

"'So rather than living cold, empty lives apart, we decided to die together and go on to whatever lies ahead. But for the record, I didn't kill Aunt Martha. I'm not a murderer. The jury was wrong. May God have mercy on their souls. Erica Fox Coleman / Richard Coleman."

Erica looked up at me waiting for my reaction. I nodded and said, "That's good. It gets the message across."

"Do you really like it?" Erica asked.

"Yes, it's good."

"All right, no more talk of suicide," Erica said.

"Thank God."

The next day I met Webster for lunch at his club on the top of the Republic Bank Building downtown. After we ate, the waiter brought us both a cigar, and we lit them up. Then we began discussing Erica's case.

"Even if you can establish that Arnold was at the motel on the day or even the night of the murder, what does that prove?"

"It proves that he had as much opportunity to kill Martha as Erica."

"So, what's the motive?"

"He hates his mother. She's a domineering bitch," I said.

"You can't prove that, and even if you did, that's not much of a motive."

"Maybe she had a lot of insurance?"

"I doubt it, but if you find that to be the case, let me know. ... So, is that all you have?" he asked.

"There are some other things. Peter and Arnold had a meeting at a strip club the other night."

"Really, that is curious. Do you have any idea why?"

"No, not at all."

"They were probably discussing your civil suit," Webster said. "I bet Peter is trying to persuade Arnold not to name the firm in the suit. He may be offering to testify against you in exchange for that concession, or maybe he's going to pay some money to settle the claim against the firm."

"That sorry son of a bitch—I can't believe the way Peter has turned on me."

"I'm just speculating, but that seems logical."

"You're probably right. Damn him."

"So, is that all you've got?"

"Well, I hate to even bring this up, but I guess we have to consider every possibility. I mean, if Erica didn't kill Aunt Martha, who did?"

"I don't know. Tell me," Webster said.

"You know the motel clerk is going to testify that she saw a man hanging around Martha's room on the night of the murder?"

"Right, I saw her statement in the DA's file."

"Well, Peter contacted Joe Weston when he got back from Barbados. He was pretty nasty and threatened to sue Joe and his firm for allowing me to speculate with Erica's trust account. Joe was pretty upset and tried to contact me, but I was still in Barbados. If he found out about Martha taking my records, he might have tried to get them back. I don't think Joe would intentionally kill anyone, but he might have confronted Martha and accidentally killed her."

"That's possible but right now it's just speculation. I'm afraid you're going to need a hell of a lot more evidence to prove it or even create some reasonable doubt."

"Well, that's all I've come up with so far."

"I guess we'll stick with our temporary insanity defense then," Webster said.

As much as I hated to admit it, Webster was right. I had nothing, not a god damn thing to help prove Erica was innocent. I began to worry about our pact. Would Erica really insist on going through with it? I was scared. I closed my eyes and prayed for inspiration. I had to figure out a way to prove Erica's innocence and extricate ourselves from our pledge of self-destruction. If I didn't, I'd have to choose between death and betrayal, and that was a choice only the Devil himself would relish.

19
Opening Statements

It was a blistering August day when the case of the State of Texas V. Erica Fox Coleman came to trial in the Dallas County Courthouse. Every seat in the courtroom was taken and dozens of people stood outside the doorway hoping to get inside. Joe and I were in the front row directly behind Erica. Arnold Collins was seated in the front row on the aisle next to Peter Phillips. The Honorable Victor King was presiding at the trial. Webster told us he was a dangerous judge because he was erratic and unpredictable, but then he admitted he never knew a judge he actually liked. At nine o'clock sharp the Judge walked into the courtroom and the bailiff yelled, "All rise!"

It had taken six days to pick the jury due to the extensive pre-trial publicity. The final jury panel consisted of eight women and four men with a good mix of racial backgrounds. The group consisted of three housewives, two government employees, two construction workers, two salesmen, a bank officer, a plumber, and a mortician. As the jury panel made its way into the courtroom, Webster and Erica watched them intently. When they had all been seated, the judge asked for opening statements.

The Assistant District Attorney assigned to the case was Ralph Blake. He was a respected, capable trial attorney and a fiery orator. Blake was tall with black hair and wore a dark blue suit. Assisting him was an intense-looking young lady attorney in a navy-blue business suit. Blake ran his hand once through his hair before beginning.

"Ladies and Gentlemen of the jury. Over the next few days, you're going to hear the story of the Fox family. It will be a tragic story of hatred and feuding which culminated in the brutal murder of Martha Collins on the night of April 3, 1980. It was on that night that the defendant, Erica Fox Coleman, realized that her Aunt had been in her condominium and discovered her sinister relationship with an attorney, Richard Coleman. Outraged that her Aunt had gone through her things and discovered her secret affair, she proceeded to go to the Starlight Motel where her Aunt was staying.

"There are no eyewitnesses as to what happened at the motel, but a few things are clear: Erica Fox hit Mrs. Collins over the head with a lamp and then held a pillow over her head until she was dead. The state will produce a witness who saw Erica Fox go to Mrs. Collins's room at approximately 9:45. This was right about the time she was murdered. We will also show that Erica Fox was so upset when she left the room, she neglected to take her purse. A clerk from a nearby 7-11 convenience store will testify that Erica Fox came into his store at approximately 10:05 frantic to make a phone call. He'll testify that she borrowed a dime from some customers and tried to call someone but was unable to make a connection. At that point, she just sank to the ground in despair and started crying.

"Now Mr. Webster will be up here pretty soon talking to you about temporary insanity. He'll try to convince you that when Erica Fox killed her aunt, it was the result of some sort of mental condition that prevented her from realizing that what she was doing was wrong. He'll tell you that when Erica confronted her aunt, they fought, and Erica reacted to the altercation by killing her aunt without conscious thought or understanding. I know all this sounds pretty ridiculous and far-fetched, but I can assure you he'll be up here in a minute trying to sell you on that idea.

"The State will show, however, that Erica Fox is a very intelligent young lady. She's a freshman at SMU, well-liked, and a good student. The state will call an expert witness, Dr. Melvin Bentley, who will testify that after extensive interviews with Erica Fox he found her to be quite normal, above-average intelligence, and well adjusted. He'll give you his opinion that Erica knew exactly what she was doing when she hit Martha Collins over the head and then held a pillow over her face depriving her of oxygen until she was dead.

"Ladies and gentlemen, the State will show you that what happened on April 3, 1980, was nothing less than cold-blooded premeditated murder. Now, I don't blame Mr. Webster for asserting the defense of temporary insanity. It's really the only thing his client could do short of confessing and negotiating a plea bargain. Consider the evidence the State will soon be introducing. There'll be witnesses who saw Erica Fox enter and leave the victim's room, then the State will show Erica's purse which was left at the scene of the crime, and finally, we'll introduce lab reports showing feathers from the murder weapon embedded in Erica Fox's fingernails and on her clothing.

"By the time the State closes it will have shown beyond any reasonable doubt that Erica Fox intentionally killed her aunt to prevent her from revealing her illicit affair with Richard Coleman. Now, it may be tempting to sympathize with Erica Fox because she was trying to protect her love relationship with Richard Coleman. It may be that Martha Collins was acting out of spite in threatening to destroy Erica and Richard's happiness, but whether or not that is true, Erica did not have the right to kill Martha Collins. In our society, we cannot tolerate people killing one another over arguments and disputes. There are criminal and civil courts in which to resolve these disagreements.

"So at the conclusion of the trial, I will ask you to

render a verdict of guilty so that a message can be sent to others who might think they can get away with murder simply by pretending to have temporarily lost their cognitive ability and understanding of what is right and wrong. Thank you."

"Mr. Webster," the Judge said.

"Thank you, Your Honor. ... Ladies and gentlemen.

"Mr. Blake has told you that Erica was trying to protect herself from the disclosure of an illicit love affair. This is puzzling since there was nothing illicit about the love between Erica Fox and Richard Coleman that inevitably led to their marriage on the day of Mrs. Collins's unfortunate death. The only person who objected to the relationship was Mrs. Collins who had no standing whatsoever to complain. In fact, she had lost an attempt to become Erica's guardian when the Court found Erica to be mature and responsible enough to be emancipated at age seventeen. Mrs. Collins's interference in Erica's life was nothing more than malicious meddling.

"Mr. Blake has suggested here today that you should be wary of a defense of temporary insanity as it is often a frivolous, contrived defense. Well, it doesn't matter what Mr. Blake thinks of this defense as it is the law and if we prove it you are compelled as jurors to render a verdict of not guilty by reason of temporary insanity. We will concede that the elements of the defense of temporary insanity are stringent as they should be. Nevertheless, we believe we can easily demonstrate that on the night of April 3, 1980, Erica Fox was so traumatized by the situation in which she found herself, that she lost all control of her actions and did not know what she was doing when she apparently took the life of her Aunt, Martha Collins.

"Now I know at first blush you say, but how could she have just totally lost it? During the next few weeks, we will bring on a host of witnesses who will testify to the long-simmering hatred and bitterness between the two branches of the Fox family. You'll learn how Martha Collins fell from her father's grace when she ran away from home as a teenager and how she was cut out of his will. We will bring in witnesses who will testify to the animosity, hatred, and feuding that became an obsession between these family members. You'll be shocked at the dirty tricks that took place and the constant attempts to subvert each other's lives.

"Finally, Erica Fox will testify and explain how sixteen years of animosity that were inflicted upon her poisoned her mind and made her feel great bitterness towards her aunt. She'll tell how evil her aunt was and how she was determined to ruin Erica's life. Finally, she'll explain the events that led up to the tragic confrontation between her and her aunt. You'll understand how sixteen years of simmering hatred suddenly exploded into a flurry of totally spontaneous and uncontrollable violence. And when we are done, I'm confident you will agree that Erica was no more responsible for Martha Collin's death than was Martha Collins herself for perpetuating nearly two decades of ill will.

"It is your duty as jurors to determine the facts of this case. The Court will instruct you on the law and how to apply the facts to the law. During the course of the trial, I would ask you to pay close attention to the definitions and instructions given to you. It is your duty to follow the letter of the law without regard to your personal opinions or predispositions. Thank you."

A commotion broke out after Webster concluded his opening statement. The judge started to bang his gavel but decided instead to call a short recess. During the break, I was able to talk to Erica for a minute.

"So, Webster did good, huh?" I said.

"It seemed like it but you never know what the jury is thinking," Erica replied.

"How are you feeling? Are you okay?"

"Yes, I'll be fine. I'm just a little scared now that the trial is underway."

"I'm so sorry, honey," I said. "I wish I could do something."

"Any word from Mr. Clark?"

"No, I called him yesterday, but he didn't return my call. Apparently, he's out of town."

"Great," Erica said.

"Maybe he's trying to track down the stewardess."

"How long do think it will take the DA to put on his case?" Erica asked.

"Three or four days."

"So we've got maybe a week left until-"

"Yeah, until you're acquitted," I said.

Erica smiled, shook her head. "You're such an optimist."

"I have faith in Webster. And you, too."

Erica looked back at the bench as the bailiff yelled, "All rise!" She took my hand, squeezed it, and then returned to the defense table.

"Call your first witness," the Judge said.

"The state calls Detective Vincent Perkins," Blake said.

The bailiff swore in Detective Perkins, and he took the stand. After going through some routine preliminary questions, he began to explain the prosecution's theory as to the events of April 3, 1980.

"We got a call about 10 p.m. about a possible homicide at the Starlight Motel in Dallas near Parkland Hospital," Perkins said. "My partner and I immediately went there to investigate reports of a woman being killed."

"And what did you find when you got there?" Blake asked.

"There was indeed a dead female, approximately fifty years old in Room 147. She had been hit over the head and then suffocated with a pillow."

"Were you able to identify the body?"

"Well, we initially thought it was Erica Fox because we

found her purse in the room, but then upon further investigation, we realized Miss Fox was only a teenager. Later on, we discovered Mrs. Collins' purse and confirmed that indeed it was she who had been killed," Perkins said.

"Were you able to locate any witnesses?" Blake asked.

"The motel manager for one," Perkins said. "She had talked to Mrs. Collins by telephone earlier when she made a long-distance phone call. She had also talked to Erica Fox when she came by looking for Mrs. Collins' room number. There was also a guest in the motel who saw Erica Fox leave the victim's room a little after 10 o'clock."

"Is that all?"

"That was it at the motel. We later interviewed a convenience store clerk and some teenagers who saw Erica at the nearby 7-11."

"Thank you, Detective Perkins. Pass the witness."

"Very well," the Judge said. "Mr. Webster."

"Thank you, your honor. Mr. Perkins, doesn't it appear rather odd to you that Erica Fox left her purse at the scene of the crime?"

"Yes, it was rather stupid," he said.

"Have you ever seen that happen before?"

"No, one time a drunken motorist ran down a pedestrian over in Oak Lawn and then smashed into a chain-link fence. His car wasn't damaged too much, so he backed up and fled the scene of the crime. There was just one problem though, he left his license plate on chain link fence."

The audience laughed.

"Yes, but there is one difference. Your drunken motorist had no way of knowing he was leaving incriminating evidence behind. On the other hand, any woman would almost immediately remember she didn't have her purse with her. For a woman to leave her purse behind would be like a man leaving without shoes."

"So, she was probably upset, she had just murdered

someone."

"Objection! Your Honor, "Non-responsive! Move to strike," Webster said.

"Objection sustained. Detective, you know better than that."

"Yes, sir," Perkins said.

"The jury will disregard Detective Perkin's last statement."

Webster continued. "Yes, she was very upset. So upset, she left her purse and ran three blocks to a 7-11 where she finally had a complete breakdown, right?"

"I don't know what you mean by breakdown," Perkins said.

"Well, tell us her condition when she was arrested."

"She was found sitting on the sidewalk in front of the Seven-Eleven."

"Was she crying?"

"Yes."

"This was late at night in not such a hot neighborhood, right?"

"Yes, it after 10:30, and no, I wouldn't walk my dog in that neighborhood," Perkins said.

"Did she try to run when the police arrived?" Webster asked.

"No."

"She was in no condition to run, was she?"

"I don't know what was going on inside her brain. All I can say is she didn't put up any struggle when she was asked to come downtown."

"No further questions at this time, Your Honor," Webster said.

"Very well, Detective Perkins, you may stand down," the Judge said. "Mr. Blake, call your next witness."

"Yes, Sir. The state calls Jayne Shah."

Mrs. Shah was called from the hall by the bailiff and

made her way up to the witness stand. She was a small woman with a pleasant smile. She appeared to be quite nervous. The bailiff administered the oath and Blake commenced his cross-examination.

"Mrs. Shah. Are you employed?" Blake asked.

"Yes, Sir. My husband and I own the Starlight Motel here in Dallas."

"I see, and do you work at the motel?"

"Yes, I'm the manager."

"And were you on duty on the night of April 3, 1980?"

"Oh yes, I'm always on duty. I live there."

"Mrs. Shah, I want you to take a good look at the young lady at the defense table and tell us if you've ever seen that woman before."

"Yes, don't you know, I saw her on the night you mentioned, April 3."

"When was it that you saw her?" Blake asked.

Erica stared at the woman, took a deep breath, and then readjusted herself in her seat.

"Let me see. It was about 9:45 or so in the evening. I'm pretty sure, you know."

"Okay, please explain where you saw her."

"She came into the office and asked for Mrs. Collins' room number."

"Did you give it to her?" Blake asked.

"Well, it is not our policy to give out our guest's room numbers, you know, but Mrs. Erica said it was her aunt and that she'd be so very upset if I didn't give her the number."

"So, you gave it to her?"

"Yes, I'm afraid I did and I'm so ashamed," Mrs. Shah said.

"Ashamed?"

"Yes, if I hadn't given it to her-"

"Objection! Your Honor. "Mrs. Shah's shame is not relevant and I'm afraid she's about to say something that would be conclusive and highly prejudicial," Webster said.

"Sustained."

"Mrs. Shah, did you see Mrs. Collins at all on April third?" Blake asked.

"No, but I talked to her on the telephone."

"I see, and what did you talk about?" Blake asked.

"I just helped her make a long-distance telephone call," Mrs. Shah said.

"What time was that?"

"About 9:30," she said.

"Do you recall who she called?"

"She said she was calling her son who was staying in Waco that night for some reason."

"Did she get through to him?" Blake asked.

"No. I don't think so," she said.

"Did you have any other contact with Erica Fox or Mrs. Collins that day?"

"No."

"Pass the witness."

"Mr. Webster," the Judge said.

"Mrs. Shah. Did Erica Fox say anything to you other than what you've testified to already?"

"No."

"Was she upset?" Webster asked.

"Yes, very upset," Mrs. Shah replied. "She was talking so fast I could hardly understand her. My English is pretty good, you know, but not that good."

"Yes, could you tell if she had been crying?" Blake asked.

"Oh gosh. Maybe, her eyes were a little red."

"Is that why you gave her the room number, because she was so upset?"

"Yes, I felt sorry for her. I thought something terrible must have happened to her," Mrs. Shah said.

"When you talked to Mrs. Collins on the phone, was

she upset?" Webster asked.

"Well, she was a trifle upset when she wasn't able to reach her son."

"I see," Webster said. "Did she say anything?"

"Only that she could never find him when she needed him."

"Did you see anyone else that night who was looking for Mrs. Collins?"

"Well, there was a man, you know, sitting in the parking lot for quite a good bit. Then he got out of his car and went to her room."

"Did he go inside?" Webster asked.

"I didn't see him go inside. You see, I don't have a clear view of that room from my office," Mrs. Shah said.

"What did he look like?"

"He was a thin man, medium height, and wearing an expensive suit. I only saw him from the back, you know, so I don't know what he looked like."

"When did you see him?" Webster asked.

"Just after Mrs. Coleman came by my office," Mrs. Shah replied.

"How long after?"

"Oh, well. Maybe three or four minutes."

"So he just disappeared?"

"Some new guests came in, and I was busy checking them in, you see, and when I was done and looked back over there he was gone," Mrs. Shah said.

Webster turned and looked back at Erica. "Pass the witness," he said.

"No further questions," Blake replied.

"Very well, Mrs. Shah. You may stand down," the Judge said. "All right it's getting late. We'll recess until ten o'clock tomorrow morning."

Erica got up, turned, and looked at me. I smiled and managed to get a half-smile in return. After she conferred with

Webster a minute, she joined me, and we left the courthouse. Although usually talkative, Erica didn't say two words to me on the way to the car. During the drive home, she sat silently, staring out the front window. Finally, I couldn't stand it so I tried to get her to talk.

"Webster did a pretty good job today on cross, don't you think?" I asked.

"Uh-huh," Erica said.

"He's setting up a pretty good foundation for your temporary insanity defense."

"You think so?"

"Yeah."

"Who do you think the man was that the manager saw?" Erica asked.

"Arnold, I'm sure. God, I wish Clark would get back to us. He must know we're running out of time."

"He's not going to find out anything," Erica said.

"Why do you say that? Don't be such a pessimist."

"I'm just being realistic. It's all going to come down to my performance on the stand."

"You'll knock 'em dead," I said.

"Maybe, maybe not. I just wish we could run away."

"We've been through this before, honey," I said.

"I know. But I'm really scared I'll get convicted. I just wish we could get the hell out of the country."

"Where would we go, anyway?"

"I've heard about a little country in Central America that is supposed to be paradise."

"Really, what's it called?"

"Belize."

"Belize? I've never heard of it."

"It's very remote and isolated. No one would ever find us there."

"How would we live," I asked.

"We could get jobs. We'd survive."

"How did you hear about it?" I asked.

"My mother was born there," Erica replied.

"You're kidding?"

"No, she had just immigrated a few years before she married my father."

"So that's probably where she is then?" I said.

"Uh-huh. I wish I could see her before I die," Erica said.

"You're not going to die," I said. "Do you want me to find her?"

"No, I need you here with me."

"God, honey. I'm so sorry. We should have gone to Belize when we were in Barbados. Why didn't you tell me your mother was there?"

"I didn't know for sure she was there. And I didn't want to spoil our vacation."

"I'd do anything to make you happy. You know that," I reminded her.

Erica smiled and wiped a tear from her eye with her sleeve. Then she scooted over next to me, took my hand, and started playing with it like she loved to do. Talking about Erica's mother made me realize I hadn't even told my parents about Erica. With so much happening it had slipped my mind.

"I wonder if my parents have heard about what's going on."

"Probably not. I doubt they cover Texas murder trials in Santa Barbara," Erica said.

"Should I call them?"

"If you feel you should," Erica said. "What do you think?"

"They'll just worry."

"They might be mad if they find out on their own before you tell them," Erica said.

"How could I possibly explain all this to them?" I said. "They'll never understand it. I don't understand it myself."

"But they have a right to know."

"I haven't talked to them in over a year."

"Why?"

"We're not close."

"Isn't it funny, I want my parents back so bad, but I can't have them. Yours are but a phone call away and you won't pick up the phone. Did something happen?"

"No, they just have their life and I have mine," I said.

"But-."

"I'm just a typical ungrateful kid, okay! I'll call them if things look bad. I'll explain everything before we kill ourselves."

"Why won't you tell me the truth. I've told you everything about my family."

I sighed. "Okay, my father isn't my real father. He adopted me when I was a baby."

"Oh, well he's pretty close to being your real father then," Erica said.

"I know and I should have been satisfied with that."

"What do you mean?"

"After I graduated from high school, I got this incredible yearning to find my real father. I don't why but it just happened."

"I can understand that," Erica said.

"I made the mistake of telling my father, my adoptive father, of my plans to try to find my real father. He went ballistic. We got into a big argument. He told me about my real father. He said he was a drunk who frequently abused my mother. I thought he was lying to me so I got really pissed off and said some things I shouldn't have. We've barely spoken since that day."

"Oh God, that's terrible, Rich. How long has it been since that happened?"

"Nine years."

"Oh God. ... It's time you two forgave each other."

I choked u. "I know, but it's hard."

Erica put her arm around me and kissed me on the cheek. We embraced.

After we got home that evening, I wasn't sleepy. I didn't want to go to bed because once the night had passed, I knew we would be just one day closer to the end. Eventually, I did turn in but instead of sleeping, I watched the minutes on the clock radio change one by one for over an hour. Still unable to sleep, I got up and went to the bathroom. Erica was sleeping soundly so I walked into the living room and looked out the window into the night. It was clear and a full moon illuminated the usually dark street. After a while, I came back to bed and watched Erica sleep. She was like an angel, so peaceful, so serene. I felt like waking her and making love to her, but she needed her rest. Tomorrow would be another difficult day. How she could sleep so soundly with the weight she had to bear, was beyond my comprehension.

The next day, the trial began again promptly at ten a.m. Blake called several witnesses; the clerk at Seven Eleven, one of the police officers who had booked Erica, and the medical examiner. Then he called the State's psychologist, Marvin Bentley.

Dr. Bentley related all his accomplishments over the years, how he had examined and tested Erica, and then Blake asked him about the results of his findings.

"So, after you had met with Erica and analyzed her tests have you been able to reach any conclusions?"

"Yes, despite a very difficult life she has been able to adjust extraordinarily well. She demonstrates a little depression but, considering what she's been through, I think that's pretty normal," Dr. Bentley said.

"Do you think she could have lost control of herself such that she didn't know what she was doing?"

"No, she is very intelligent and has a lot of drive and determination. She's not only totally in control at all times but she has the type of personality that controls other people."

"You don't think that anything could have happened to her to make her snap and act without an understanding of what she was doing?"

"No, sir. Absolutely not. Not this woman."

"So, do you think she was temporarily insane when she murdered her aunt?"

"Objection," Webster said. "The question assumes a fact yet to be established, is inflammatory and highly prejudicial."

"Sustained."

"So, do you think she was temporarily insane when she suffocated her aunt?"

"Objection," Webster said. "Assumes-"

"She's admitted by pleading not guilty by reason of insanity that she suffocated her aunt," the Judge said. "Objection overruled. Let's get on with it."

"You may answer Dr. Bentley," Blake said.

"No, she did it knowingly and intentionally."

"Thank you, doctor, pass the witness."

"Mr. Webster," the Judge said. "Your witness."

"Thank you, Your Honor."

"Dr. Bentley, now your evaluation of Erica was done after she met and fell in love with Richard Coleman, is that right?"

"Yes."

"What did Erica tell you about her relationship with Mr. Coleman," Webster asked.

Dr. Bentley laughed. "She told me she seduced him. That's what I mean about her being a controlling person. She wanted him so she seduced him into a rather dangerous relationship."

"After the seduction how did the relationship go?"

"Very well. They filled a void each had in their lives at the time."

"So, do you think Erica was mentally better off after

meeting and falling in love with Mr. Coleman than she was, let's say, right after her father's death?"

"Oh, most definitely," Dr. Bentley said.

"So, you never examined the Erica Fox that was lonely, depressed, and full of programmed hatred for Martha Collins, did you?"

"Objection," Blake yelled. "The question assumes facts not in evidence."

"Your honor," Webster said. "I'm just rephrasing the doctor's testimony. He's an expert witness. I'm allowed a little latitude."

"Overruled," the judge said.

Webster said, "You examined the girl who had suddenly found love and happiness in Richard Coleman, isn't that right?"

"Well, it's not that simple, but I see your point," Dr. Bentley said.

"Let me ask you, doctor," Webster said. "Knowing Erica's family history the way you do, don't you think it was a pretty traumatic jolt to her when Aunt Martha, the family villain, appears and threatens to take away the love and happiness in her life?"

Dr. Bentley started to answer but Webster interrupted him.

"Don't you think all those memories of fear, hatred, and anxiety suddenly erupted in her mind? Don't you think she was devastated by the thought of a return to the loneliness, depression, and despair that was her life prior to meeting Richard?"

"Objection!" Blake yelled. "Counsel is not allowing the witness to answer the questions."

"Sustained." the Judge said. "Mr. Webster."

"I apologize, your honor," Webster said and then looked at the witness. "You may answer."

"I'm sure she was," Dr. Bentley said.

"And when Erica actually saw Aunt Martha and she refused to back off from her threats to blow the whistle on Richard Coleman, don't you think it's possible Erica snapped? Don't you think she might have totally lost it? Isn't that why Martha Collins is dead?"

"Objection," Blake said. "Mr. Webster is testifying again, your honor."

"No, Your Honor. I'm simply posing a hypothetical question to an expert witness."

The judge thought for a moment, then nodded. "Overruled, but let the witness answer each question, Mr. Webster."

"Yes, Sir," Webster said. "You may answer Dr. Bentley."

"That's an interesting theory but not one I would adopt."

"But it is possible?"

"Anything's possible," Dr. Bentley said.

"Thank you, doctor. No further questions."

Webster's cross-examination of Dr. Bentley lifted my spirits incredibly. For the first time in days, I saw Erica smile. The knot in my stomach that I had feared was permanent, momentarily eased. The press and the gallery seemed for the first time to show a little sympathy for Erica. It was a good moment, a very good moment. Unfortunately, it was soon forgotten when Arnold Collins took the stand.

"What kind of woman was your mother?" Blake asked.

"She was a very kind, loving, and understanding woman."

"When you were growing up, could you talk to her?"

"Oh yes, she always had time for me. I always discussed my problems with her."

"What about this feud between your mother and her father?"

"It's really been blown out of proportion. My mother and

grandfather had a falling out, but she wasn't bitter. She always said she didn't want her father's money anyway. She thought money corrupted and made otherwise good people become evil," Collins said.

Erica laughed and then covered her mouth to stop herself. Webster smiled.

"Objection. Your Honor," Blake said.

"Mr. Webster, please control your client," the judge replied.

"Yes, sir. I'm sorry," Webster said and then whispered something to Erica.

Blake said, "Do you think your mother would have ever intentionally done anything to hurt Erica?"

"No, she loved Erica," Collins said. "She always said the family was of paramount importance. She even invited Erica to live with her when her father died."

"Let's move to the day of the murder. Did you know your mother was going to Dallas?"

"No, I was at an Alumni meeting and dance in Waco. I didn't hear anything until after she had been murdered."

"Did you go to Dallas that night?"

"No, I stayed all night at the La Quinta Motel."

"Were you alone?"

"No, I was with a friend," Collins said.

"No further questions, pass the witness," Blake said.

"Mr. Webster," the Judge said. "Your witness."

"Thank you, Your Honor. ... Mr. Collins. You represented your mother when she filed an objection to Erica's petition to be emancipated, isn't that right?"

"Yes."

"Erica was seventeen, wasn't she?"

"Yes."

"And Erica wanted to stay in Dallas and attend SMU, isn't that right?"

"Yes."

"Why did your mother object to Erica's express wishes?"

"She didn't think a teenager should be alone in a big city. She was worried about her and for good reason, I might point out," Collins said.

"Was that really it, or was she doing what she had done for the last twenty years, trying to cause her brother grief over the disinheritance. Except, of course, her brother was dead, and Erica was the only target left."

"That's not true."

"She was a bitter woman, wasn't she?"

"No, not really."

"How much money did she lose when she was cut out of her daddy's will?" Webster asked.

"A little over two million dollars."

The crowd stirred, and the judge sat up straight in his chair. Arnold took a deep breath.

"How old were you when this happened?"

"About twelve or thirteen."

"Was your mother angry?" Webster asked.

"Well, wouldn't you be?" Collins said.

"You remember that day well, don't you, Mr. Collins?" Webster said. "Did she yell, scream obscenities or throw around the furniture? All of the above?"

Collins frowned and glared at Webster. "I don't know. I left shortly after she found out."

"Where did you go?"

"A friend's house."

"You couldn't take it, huh?" Webster said.

"No, that wasn't it."

"Did your mother do anything about the disinheritance?" Webster asked.

"She consulted an attorney but was told it would be very expensive to contest the will."

"In fact, wasn't she told that since there had been a

long-standing estrangement between her and her father, it was unlikely she would be successful?"

"I don't know what she was told, " Collins said.

"But you're an attorney, isn't it unlikely she would have been successful?"

"Objection!" Calls for a legal conclusion and it's irrelevant anyway," Blake said.

"I'll allow it," the judge said.

"Perhaps," Collins said.

"So did she ever forgive her father?"

"How do you forgive someone who is dead?" Collins asked.

"By leaving the rest of the family alone," Webster replied.

"I don't know what you mean."

"How often would your mother talk about your grandfather."

"I don't remember."

"How often did she curse him?"

"I don't know," Collins said.

"It was every day, wasn't it," Webster said. "She was obsessed, wasn't she?"

"No, she wasn't obsessed. She just had trouble dealing with it."

"Oh, I see. Did she go to her brother, Franklin, and ask him to give her half of the inheritance?" Webster asked.

"Yes."

"When he didn't give it to her, did she have trouble dealing with that?"

"Of course, she did," Collins said. "It was half her inheritance, and she wanted it. She was entitled to it."

"How did you feel about it?" Webster asked.

"I thought Mother should have had the money. She worked so hard, but she couldn't earn a decent living. It's tough for a single mother in our society. Yes, we could have used the money, there's no doubt about that. But what was particularly galling was to watch Uncle Franklin blow it."

"Did your mother complain about Franklin's gambling?"

"Well, yes, that upset her," Collins said.

"How about his propensity for women and fancy cars?"

"Obviously, she didn't like that much either."

"So, do you admit there was some hostility between your mother and Franklin," Webster said.

"I think that's obvious, but it wasn't an obsession. It was just natural for her to be disappointed."

"Did your mother ever seek counseling or psychiatric help for her obsession?"

"Objection," Blake yelled. "The witness testified there was no obsession."

"Withdrawn. Did your mother ever seek counseling for her disappointment?"

"No," Collins said.

"That's too bad."

Blake stood up and yelled. "Objection, Your Honor."

"Withdrawn," Webster said.

"So, you testified your mother was a model parent."

"Yes, she was a good mother."

"She was able to keep her frustration at losing her inheritance from affecting your family life."

"Yeah, pretty much."

"What about the divorce?"

"What about it?"

"How did she take it?"

"Objection! Your Honor. Irrelevant," Blake said.

"Your Honor, the witness testified about how wonderful his mother was. I have a right to impeach him."

"I'll allow it but you better be leading somewhere," the Judge said.

"Thank you, Your Honor. ... Mr. Collins, you may answer the question."

"Obviously, it wasn't pleasant."

"Isn't it a fact your life was a living hell?"

"No."

"Your mother was overbearing, always interfering in your life, wasn't she?"

"No."

"She took all her frustrations from the loss of her inheritance and the divorce out on you, didn't she? She made your life a living hell, didn't she?"

Arnold didn't answer immediately. He took a deep breath. "It wasn't like that. She wasn't a happy woman, but she was still a good mother."

Webster paused; he knew he was running up a dead end. "You didn't have a fairy tale childhood as you testified earlier, did you."

Arnold shrugged and replied, "Not exactly."

"So, it's your testimony that you didn't go to Dallas on the night of the murder."

"Correct."

"What if I were to tell you I've got two witnesses that saw you at the motel on the night of the murder."

"That's possible."

"Pardon me?" Webster said.

"I said I didn't go to Dallas from Waco. My flight to Waco went by way of Dallas. Since I had an hour layover between flights, I went to my mother's motel hoping to catch her. Unfortunately, I missed her. If someone saw me at her motel it was in the afternoon."

"Objection, Your Honor," Blake said. "This whole line of questioning is irrelevant. The defendant has pleaded not guilty by reason of insanity."

"Your Honor," Webster said. "It's important that we know where Mr. Collins was at the time of the murder. We believe he may have been at the hotel when she was murdered. If he was there, then he would have seen the defendant and could testify as to her mental condition."

"I think you've gone far enough with this line of questioning," the Judge said. "If the witnesses you speak of confirms that Mr. Collins was at the motel near the time of the murder then I'll allow you to recall him and continue this line of questioning. So, at this time, I'm sustaining the objection. Let's move on."

"Okay, you testified you were with a friend on the night of the murder. What kind of a friend? Casual or- "

"We live together in Odessa. We actually met while we were both attending Baylor," Webster said.

"Really, is she available to corroborate your testimony?"

"Yes."

"What's her name?"

"Well, actually his name is Ralph."

Whispers broke out in the Gallery, and Erica looked over at me and smiled. It was obvious from the look on her face this was the first she'd heard of Arnold's homosexuality.

"Oh, I see," Webster said and then thought a moment. "Did your mother know you were gay?"

"Of course."

"Did she approve?"

Blake jumped up and yelled, "Objection! Your Honor. This line of questioning is totally irrelevant."

"Sustained," the judge replied.

"All right . . . does Ralph have a last name?"

"Yes, Benitez."

"I see. Did you talk at all to your mother that night?" Webster asked.

"No."

"Did Ralph talk to her?"

"Not to my knowledge."

"Where is Ralph right now?"

"He's back in Odessa. He wanted to come to the trial,

but he had to work."

"So, you're sure you two were together in Waco the entire evening?"

"Yes, our flight arrived at about 6:30. We went straight to the motel and then to the reunion."

"Where was Ralph when you went to see your mother in Dallas?"

"He stayed at the terminal."

"And you two took off from Dallas together and arrived in Waco at 6:30 p.m."

"Correct."

"Pass the witness," Webster said.

By the end of the day Blake had called his last witness and the judge recessed the case until the following morning. Ever since we had learned of Arnold's stop in Dallas and his homosexuality, my mind had been working hard to analyze this new information. Webster had immediately picked up on the possibilities that opened up with a new player in the game. Unfortunately, due to the insanity plea, the judge wouldn't allow Webster to delve too deeply into how Ralph and Aunt Martha got along.

I couldn't imagine Aunt Martha being thrilled about her son being gay. She must have been quite distraught about it, and knowing her, she would have done everything in her power to keep Ralph and Arnold apart. Suddenly we had another prime suspect in Aunt Martha's murder. The only problem was proof. Right now, the idea that Ralph had killed Aunt Martha was pure speculation. Arnold had testified that Ralph had been with him on the flight to Dallas, but he could be lying either because he was a co-conspirator, or he wanted to protect his lover.

Should I launch an all-out investigation of Ralph or leave it alone? I was feeling better about how things were going. It seemed the momentum of the case had shifted these last two days, yet if the real killer could be identified, then that would eliminate the possibility of an adverse verdict. I decided, for Erica's sake, I had to try one more time to find the truth. On the way home I stopped at the first phone booth I saw and called Mr. Clark. I asked him to do a complete background investigation on Ralph Benitez and report back to me immediately. He promised to get right on it.

20
Broken Promise

That night Erica was in an amorous mood. She made a candlelight dinner, and we danced to some slow jazz on the radio. It seemed that she had buried the trial somewhere deep in the recesses of her mind so that she could enjoy the final moments of her life. No matter how optimistic Webster or I felt she seemed to be preparing herself for the worst. Each moment had become a precious commodity to her. Sex between us had always been great, but ever since the night, Erica was arrested our love life had intensified and become much more physical. I was so exhausted when she was finished with me, I slept all night for the first time in weeks. The next morning Erica had to shake me hard to get me to wake up.

"Is it time to get up already?" I said. "I'm still tired from last night."

She smiled. "What's wrong, am I too much for you?"

"Last night you were. What in the hell got into you?"

"We may only have a few days left; we better make the best of them."

"A few more nights like that and I won't need the cyanide."

Erica laughed. Then she climbed on top of me, ran her hands through my hair, and said, "Maybe we can sneak into the bathroom at lunch."

"Oh, good idea. Maybe we should invite the press in

too. They'd like to watch us make love."

Erica sat up and smiled. "Sure, why not."

"I love you," I said.

"Me. too. How many more days do you think we have?"

"Until what?"

"Until the jury decides my fate?"

"You mean, our fate," I said.

"Right."

"I don't know, probably two or three."

"We should bring the cyanide tomorrow just in case."

"Erica," I said, as I pushed her off me. "We can't kill ourselves. Get real."

"But we have an agreement."

"I know, but I can't commit suicide, and I can't let you do it either. I love you too much."

"Rich, you promised. You can't do this to me now. I've already prepared myself to die for you."

"I know it would be romantic, and I sure as hell don't want to live without you, but even if you're convicted, we can appeal. You may not ever go to prison," I said.

"I can't take that chance. I'd rather die than live like a rat in a cage."

"I won't let you kill yourself, damn it!" I yelled.

"How will you stop me?"

"I'll tell them you're suicidal. They'll search you when you get to court and keep a close eye on you."

"You bastard!" Erica screamed and then slapped me across the face.

"Erica!" I yelled as I watched her storm through the bedroom door. "Erica! Come back here."

I fell back into the bed and took a deep breath. I was overwhelmed with guilt for breaking our pact. There had to be a way out of this. It was too early to give up. There still was hope. Finally, I got up and went into the living room expecting to see Erica sulking on the sofa. I looked around but the room was empty. After checking the bathroom, I assumed she went to the courthouse without me.

"Damn," I said, and then went back into the bedroom to get dressed.

When I got to the Dallas County Courthouse I parked underground as usual. After walking through the tunnel between the parking lot and the courthouse, I was met with the usual mob of reporters wanting my opinion as to how the trial was going.

"Mr. Coleman, where's Erica this morning?" a reporter asked.

"I don't know. I assume she's inside."

I pushed my way through the crowd and walked through the glass doors into the basement of the courthouse. After waiting for an elevator, a minute, Webster came up behind me.

"So, where's Erica?"

"I imagine she's upstairs in the courtroom."

"Well, this pressure has to be getting to her," Webster said.

"She was taking it pretty well until this morning."

The elevator door finally opened, and we stepped inside. It didn't seem like such a good idea to tell Webster about our little pact. If Erica was upstairs and he knew she was suicidal he might be compelled to do something about it. Perhaps I had been wrong to break our pact. How could she want me to die? If I were on trial I sure as hell wouldn't want her to die. When the elevator door opened my heart started to beat faster and faster. I longed to see her pretty face, embrace her and tell her I was sorry. Quickly I made my way to the courtroom and went inside. I couldn't stand the thought of her being angry with me. We had to makeup, we just had to. I scanned the big room looking for her.

"She's not here," Webster said.

"Maybe she went to the ladies' room."

"What did you two argue about, anyway?"

"Oh, nothing of any significance. She just wanted me to do something that I didn't want to do. You know how she has to always have her way. It was no big deal."

"Maybe it was to her."

"She'll be here, I'm sure she's just stewing somewhere. She'll be here before the case reconvenes."

It was a lie, but what could I say? Suddenly I realized Erica was gone. My betrayal had devastated her. I felt ashamed. The last thing in the world I had ever wanted to do was to let Erica down. I loved her dearly. Now, suddenly I realized I was prepared to die for her. Why had I let her get away? "Oh, God. Please help me," I said softly.

"What?" Webster said.

"Nothing."

I spotted Joe coming into the courtroom. I went over to him and explained the situation. He said he'd go back to the condo and see if she was there. He left just as the court reporter entered the room. This meant the judge was about to take the bench. Webster gave me a distressful look and then sat down at the counsel table. I closed my eyes and prayed. Finally, the door to the judge's chamber opened and the bailiff said, "All rise."

Everyone stood up as the judge took the bench. His attention was immediately focused on the empty chair next to Webster."

"Mr. Webster, where is your client this morning?"

Webster stood up and looked over at me. "Your honor. I don't frankly know. She and Mr. Coleman had a little argument this morning, and she ran off. We were expecting her to be here this morning, but we frankly don't know where she is. Perhaps she got caught in a traffic jam on Central Expressway."

"Well, I suspected that little lady would skip town sooner or later. That's why I set her bond so high. Mr.

Coleman, do you have any idea where your wife is?"

I stood up and said, "No, sir. I'm sure she'll be here shortly. I've sent someone to look for her."

"Well, I'm going to recess the case for one hour. If she's not here by eleven o'clock I'm going to issue a warrant for her arrest and revoke her bond."

"Your Honor," Webster said. "I think that's a little premature. Mrs. Coleman may be sick or she might have gotten into an accident or something."

"You're right, counselor," said the Judge. "I want to be reasonable. I'll give you until tomorrow morning at 10 a.m. If she's not in this courtroom ready to proceed, then I'll issue the warrant and revoke her bond. Is that understood?"

"Yes, Your Honor," Webster said.

From the courthouse, I went directly home. I was expecting to see Joe there, but he was nowhere to be seen. After I checked her closet and found her suitcases and clothes gone, I called the bank to check Erica's bank account. Sure enough, she had drained it of the seven thousand two hundred twenty-two dollars that had been on deposit the day before. It was ten forty-five. I figured she had an hour and a half jump on us. The logical place for her to go was the airport. I grabbed a photograph of her and went to Love Field.

After parking in short-term parking, I entered the airport and started searching. It seemed logical that she would be headed overseas so I went to the international portion of the terminal first and started showing everyone Erica's picture and asked them if they had seen her. After stopping at the Braniff, American, and Delta ticket counters I turned to leave only to find myself staring Detective Perkins and two police officers in the face.

"Going somewhere, Mr. Coleman?"

"No, I'm looking for Erica. I figured she's headed overseas. I wanted to stop her."

"Really? Or did you two plan this escape?"

"You think I'm crazy? We've got a million-dollar bond up for godsakes. I just want to find Erica and talk some sense into her."

Detective Perkins smiled. "You know Mr. Coleman if Erica doesn't show up by ten tomorrow this may be the first murder trial in Dallas County history that makes a profit."

"Don't count your money yet. I've still got twenty-two hours to find her."

"Did she have a passport?" Perkins asked.

"Yeah, she does a lot of traveling."

"Great. She's probably halfway to Argentina by now."

"Argentina? Why would she go there?" I asked.

"A person with money can disappear in Argentina."

"But Erica doesn't have much money, most of what she had is all tied up in the bond."

"Well, if she contacts you, don't even think about sending her money or I'll slap your ass in jail as an accessory. I've already warned your friend."

"What friend?"

"Mr. Weston, we intercepted him leaving the airport about fifteen minutes ago."

"Oh, right. I asked him at the courthouse to go look for Erica. I guess we all came to the same conclusion."

"It was pretty obvious she had decided to run when she didn't show up in court today," Perkins said.

"I'm going to do everything in my power to get her back here by 10 a.m. tomorrow," I said. "She just got scared. This whole thing has been very hard on her."

"It's going to get a lot harder if her bond is revoked," Perkins said. "I don't think she'll like the accommodations at the Dallas County Jail."

Detective Perkins and his men turned and walked away. After they had disappeared around the corner, I resumed my search. Having no luck on international flights I decided she might have flown somewhere in the U.S. first and then flown out of the country. If she were going to South America, she'd have to go to Miami, so I went to each of the gates with flights there. After visiting the Continental and American gates I stopped at Gate 4A occupied by Braniff Airlines. A young lady was busy on a computer as I approached. I showed her Erica's picture. She stopped working and took a good look at the photograph. "Well, I think you're in luck. I do remember seeing her about an hour ago. Lets' see, flight 287 to Miami. She should be arriving in another twenty or thirty minutes."

"When's your next flight to Miami."

"It boards in twenty-two minutes."

"Can I get a ticket?"

"You'll have to go out to the ticket counter. I don't sell tickets here. You better hurry."

"Thank you so much. I've got to find her."

"Good luck."

It took a while to get my ticket, but I got back to the gate just in time to board. The ticket agent, who had helped me earlier, smiled and waved as I ran down the ramp. Once settled in my seat, I tried to relax and think. What would I do once I got to Miami? I had no idea where Erica was going: Barbados, the Cayman Islands, Argentina. I tried to put myself in Erica's shoes. Where would I go if I were desperate, alone, and with very little money? After careful consideration, I decided it would be Barbados. We had been there, she loved it, and she'd feel comfortable there at least for a while until she could sort things out. Thinking I had solved the puzzle, I let myself relax and fell asleep. Soon I was in the midst of a nightmare about the trial. Erica had been convicted and we had taken the cyanide. I woke up abruptly shaking and sweating profusely. People were looking at me. The stewardess asked if I was all right. I told her I was fine, but from the look on her face, I wasn't very convincing.

When we finally started our descent into Miami, I

began to get anxious. There was a slim possibility that Erica would have to wait for the next flight to Barbados and she could conceivably be there when I arrived. I prayed to God that would be the case. When the plane finally landed, I asked the attendant at the gate if she could check on the next BWAI flight to Barbados. She punched something into her computer and waited.

"Okay ... the next flight leaves in twelve minutes from Gate 23 N."

"Oh, shit, " I said and started running. Having taken the flight to Barbados I knew where the gate was situated. It was quite a distance, so I knew I had to run. Before I got to the gate, I had to pass through security, buy a ticket and get to the gate before the plane took off. As I approached the metal detectors a security guard intercepted me.

"What's the big hurry, sir?"

"My wife, I'm going to miss my wife."

The security guard took his time waving his metal detector all around me and then nodded that I could go on. When I finally reached the ticket office, there were just six minutes until the plane took off. The agent reluctantly issued me a ticket although she said she doubted I would make it in time. I ran as fast as I could toward the gate. Unfortunately, the international gates were at a remote location in the airport, and I had to board a tram to get to them. As I approached the tram the door was closing. I pounded on the door, but it was too late.

When I finally got on the next tram and arrived at the gate, the plane was taxiing down the runway. I went over to the window and watched it leave the gate area. "Damn it," I said.

I watched the plane get in line to take off, then I rushed over to the gate where a clerk was working and asked, "When is the next plane to Barbados?"

The clerk looked up. "Four-thirty, sir."

"I missed my flight. Can I get on the next one?"

"I think so, let me check," the clerk said as she started typing on her computer. "Yes, I've switched you to the next flight."

"Thank you."

Dejected, I went over to a chair and sat. It was two forty-five so that meant I had nearly two hours to wait. The worst thing was that Erica would have nearly two hours to get lost in Barbados and I was running out of time. If I didn't find her soon, we'd never make it back to Dallas by ten the next morning. I started to think of where Erica would go in Barbados. I figured she go to the Ginger Bay Beach Club. If she wasn't there when I arrived, I thought I'd find her at St. John's Catholic Church in the chapel praying. As I was thinking I felt a hunger pang in my stomach, so I figured I'd go get a bite to eat while I waited. As I walked by a lounge, I noticed a TV was on and I saw Erica's picture flashed on the screen. I went over to the TV and listened to the report.

It amazed me that the stations in Miami had already picked up the story. It was the money I figured. How often does someone lose a million dollars overnight? After listening to the story, I realized I was now a fugitive from the law. The reporter had stated that an arrest warrant was out for both Erica and me. I continued on toward the snack bar. When I got close, I noticed there were two policemen standing near the cash register. I stopped. Making a quick change of direction, I headed back to the gate.

I found an inconspicuous spot in the corner and waited. I scanned the waiting area for anyone who might look suspicious. After a long agonizing wait, the flight was finally called, and I boarded the plane to Barbados. Once in the air, I began to relax. Fortunately, it was a dinner flight, so it wasn't long before the food arrived. Not having eaten since breakfast I was famished and quickly devoured the small tray of food provided, drank a cup of coffee, and waited. It would only be a few more hours and I would be in Barbados.

It was dark when the plane landed. After I went through customs, I got a cab and went to the Ginger Bay Beach Club. I paid the cab driver and then went inside and straight to the front desk. A tall, dark, Latin man with a mustache stood behind the desk doing some paperwork.

"Excuse me, I wonder if my wife has arrived yet? Erica Fox. It may be under Erica Coleman."

The clerk looked up and then grabbed the guest register. He searched it for a moment, then looked up and shook his head. "Sorry, sir. I don't see anyone under either name."

"Are you sure?" I asked. "Here's a picture of her. Have you seen her here today?"

The clerk squinted to get a good look at the picture and then shook his head again. "No, sir. I haven't seen her."

"How long have you been on duty?"

"All day, if I'd seen a woman such as this, I surely would have remembered her," he said and then went on about his work.

Stunned, I closed my eyes. What was I to do now? In twelve hours, Erica would lose a million dollars, but that wasn't what was really bothering me. What if I never saw her again? What if she vanished? Perkins had said it was easy to disappear in Argentina. Maybe she was already gone forever.

I stood paralyzed before the front desk. Then I remembered the church. Maybe she went directly to the church to pray. I turned quickly, nearly knocking a lady down, and ran from the hotel. Someone was getting out of a cab so I jumped in and told the cab driver to take me to St. John's Catholic Church. He took the money from his last fare and then took off. When we arrived, the churchyard was deserted. I walked briskly up to the door and opened it. It was dark with only a few candles illuminating the church edifice. I closed my eyes and prayed that Erica would be inside, kneeling before the altar of God. As I approached the Chapel door, I placed my right arm on the doorknob and pulled it toward me. Once inside I quickly scanned the room hopefully, but my hopes were quickly dashed as I realized Erica was not there.

Devastated, I began wandering the streets of Barbados hoping somehow, I'd run into Erica. If I could just find her, I could charter a flight back to Dallas and make it by ten. After another hour of searching, I gave up and went into a bar. It was crowded with tourists, but I managed to find a table. It wasn't long before the barmaid came by to get my order. I smiled and ordered a rum and Coke. I wondered where Erica was. Was she also in a bar, alone in some strange land? Was she frightened? Was she thinking of me? I missed her terribly.

As the evening wore on, the barmaid made numerous trips to my table. Before long I was joined by a couple young ladies who talked me into buying them a drink. We talked and drank for quite a while. I was getting so drunk my head began to spin. When the bar finally closed, the two women helped me back to the Club where I checked in for the night. They wanted to join me in my room, but I said no, gave them a hundred bucks each, and went to bed.

In the morning I had a bad headache. After taking a long shower I went to the restaurant where I had proposed marriage to Erica. As I sat at the same table where we had made the ultimate commitment of love, I wondered if I'd ever see her again. Where could she be I said to myself. Where would my little darling go to hide from the world? Suddenly a tingling sensation came over me. Why had I been so stupid? How could I have not known where she would go? It was obvious. She was searching for her mother. She was in Belize.

21
Belmopan

Getting to Belmopan, the capital of Belize, from Barbados was not an easy task. First I had to fly to Caracas, then to San Pedro Sulsa, Honduras and finally Belmopan, Belize. Somewhere over the Caribbean, between Barbados and Caracas, Erica lost her million dollars. But that was history. My only concern now was finding her and getting her back to Dallas so she wouldn't be a fugitive from the law the rest of her life. The small plane landed in a torrential downpour. Not being prepared for damp weather, I got soaked between the plane and the customs office. As I looked at the old rusty hanger that housed the custom's building, I wondered how in the hell I was ever going to find Erica in this strange land.

It occurred to me that Erica must have passed through this same customs office. If that were true one of the custom's officers might remember her. While I was being processed, I showed the agent my picture of Erica and asked him if he had seen her in the last few days. He said no but pointed to another agent who had been working the day before. When my paperwork had been completed, I walked over to where the other man was working.

I held up Erica's picture and said, "My wife was supposed to have come through here yesterday or this morning and I wondered if you might have seen her? She was supposed to have left me a note before she left but she didn't do it. I'm really worried about her."

"Oh, yes, a very pretty lady. She came here yesterday afternoon on a flight from Cozumel."

"Really? . . . Oh, I'm so relieved. She must be at the hotel then. I'm surprised the desk clerk didn't know she had checked in. Thank you so much."

As I left the airport, I was mobbed by cab drivers wanting to take me into town. After carefully inspecting all of them I picked the least scrungy of the lot and had him take me to the best hotel in town. It was my fervent hope that this would be the place where I would find Erica. Following a wild ride through the narrow streets of Belmopan, we arrived at the Embassy Garden Hotel.

After getting settled in my hotel room, I collapsed on the bed and closed my eyes. A sharp hunger pain reminded me I hadn't eaten in thirty-six hours. The thought of eating had scarcely crossed my mind since Erica had disappeared. I decided I'd better get some food to keep up my strength. The hotel restaurant and bar were filled with customers unwinding after a hard day. I made my way into the crowded room and found a small table. Before long a waitress stopped and took my order.

Now that I was here in Belize, I wondered how I would find Erica's mother. That's where I figured I'd find my angry wife. Why had I betrayed her? I prayed she'd forgive me. I knew her mother's name was Carmen, but I wasn't sure if she would be going by her married name, Fox, or her maiden name, Ramirez.

A sense of helplessness overcame me. I recalled the day I had left home after fighting with my father. I was just seventeen and after storming out of the house, I felt very scared and alone. But this time the tables had turned. Erica had left me-or had she. Perhaps she was simply running for her life? She had wanted to run away with me, but I had refused. I had convinced her to stay and face the murder charge.

As I was reminiscing, the idea occurred to me that perhaps I could find the Belize equivalent of a private investigator to help me out. After dinner I inquired at the front desk and was referred to a man named Raul Price. The next morning, I took a cab to Mr. Price's place of business and went inside. The office was in an old adobe building and was cluttered and generally unkept. Mr. Price was half asleep in a chair by the window.

"I understand you're a private investigator," I said.

"Yes, that is correct. You have need of my services?"

"Yes, as a matter fact, I do. It's my wife. She's here looking for her mother, and I've lost track of her. I need to find her."

"What's her name?"

I told him and explained the situation.

"Okay, no problem. I'll need five hundred dollars up front."

"Do you take American Express?"

"No, only cash."

I pulled a wad of 100 dollar bills out of my pocket and carefully counted out five of them.

"Can I get a receipt?"

"Okay," Raul said, picking up a piece of scratch paper and writing out a makeshift receipt.

Reluctantly, I took the receipt, wondering if I had just thrown away $500. He smiled and said, "Okay, I'll find her. What hotel are you at?"

"The Embassy Garden."

"Okay, you go back to your hotel, and I'll call you when I know something."

"How long do you think it will take?"

"I don't know, maybe a couple of days. Don't worry, I'll find her."

It seemed weird just turning over my search to a

perfect stranger. What was I supposed to do while I waited? I needed some clothes since I hadn't been able to pack anything before I left Dallas. I went to the concierge and was referred to a clothing store down the street where I bought a few things. When I got back to the hotel, I decided I'd better call Erica's attorney to advise him of the situation and find out what had happened after Erica had skipped out in the middle of her trial. I waited until it was about 12:15, hoping to catch him at his lunch break. It wasn't easy getting through to Dallas from Belize, but eventually I made a connection.

"Have you found Erica?" Webster asked.

"No, but she's down here. I've got a private investigator looking for her right now. What's happening in the trial?"

"The judge made us continue on," Webster said. "I've got maybe another day until I run out of witnesses. If Erica isn't back here by tomorrow afternoon, I may have to let the case go to the jury without the benefit of her testimony. That would almost guarantee she'd be convicted."

"I know, I've been searching frantically for her these last two days."

"You know they've got a warrant out for your arrest too."

"Yeah, I heard that on a TV news broadcast in Miami," I said. "Detective Perkins saw me at the airport. He didn't buy my story obviously."

"I guess not. He told me he thinks Erica panicked during the trial and you covered for her while she got away. Then you took advantage of the first opportunity to follow her."

"What about the million-dollar bond? Why would we walk away from that?"

"He figures Erica finally realized her freedom was more valuable than money. Besides, with your talent for making money, you could make her another million pretty easy, right?" Webster said.

"I don't know about that, but that's the first intelligent

thing I've heard Perkins say. Erica's freedom is more important than money, but there's no guarantee that she wouldn't get caught even if she became a fugitive and went into hiding."

"That's right, so I hope you find her and can talk some sense into her," Webster said.

"I'm going to try like hell, if I get the chance."

"Okay, keep me posted. I'll stall as long as I can, but after tomorrow afternoon it may be all over."

"I'll call you if I find her and let you know when we'll be arriving," I said.

"Fine, good luck."

While I was killing time, I decided to call my mother to explain to her what was going on. I knew by now she must have heard about Erica, the trial and the warrant out for my arrest. It had been a long time since we had talked, and she didn't even know I had gotten married. I had a lot of explaining to do. She was relieved to get the call and offered me her usual motherly support and understanding. I promised to stay in touch.

An hour later I hung up the phone and collapsed on the bed. Since there was nothing to do but wait, I fell asleep and began to dream. In my dream I was floating above my body. I could see myself and Erica lying next to each other in the morgue. We were pale and stiff and two men in white coats were standing next to us talking. I couldn't hear them, but I could see their lips moving. I looked around and I saw Erica floating above me. She was smiling and beckoning me to catch up with her. After I took one last look at my mortal body, I ascended to her and took her hand. We couldn't talk but our minds seemed to communicate with each other without difficulty.

As we gazed into each other's eyes we were suddenly drawn into a swirling tunnel of smoke. It was dark and we were battered about so violently we held on to each other desperately, fearing eternal separation. At the end of the tunnel, we were dropped into a fiery inferno. We wailed in utter agony from the intense heat. Our skin blistered and our hair caught on fire. Finally, beyond the inferno, there was nothing but cold darkness as we fell down into the bottomless pit. With our senses useless in this stark environment, it seemed like hours, months, days, decades that we fell into nothingness. We were terrorized by thoughts of the destiny that awaited us at the end of our journey. Many times, we tried to cry out to God to save us, but our voices were mute. A somber, hopeless sensation engulfed us.

The telephone rang, waking me from a deep slumber. I picked up the receiver and said, "Hello."

"Mr. Coleman. This is Raul. I've got good news for you. I've found your wife and mother-in-law."

"Huh?"

"Your wife, I've found her."

"My wife? ... Oh, my God! Thank you! Where is she?"

"Erica's mother is living in a small house on the outskirts of town. Get a taxi and have them drive you to 555 Hope St. I'll be waiting for you."

"Does Erica know you've found her?"

"Nobody knows but you and me."

"Good, she might run if she thinks she's being followed, so don't get too close to her."

"I won't, but just get over here as quick as you can."

It was so great to get Raul's call. I immediately went downstairs and asked the desk clerk to call me a cab. It was raining as usual, so I stood just inside the doorway and waited. Finally, a beat-up 65' Ford Fairlane drove up, and the driver waived to me to get in. After a quick dash to the cab, I jumped in the back seat. As the cab sped through the narrow streets of Belmopan, I prayed that Erica would be there with her mother. It was a dark day, and it was difficult to see very far ahead. The cab driver stopped, opened his window, and yelled at a man with an ox pulling a wagon across the street blocking our path. In a minute we were on our way again only to be forced to stop, this time for a small military convoy just coming into town. Finally, we started moving again and before long turned onto Hope Street. The cab driver drove down the street and stopped at number 555. After paying the cabby, I got out.

The white stucco house nestled under a canopy of trees was old and run down. Weeds grew high above where flowers once grew. A '72 Chevy Pickup was parked in the gravel driveway with its hood up. I looked to my left and saw some children playing and then to my right and saw a blue sedan. A man got out and waved to me. I figured it was Raul, so I walked over to him.

"Do you know if she's still there?" I asked

"I don't know, you said not to get too close," Raul replied.

"Right, I'll go and find out if she's there. Do you know who lives in the house?"

"A woman named Carmen Ramirez," he said.

"Does she own it?" I asked.

"No, she has been a tenant there about eighteen months."

"I see. Well, I'm going to go to the door. Wait for me, okay?'

"I'll be right here."

It felt strange approaching this little house in this unfamiliar country, so I approached cautiously. When I got to the front door I knocked gently. There was no response, so I knocked again much louder. This time I heard voices inside and could hear the footsteps of someone coming to the door. The front door opened, and an attractive middle-aged woman appeared.

"Yes, what do you want?" she said.

"Mrs. Ramirez?"

"Yes, who are you?"

"I think you know who I am," I said.

She just stared at me and replied, "I don't know what you're talking about."

"You used to be Carmen Fox, isn't that right?" I asked.

"No, you've got me confused with someone else."

"Then why did your daughter from Dallas come visit you yesterday?"

"I don't have a daughter."

I started laughing. "Then why do you look so much like my wife? Where is she? Tell her to get her cute little ass out here or I'm coming in to get her."

Erica pushed her way in front of her mother and said, "How did you find me?"

"It wasn't easy, believe me. It seems like I've traveled halfway around the world looking for you."

Erica glared at me. "Well, you can just turn around and go right back to Dallas."

"Not without you. Why did you run out on me like that?"

Erica took a deep breath. "I finally realized you didn't love me."

"What? I don't love you. How can you say that? I've never loved a woman more than you."

"Then why did you break our pact?" she asked.

I looked at Erica and shook my head. "My life is all I have, and I didn't think at the time I could end it even if I lost you. But since you left me, I realized I was wrong. If you'll come back to Dallas, I'll honor our agreement."

A smile came over Erica's face, and she opened the door and ran into my arms. Holding her again was such a relief. We kissed. Her lips felt so warm and succulent I didn't want the moment to end. Her mother coughed. We let each other go reluctantly and smiled at her, still holding hands.

"If you ask me, you're both crazy," Ms. Ramirez said. "Don't go back to Dallas. They'll never find you down here. Why don't you just stay with me for a while? Belize is not such a bad place to live."

"I found you," I said. "Besides, I checked it out, and Belize used to be a British Colony so there's an extradition treaty. If Erica's convicted in Dallas, they could come get her down here. If we were going to hide, we'd have to go somewhere else."

"Then go somewhere else. Don't go back to Dallas whatever you do."

"It's up to Erica. I'll do whatever she wants as long as we stay together," I said.

Erica put her arms around me and kissed me again. Then she pulled away, smiled and said, "I missed you so much. I can't believe you found me."

"I can't believe you blew off the million dollars that I worked so hard to make for you."

"I know, I'm sorry. I got so scared. I didn't think you really loved me. Here I was about to get convicted of murder, and I was all alone. I figured if I were going to escape, I'd have to do it then. I wouldn't have another opportunity. The money suddenly wasn't important anymore."

"I was sick when you disappeared," I said. "If you had told me you wanted to escape, I'd of gone with you,"

She laughed. "Would you have? Or would you have tried to talk me out of it."

I nodded, "You may be right. I guess I haven't been much comfort to you."

"Yes, you have," she said. "I asked an awful lot of you. Maybe I expected too much. Someday I'll explain."

"Explain what?"

"It's complicated. Now's not the time."

"Why don't you two come inside?" Mrs. Ramirez said. "The mosquitos are going to eat you alive."

We went in the house. Erica and I sat on the sofa, hand in hand, while Mrs. Ramirez prepared us something to drink. The house inside was very clean and neat. In one corner of the room was a ten-inch statue of the Virgin Mary and a number of glowing candles. A dozen pictures adorned the wall to our right. One of them was a picture of Mrs. Ramirez and her husband, Franklin Fox. They were a handsome couple. I thought what a shame it was that their marriage was doomed from the very start.

"So, did you have a hard time finding your mother?" I asked.

"No, mother sent me a letter when she read about my trial in the newspaper."

"Your trial was in the newspaper down here?"

"No, I go once a week and get the New York Times from the hotel," Mrs. Ramirez said. "I like to keep up on what's going on in America."

"You never mentioned to me that you had heard from your mother," I said.

"Well, the letter came in the day we had our fight," Erica replied. "When I came back to get my things, it was there. It was almost like a message from God. I mean, I had no idea where to run until I came home, and there was mama's letter. It was amazing."

"You told me you suspected your mother was in Belize?" I said.

"Yeah, I knew that was quite possible, but I would never have found her had it not been for the letter," Erica said. "I can't believe you were able to find us."

"I needed the help of a private investigator. He's outside. I guess I better tell him he can go."

"He's outside right now?" Erica laughed.

"Yeah, the poor guy's been out there for twenty minutes."

I went outside and waved to Raul. He got in his car, drove down to the house and opened his window. I thanked him and he left. When I went back into the house Mrs. Ramirez handed me some fruit punch and then she sat down in a chair across from us and smiled.

"I wish I could have been at your wedding. Erica has told me all about it."

"She was a beautiful bride, and the old church in Barbados was very quaint. The only thing missing were about two hundred guests." We all laughed.

"Oh well, God was your witness," Mrs. Ramirez said.

"So, were you surprised to see your daughter show up at your doorstep?" I said.

"Oh yes, what a wonderful surprise. I've really missed her."

"Erica has been dying to find you. She's talked so much about you; I almost feel like I know you."

"You're going to get to know me very well," she said. "Now that Franklin's gone there's nothing to keep Erica and me apart."

"That's right, we should bring mother back to Dallas with us," Erica said.

"Oh, you're not going back to Dallas, are you?" Mrs. Ramirez said.

"I have to. I don't want to be on the run the rest of my life. Anyway, I think the jury will let me off."

"Well, if we don't get back to Dallas tonight it may be too late. Webster said he couldn't drag the trial out beyond tomorrow afternoon. If you're not there to testify, then it will be all over."

"We better go then," Erica said. "I've got to convince the jury that I was crazy when I killed Aunt Martha."

"But you said you didn't kill her?"

"I know, but this is a game we have to play. Everyone has made up their mind that I killed her. So I've got to play along with them, but convince them I didn't know what I was doing when I supposedly killed her."

'I don't understand," Mrs. Ramirez said.

"Don't worry about it, mother. It'll all work out."

"Maybe we should bring your mother to testify?" I said. "She certainly could give the jury some insight into Aunt Martha's dirty tricks."

"Oh, we shouldn't get her involved," Erica said.

"I'd love to testify against that bitch. She's half the reason Franklin and I got divorced. She was a very wicked lady."

"Good, then it's settled. We'd better get going," I said.

22
The Performance

By the time we got to the airport, there was only one flight going out that night and it was to Cozumel. We checked with the ticket agent and found out that we could go to Cozumel and from there to Mexico City. From Mexico City, we could get an early flight and be in Dallas by noon. It was our only hope so that's what we decided to do. It was a long, rough night, but at 12:07 p.m. we landed at Love Field. Joe was waiting for us at the airport.

"Why in the hell did you two come back here?" Joe said. "I didn't figure I'd ever see either one of you again."

"We've got to prove Erica's innocence," I said. "We don't want to be fugitives for the rest of our lives."

"Better fugitives than dead," Joe said.

"What are you talking about?" I asked.

"Never mind, I promised Webster I'd get you to the courthouse by 1:30. We need to get a move on."

"What happened to you the other day? Detective Perkins said he saw you at the airport."

"Right," Joe said. "He did. I figured that's where Erica was headed, and if I waited around for you, she would be long gone. Unfortunately, I didn't find her. I searched all the gates, but she must have already left. Then I ran into Perkins and, of course, he gave me the third degree."

Joe drove us immediately to Erica's condo where we changed and then went directly to the Courthouse. Webster was standing over the defense table when we walked in.

"Thank God," Webster said. "I can't believe it."

"I'm really sorry about running out on you the way I did," Erica said. "I don't know what to say."

"Well, there's no time to worry about that now. I guess you know you've seriously jeopardized your case by disappearing the way you did. Not to mention losing your million-dollar bond."

"I know," Erica said.

"Are you ready to testify?" Webster asked.

"Yes, my mother wants to testify too."

Webster nodded. "Right, that's what Rich said over the phone, so I've prepared some questions for her. We just finished up with Dr. Beckman this morning. He did a great job explaining temporary insanity and how you were mentally programmed all those years to think your aunt was the devil himself. He testified that the threats from your aunt triggered an outburst over which you had absolutely no control. He felt that when you killed your aunt, you were completely mad and out of control."

As we were talking the prosecutor walked in and gave us a hard stare. Then he went over to the bailiff and said something to him. When he was done, the bailiff came over to us.

"Mrs. Coleman?"

"Yes, Erica said."

"You'll have to come with me after today's session, your bond has been revoked. You'll have to stay in the county jail for the duration of the trial."

Erica looked at me anxiously and then turned back to the bailiff and said, "Yes, I understand."

"Mr. Coleman, I have a warrant for your arrest, but perhaps your appearance today may give the judge reason to revoke it. Perhaps Mr. Webster can bring the matter to the Judge's attention. If not, I'll have to arrest you after today's session."

Webster said, "Yes, I'll discuss that with the judge. Thank you."

After the bailiff's words sunk in, I had second thoughts about our return to Dallas. What if the judge decided to be an asshole and lock me up as well as Erica? Maybe Joe was right, we should have stayed in Central America. Oh, God! Had we made another mistake? As I was lamenting our decision, the door to the judge's chamber opened. The bailiff stood up and yelled, "All rise!"

The Judge entered the courtroom, took his seat, and said, "Well, Mrs. Coleman, so nice of you to attend the last few days of your trial. We've missed you. Would you like to enlighten us as to where you've been?"

"Yes, Sir," Erica replied and then proceeded to explain to the judge the situation with her mother.

"Well, if you think just because you came back here today, I'll reverse my decision to revoke your million-dollar bond, forget it. It's gone," the judge said. "Even if you're not convicted, you won't get the million dollars back, I promise you. I hope visiting your mother was worth it."

Erica looked at her mother. "It was," she said.

Webster stood up. "Your honor, in light of Mrs. Coleman's voluntary return to this courtroom, and since she's already forfeited a million dollars, I would respectfully request that she be released after today's session on her own recognizance. There's no reason to lock her up."

"I'm afraid not, counselor," the Judge said. "Your client has already shown contempt for the law and this court when she fled the country. She won't have that opportunity again."

"Very well, your honor. In light of the fact that Mr. Coleman found his wife and brought her back to Dallas, I would respectfully request that the warrant out on him be dismissed. He obviously was not aiding and abetting Mrs. Coleman's flight but was diligently trying to stop it."

"On that point, I would have to agree," the Judge replied. "All charges against Mr. Coleman are dismissed and the warrant for his arrest is hereby revoked. Now, let's get on with the trial. Mr. Webster, call your next witness."

"The defense calls Erica Fox Coleman."

Erica stood up and looked over at me for encouragement. She looked stunning in her grey satin shirt with French cuffs and black knit skirt. She tossed her long black hair and then walked to the witness stand. The bailiff administered the oath and she sat up and smiled at Webster as he approached her.

"Now Mrs. Coleman you have been charged with the murder of your aunt, Martha Collins. Do you understand that?" Webster asked.

"Yes."

"Do you have any recollection of killing Mrs. Collins?"

"No, not of actually killing her," Erica said.

"Do you dispute the allegation that you killed her?"

"I don't remember doing it but I know I was there after it happened. I can remember seeing Aunt Martha lying there on the ground. Her eyes were open, and she looked awfully pale."

"What did you do when you saw her like that?" Webster asked.

"I shook her hard and tried to get her to breathe but she just stared at me," Erica said.

"So when she didn't respond, what did you do?"

"I was scared. I went outside to get help, but then I realized that everyone would think I had done it. I didn't know what to do. While I was standing in front of her room trying to figure out my next move, I heard some kids coming so I just instinctively ran."

"Where did you run?"

"No place in particular," Erica said. "I just started running down the street. I ran for a good ten minutes until I saw a Seven-Eleven, so I decided to stop and call Rich."

Webster continued to question Erica about the night of the murder. Then he had her explain everything from when she first met Rich to the day they returned from Barbados. Erica was a good witness. She sat up proudly in her chair and looked the members of the jury in the eye. They listened intently to her story. I noticed the male members of the jury watching her very closely, smiling and occasionally laughing at how she manipulated me into doing exactly what she wanted. The female members of the jury panel seemed equally intrigued, but they reacted more to the million dollars I had made for Erica and our secret romance. I even noticed one of them shed a tear when Erica described our wedding day. Then Webster asked Erica about her childhood.

"Now before you met Richard Coleman, were you happy?"

"No, I was miserable."

"Why?"

"I thought my mother had deserted me," Erica said. "I didn't realize she had been driven away by my Aunt Martha."

"How did she manage to drive your mother away?"

"Mother was from Belize. She immigrated to the U.S. and got a job as a waitress at the country club daddy belonged to. That's where they met and got to know each other. Much to Aunt Martha's displeasure they got married. She always felt that my mother was beneath Franklin and that he had disgraced the family by marrying a penniless immigrant. Although Daddy told her often it was none of her business, she tried to sabotage the relationship at every opportunity."

"Can you give us some examples of how she would do that?" Webster asked.

"She would frequently call mother supposedly to talk but would end up insulting her and making her feel like she was the scum of the earth. Many times, I would come home, and mother would be crying after a telephone conversation with Aunt Martha."

"Anything else that comes to mind?" Webster said.

"At family gatherings, Aunt Martha would treat her mother like she was a hired maid. She would order her around and show her no respect whatsoever. One time she had a family dinner, and there wasn't room enough for everyone to eat together so the children were fed in the kitchen. Aunt Martha made mother eat in the kitchen with us children while the rest of the adults ate in the dining room."

"How did your father react to this situation," Webster asked.

"Daddy was very tolerant of Aunt Martha's behavior," Erica said. "I don't know why exactly. Maybe he felt guilty because my grandfather had given him the family fortune and gave Aunt Martha nothing. Anyway, he just laughed off all the insults and abuse that my mother had to take."

"He did nothing to protect her?"

'No, not that I could see," Erica said.

"Could you describe your father and Aunt Martha's relationship?"

"Daddy hated Aunt Martha, but as I said, he wouldn't tell her that to her face. She was family, so he always treated her with respect. Many times, though when he'd come to tuck me in at night, he'd tell me not to pay attention to her. He said she was a mental case."

"So, is there anything else you remember about your Aunt?"

"Yes, she was always trying to borrow money from Daddy. I can remember waking up one night and hearing my father screaming on the telephone at her. She wanted money, and he wouldn't give it to her."

"Did your father ever give her money?"

"The next day I asked him why he didn't give her the money and he said if he gave her money once she'd be back for more every week. He didn't want to set any precedents."

"So how did your Aunt Martha treat you?"

"Like I didn't exist. She never remembered my birthday, and at Christmas, if I got a candy cane, I'd be lucky. Of course, her little darling Arnold, she treated him like a king."

"So how did you feel when your mother left?"

"I was crushed. I couldn't eat or sleep for weeks. My grades at school crashed."

"So how did you cope with the situation?"

"Daddy and I became very close," Erica said. "He tried to fill the void that was created when mother left but I fell into a deep depression. I've never told anyone this before, but I even tried to commit suicide once."

"You did?" Webster said.

"Yes, it was four or five weeks after mother had left. Aunt Martha had been over and had made an ass of herself as usual. At dinner, she went on and on about how my mother was a tramp and how much better we both were without her. I couldn't believe Daddy was just letting her foam at the mouth the way she was. I got mad and started screaming at Aunt Martha. I told her to shut up and never to talk bad about my mother again. She was outraged that I would talk to her that way, so she slapped me across the face."

"She slapped you?" Webster said.

"Yes, and Daddy didn't do anything about it. He just sent me to my room."

"So, what did you do?"

"I decided there wasn't any reason to live," Erica said. "My mother was gone forever, and my Daddy didn't love me enough to protect me from that bitch, so what was the point of living. I knew Daddy had some pain pills in his bathroom cabinet, so I went in and got them. I took ten or fifteen of them."

"Obviously, you weren't successful," Webster said.

"Yeah, I picked up the wrong bottle. I got the muscle

relaxers instead of the pain pills. Two days later I woke up relaxed as hell."

Laughter came from the gallery. The Judge started to pick up his gavel, but it quickly died down.

Webster smiled. "So, in a year you went from a deep suicidal depression to complete joy and happiness, right?"

"Yes, a total emotional turnaround," Erica said.

"So, what happened when you came back from Barbados?" Webster asked.

Erica explained what happened. The jury continued to watch her intently. She broke down several times, crying softly. Webster asked her if she needed a break, but she said no. The juror who I had seen wipe a tear from her eye earlier, was visibly upset. Several male jurors shook their heads. It was a good sign. Erica was getting a lot of sympathies, I thought, or maybe it was disgust over the appalling situation she had gotten herself into. I wasn't sure.

"So how did you feel?"

"I was scared. My life was a dream, and I knew Aunt Martha could destroy it in a minute. You just don't know what unpleasant memories rushed through my mind at that moment."

"Memories of your childhood?"

"Memories of the mental torture Aunt Martha had inflicted on my mother and father. I knew how evil she could be, and I feared she'd do everything in her power to destroy Rich."

"So, what did you do?" Webster asked.

"There was nothing I could do. I had no idea where she was staying. The police wouldn't tell us anything." She went on to explain how Rich went to the office, and then she got a phone call from Aunt Martha.

"Oh really? Why had she called?" Webster asked.

"She said she was calling to make sure I was all right, but I knew it was a lie. She just wanted to let me know she was about to ruin my life."

"What did you do?"

Erica explained her confrontation with Aunt Martha on the phone.

"All I could do was try to call Rich at the office to tell him about Aunt Martha's call. Unfortunately, the answering service picked up the call."

"What time was this?" Webster asked.

"About nine-fifteen when the cab finally came and nearly nine-thirty when I got to the motel."

Erica recalled her confrontation with the motel manager and repeated what happened in the motel room when she found Aunt Martha. Webster asked her to explain how she got fibers from the pillows under her fingernails. It seemed plausible to me, but I wondered what the jury thought about her explanation. I watched them as she talked, but there was little visible reaction to the testimony. I thought this to be a bad sign.

"So, you have no memory whatsoever of seeing your Aunt alive that evening."

"No, the only memory I have is of her lying there dead on the floor."

"Pass the witness."

"Mr. Blake, your witness," the Judge said.

Blake got up, took a deep breath, and looked at Erica. Then he began a long series of questions about Erica's schooling, grades, acceptance into SMU, love of her father, and other things designed to show her as a normal well-adjusted teenager. Erica was not intimidated by Blake at all and answered his questions calmly and with little emotion. Then he turned to the night of the murder.

"Mrs. Coleman. How did you feel when you discovered your home had been ransacked by your Aunt?"

"I was pissed off."

"Because she had violated your home, right?" Blake

said.

"Yes."

"And because she was threatening to destroy the life you loved, right?"

"Yes."

"So, you wanted to stop her?"

"Of course."

"At whatever cost you had to stop her?"

"What do you mean?"

"No matter what it took, you were going to stop her from ruining your life, isn't that right?"

"If you're suggesting I was going to kill her, no. No way. I'm not a murderer. That wasn't an option."

"That wasn't an option, but she was going to ruin your life. Didn't you want to protect yourself from her?"

"Sure, but I'm not a killer. I was just going over there to talk some sense into her."

"Come on, Mrs. Coleman. This is the West Texas Bitch we're talking about. You knew you couldn't talk any sense into her, didn't you? There was just one way to save yourself, and that was by killing her, wasn't it?"

"I never planned to kill her. It had never crossed my mind."

"How do you know that?" Blake said. "You don't remember if you killed her or not, do you?"

"No, I don't remember that, but I know I never made plans to kill her," Erica said.

"Okay, but you could have made up your mind to kill her once you realized she wasn't going to be reasonable, right?"

"I suppose. Anything's possible."

"Your daddy was right about one thing, wasn't he?"

"What's that?" Erica said.

"Erica always gets her way. You got what you wanted didn't you?" Blake said and then shook his head in a dramatic show of disgust. "No further questions."

"Mr. Webster, redirect?" the Judge said.

"No, Your Honor."

"Then call your next witness."

"The defense calls Carmen Ramirez."

Erica turned to watch her mother take the stand. They smiled at each other as Carmen went by. Then Webster approached the witness stand and began his questioning.

"Mrs. Ramirez, tell us how you met Franklin Fox?"

"Well, my family had just immigrated to the United States. My father was an engineer and Texas Instruments sponsored his immigration to the U.S. When we arrived, I was very lucky to get a job at the Dallas Country Club as a waitress. About a month after I started work there, I met Franklin. It was a Saturday night and I had just served some dessert to some guests when I noticed Franklin staring at me. He was so handsome; I was quite embarrassed to have him stare at me that way."

"Did you speak to him?"

"Not at that moment, but later when I got off work, he was waiting outside the kitchen for me. I was quite shocked. He took me for a ride in his Porsche to White Rock Lake. We kissed and then took a walk in the moonlight. It was wonderful."

"So how long did you date before you got married?"

"We had to keep our relationship a secret because Franklin's mother and father would not approve of Franklin dating a Latin immigrant. I guess we dated six or eight months before we finally got enough nerve up to announce our engagement," Carmen said.

"What about Franklin's sister, Martha? Did she approve of the relationship?" Webster said.

"No, she was against it from the beginning. It became an obsession with her to prevent Franklin from seeing me."

"How do you mean?"

"She told Franklin he shouldn't associate with such a lowly person as me. Then she convinced Franklin's father to offer me money to leave him."

"How much money?"

"Ten thousand dollars."

"Did you take it?"

"No, I only take money if I've earned it. My family is very proud."

"Is that all?"

"No, she threatened me. She said women like me had accidents, and that I better watch my step."

"Did she ever physically hurt you?"

"No, she was sugar sweet when we were in someone's company, but just as soon as we were alone everything changed. She would scold me for seeing Franklin. She accused me of being after his money. She warned me not even to think about marrying him."

"But you didn't listen?"

"No, Franklin said not to pay any attention to her. He said she was just a bitter woman but was harmless."

"Did you believe she was harmless?"

"No, when she knew I was alone she'd call the house four or five times in a row and not say anything. It would scare me half to death. Then she'd send me candy and flowers."

"Oh, she realized she had been wrong?"

"No, the flowers were always dead, and the candy would be full of worms."

"You're kidding?!" Webster said.

"No, then there were the letters."

"Letters?" Webster said.

"Yes, at least once a week I'd get hate letters. They would go on and on for pages and pages defaming and ridiculing me."

"Were these handwritten letters?"

"No, they were usually typed. A couple of times they

were cut out letters . . . you know, from magazines."

"Did you show them to Franklin?"

"No, he had a bad temper, and I was afraid he'd do something rash."

"Did you ever confront Martha about the letters and flowers and stuff?"

"Yes, but she denied it. She said she had better things to do than play games with a slut like me."

"Did you ever do anything to get back at her?"

"No, I figured once we were married, she'd leave me alone."

"Were you correct in that assessment?"

"No, it got worse after we were married."

"How so?"

"She quit being nice to me in public. She didn't pass up any opportunity to berate me or humiliate me in front of family and friends."

"Did the phone calls, letters, and hate gifts continue?"

"Yes, but I tried to ignore them. If I got a letter or gift in the mail, I would just throw it away."

"Did anything change after Erica was born?"

"Yes, Martha got married and moved to Odessa. That was the happiest day of my life when she left town."

"How did Martha and Erica get along?"

"Luckily, Erica didn't see much of her aunt. She would only come to visit once or twice a year. Erica tried to be nice to her, but she would usually rebuke and chastise her at every opportunity. Erica grew to hate her aunt. I'm afraid I encouraged the hatred. In fact, when she was older, I told her about what her aunt had done to me."

"You told her everything?"

"Yes."

"What was her reaction?"

"She was horrified. She would barely speak to her aunt after that."

"So, we've heard talk of how Martha drove you away from your husband. Is that true?"

"Yes and no. I can't blame it all on Martha. It was partly Franklin's doing. You see, he liked other women, and he didn't always respect our wedding vows. I wasn't aware of it, but when Martha found out about one of his affairs, she immediately told me and rubbed my nose in it. She knew I wouldn't tolerate infidelity."

"So, did you confront Franklin with it?"

"Yes, and he said if I divorced him, I would never see Erica again. It was horrible. We began fighting all the time. Then one day he hit me. A hard slap across the face. My eye swelled up and turned black and blue. We told everyone I had been hit by a snowball. I could have lived with that, but when it happened a second time, I decided our marriage was over and left."

"Just like that?"

"Well, a week in the hospital gave me a lot of time to think."

"How could you just leave your child?" Webster asked.

"It wasn't easy. She was my life, my very reason for living. But the bickering and fighting were killing her. I knew Franklin wouldn't let me take her with me, so I thought it best that I just leave."

"But why didn't you say goodbye to Erica?"

"If I would have said goodbye then I would have had to tell her why I was leaving. I didn't want her to hate her father. She was going to have to live with him for some time. I thought it best she hates me rather than him."

"Thank you, Mrs. Ramirez. Pass the witness."

"Mr. Blake," the Judge said. "Your witness."

"Mrs. Ramirez. All of these hate letters were unsigned, right?"

"Yes," Carmen said.

"Then how did you know they were from Franklin's

sister?" Blake asked.

"There was nobody else who hated me."

"What about your father and mother-in-law? I thought they didn't approve of the marriage."

"They didn't at first, but after we were married, they grew to accept me. They were always if not warm, very civil."

"But these letters could just as well have come from them, couldn't they?"

"It's possible."

"Or they could have come from someone else, perhaps an ex-lover or someone you offended and perhaps didn't realize it?" Blake said.

"No, they were from Martha," Carmen said. "I am certain of it. Only a bitter hateful person could do the things she did. I've never known anyone like that other than her."

"You say you love your daughter, is that right?"

"Absolutely."

"And you'd do anything to protect her?"

"Of course."

"Including making up this story about hate letters and dead flowers," Webster said.

"No, it's the truth."

"Why should the jury believe you? I'm sure you don't have any of these letters, do you?" Blake chuckled.

"Yes, I do. I have them all."

"You do?" Webster said.

"Yes, I brought them with me," Carmen said. "Would you like to see them?"

"No, that won't be necessary," Blake replied. "Mrs. Ramirez, now you know your daughter quite well obviously?"

"Yes."

"She's very intelligent, isn't she?'

"Yes."

"She's always very alert and on top of things, isn't she?"

"Oh, yes," Carmen said. "She's always been very much in control of her life."

"Do you think she has been insane?"

"No, of course not."

Then a clamor broke out in the courtroom and the judge picked up his gavel and banged in on the bench. "Order."

"Objection. Your Honor. She's not a psychiatrist?" Webster said.

"Overruled."

Blake smiled. "You taught her what's right and wrong, didn't you?"

"Yes."

"Do you think she understands the difference between what's right and what's wrong?"

"Yes, she's a good Catholic girl."

"No further question, pass the witness."

"Redirect, Mr. Webster?" the Judge said.

"Yes, thank you, Your Honor," Webster said.

"Mrs. Ramirez. When you say your daughter has never been insane what do you mean?"

"I mean she's no lunatic."

"Okay, but she's a normal human being, right?"

"Yes."

"Objection. Leading," Blake said.

"Sustained," the Judge replied.

"Does she have her emotional ups and downs just like all of us?"

"Of course."

"Do you think it's possible that she could ever be under so much stress that she might lose it?" Webster said.

"Lose it? I don't understand.," Carmen said.

"Well like if you were to drive too fast you can lose control of your car, right?"

"Yes."

"Well, could things have gotten so bad for Erica that she might have lost control of her life, just for a few moments?"

"Oh, yes. I see what you mean. Yes, that could have happened to her."

"And do you think if there was a time where she wasn't in control that, at that moment, she might not have recognized right from wrong?"

"Uh-huh," she said. "That could happen."

"You heard your daughter testify she once tried to commit suicide, right?"

"Yes."

"Do you think she was sane when she did that?"

"No, I guess not."

"Everyone has moments of insanity," Webster said.

"Objection," Blake said. "Counsel is not a psychiatrist."

"Withdrawn," Webster said.

"So, if what you just described constituted the elements of temporary insanity, then would you admit it could be possible for your daughter to be insane . . . at least temporarily?"

"Objection," Blake yelled. "The questions are ambiguous and calls for a legal conclusion."

"I think you opened the door," the judge said. "Overruled. You may answer the question."

"Yes, it's possible she was for a moment," Carmen said.

Webster said, "Mrs. Ramirez. You said you had some letters."

"Yes," she replied.

"May I see them?"

"Of course," she said and then opened her purse and pulled out a stack of letters with a rubber band around them.

"Your Honor, I would request a short recess so that the prosecution and I might examine this new evidence," Webster said.

"All right, we'll recess until 3:30," the judge said.

"All rise," the Bailiff bellowed as the judge left the bench.

While Blake and Webster were reading the letters, the bailiff came over to take Erica into custody. Before he could take her away, I ran over and embraced her. Webster motioned to the bailiff to give us a moment. He backed off for a moment but watched us carefully.

"I'm so sorry you're going to have to go to jail," I said. "I'm sure it will be just a day or two."

"It's all right. I'll live," Erica said. "I'm just worried about how I'm going to get the cyanide past the guards."

"There's no way. We're not going to need it anyway. Your mother did a good job of showing what kind of mental torture your aunt put you through. I wouldn't have blamed you had you actually killed her."

"I don't know."

"Don't worry. You both did great. I'm sure the jury will find you not guilty."

"Yeah, but mama said I couldn't have ever been insane. Don't you think that will hurt me?"

"Oh, that was just legal semantics. Don't worry about that."

"I'm scared."

"I know," I said as I gave Erica a squeeze. "We're going to get through this."

The bailiff motioned that our time was up. He came over and put his hand on Erica's shoulder.

"Don't forget your—"

She paused in mid-sentence not wanting to say the word cyanide in front of the bailiff. I got her message through, loud and clear.

Erica whispered. "You won't forget our pact, will you?"

"No, but I told you we won't need it."

"Bring it just in case."

"I will, I love you."

"I love you too," Erica said and then went with the Bailiff through a door in the back of the courtroom.

As the door closed, I realized I may have held Erica for the last time. Our fate was now in the hands of twelve strangers. It didn't seem right. Neither of us had done anything terribly wrong. No one had been hurt by our little romance and I knew that Erica was innocent. A lonely, helpless feeling overcame me. I understood clearly then how Erica had been right all along. I couldn't live without her. If we couldn't be together then death was our only option.

Erica's mother and got something to eat during the break. We talked about Erica and how wonderful a woman she was. Her mother told me more about Erica's childhood and how devastated she was to have to leave her. As we talked, I couldn't help but think how she would feel if she knew of our pact. If only there was a way, I could keep her away from the courthouse on the day of the verdict. She had experienced enough agony in her life without seeing her daughter die before her eyes. After fifteen minutes, the trial resumed.

"Mrs. Ramirez, at the break we looked over the letters you brought with you and I want to ask you about one of them," Webster said and then handed a letter to Mrs. Ramirez.

"Yes," Mrs. Ramirez said. "This was a letter I received on April 3, 1961."

"Objection, Your Honor," Blake said. "If Mr. Webster is even thinking about having Mrs. Ramirez read this letter, I would have to most strenuously object. He can't possibly prove its authenticity nor that it came from the decedent."

"It doesn't matter," the Judge said. As long as Mrs. Ramirez received it and thought it was from the decedent then it would have contributed to her state of mind and the state of mind of her daughter as influenced by her mother. The jury can decide if it's credible or not. Therefore, your objection is overruled."

"Thank you, Your Honor," Webster said. "Go on, Mrs. Ramirez."

"Well, like I said I received this letter by mail on April 3, 1961. It was a letter warning me that I was going to be poisoned," Carmen said.

"Would you read it to us?"

"Sure."

"'Dear Whore,

You are a hard-headed daughter of the devil. Don't complain that you haven't been warned. You won't know when to expect it. It's a clear, odorless brew. It could be today, tomorrow, or next week. You won't know when, but one day soon, you'll suddenly feel nauseous, you'll double over in pain and collapse. Your head will be spinning, your vision blurred. You've never known the misery you'll feel before it's over. You'll be praying for the good Lord to take you away rather than make you endure the wrath of the poison. Let this unholy alliance go while you still can. Disregard this warning at you own peril.'"

The gallery was shocked by the letter. Several gasps came from the jury box as Mrs. Ramirez read it. A general commotion arose in the Courtroom. The judge banged his gavel to restore order. Webster had Carmen read several of the other letters and then asked the judge to allow them in evidence. Blake protested but the judge let them in. After Webster rested Blake called Dr. Bentley back on to try to discount the effect of the letters and other evidence of hatred for Aunt Martha. Finally, both sides closed late Friday afternoon and gave final arguments. After the judge had instructed the jury on its duties, he sent them home.

"All right," the Judge said. "Ladies and Gentlemen of the jury, you have your instructions. First thing Monday morning I want you back here to start deliberations. Do not talk to anyone about the case over the weekend. Thank you. You're dismissed."

The jury retired and the courtroom began to empty. Webster came over to me and smiled.

"Well, it's out of our hands now," he said.

"What do you think?" I asked.

"I feel good. It's just so hard to assess what's going on in each of the juror's minds."

"I know. They were hard to read."

"So, what are you going to do this weekend?" Webster asked.

"Well, Carmen and I are going to spend the time getting to know each other. We've got something very special in common."

"Yes, you do," he said "Keep your chin up."

"I will. Thanks for your help. You did a terrific job."

"Well, I hope you're right."

23
The Verdict

That weekend was the longest two days I've ever experienced. It wasn't until after midnight that I finally fell asleep and then I woke up at 4 a.m. wide awake. On Saturday morning Clark called me with the rundown on Ralph Benitez. He found out that Arnold and Ralph had been teammates on their high school swim team. They became best friends, but no one suspected they were anything more than that. They were roommates at Texas Tech for four years and upon graduation, they went to Baylor. Arnold went to law school and Ralph enrolled in an MBA program. Clark didn't have any information on how and when their relationship changed or how Arnold's mother found out about it but he did give me the name of a person he thought could fill me in.

That person was Arnold's ex-girlfriend, Amanda Miller. Clark advised me she was a waitress at Steak and Ale in Lubbock. That afternoon I took a Southwest flight to Lubbock to talk to her. I picked her up from work, and we drove to Denny's and had a cup of coffee.

"So, how long did you two date?"

"About six months," Amanda said.

"Did you meet Ralph?" I asked.

"Yeah, sure. He was always hanging around with Arnold. I never liked him much. He was very critical and judgmental. I told Arnold he ought to find a new roommate."

"What was his reaction?"

"None," Amanda said. "He just blew it off. He said I was too hyper-critical."

"Did you meet Arnold's mother?"

"Oh, yes, many times. She and Arnold were very close. He wouldn't do anything without consulting with his mother first. It was actually kind of annoying, but I knew better than to interfere with that relationship."

"Why?" I asked.

"It was obvious mama was number one in his life, and no one was going to be taking over that position," Amanda said.

"We're you all right with that?"

"Oh, I didn't like it much, but I learned to live with it. There wasn't any use in fighting it. If I wanted Arnold, I had to take his mother too. They were a package."

"So, what happened to break you two up?" I asked.

"During the summer after our freshman year, Arnold suddenly seemed to lose interest in me. He and Ralph had gone on a hiking and fishing trip to Colorado. They did some backpacking and horseback riding in the backcountry for several weeks. Everything was fine when they left, but Arnold wasn't the same man when he returned."

"Did you confront him about it?"

"Yes, he said he had done a lot of thinking while he was in the backcountry and decided he and I weren't meant for each other. I never saw it coming."

"When did you suspect your rival was Ralph?"

"Almost immediately," Amanda said. "Ralph seemed to be gloating over our break-up. At first, I just thought he was just being a prick as usual, but then I realized it was more than that."

"Did you confront Arnold with the fact that you knew he was gay?"

"Yes."

"Did he deny it?" I asked.

"At first he did, but after a while, he confirmed that he liked Ralph sexually."

"Did Mrs. Collins find out that her son was gay?"

"Oh yes, she called me one day and asked me what had happened between Arnold and me. I told her the same lie that Arnold had told me, but she didn't accept it. She knew there was something else. Finally, I had to tell her the truth."

"How did she react?" I asked.

"She was shocked at first," Amanda said. "She said I must be mistaken."

"Did she confront Arnold with it?"

"Yes, almost immediately. He denied it at first just like he did with me, but then he finally admitted it."

"How do you know this?"

"He told me afterward. We're still friends. I was obviously devastated when he dumped me for a man, but I've gotten over it now pretty much. At least I found out before we got married."

"So, did Mrs. Collins do anything about the relationship between Arnold and Ralph?"

"Yes, she tried to get Arnold to go to a shrink. She couldn't stand the thought of her son being gay."

"Did he go?" I asked.

"No, he refused, so she began to work on Ralph. She did everything in her power to make him miserable. I guess she figured he'd get tired of it and break up with Arnold."

"Do you know what kind of things she did?"

"No, Arnold wouldn't tell me. He was totally humiliated by his mother's behavior, yet he was so much under her spell he couldn't break his relationship with her. It was pretty sad actually."

"Well Amanda, you've been a big help. This sheds some light on the situation. I think perhaps we're getting closer to the truth."

"So you think Arnold killed his mother?"

"Maybe, but I'm thinking Ralph is more of a possibility. He must have quickly come to the realization that he and Arnold would never have any peace with Martha continually meddling in their affairs. She was an expert at harassing and terrorizing her enemies until they gave up or fled. She drove away Erica's mother, and she was obviously hell-bent on driving away Ralph. Arnold testified Ralph was at Love Field on the day of the murder. I wonder if he really was on the plane to Waco with Arnold. Arnold may be lying about that to protect him."

After our meeting I had the taxi driver drop Amanda back at her apartment. Then I had him take me directly to the airport. On the way to the airport, I pondered how I could prove that Ralph was the killer. Then I remembered we had sent pictures of Arnold to all of the guests of the Starlight Motel. We needed to do the same thing with Ralph's picture. If anyone saw him, then we would know Arnold was a liar and Ralph was most likely the murderer. When I got back to Dallas, I called Suzie.

"So, you think Ralph killed her?" Suzie said.

"He had good reason to."

"So, what do we do?"

"I need you to find a picture of Ralph and send it to the people on the Starlight Hotel guest list as we did for Arnold."

"But we won't get a response by Monday," Suzie noted.

"Send it overnight mail. They should have it by Monday morning. The jury may be out for a week. If we get lucky and someone calls us we might be able to prove Ralph is the killer. With this new evidence, Webster can ask the judge to reopen testimony, abandon the temporary insanity defense and prove Erica is innocent."

"Okay, whatever you say, but I think it's too late."

On Sunday I went to Mass with Carmen and we both prayed for God's help in extricating Erica from her plight. That night I doubt I slept ten minutes and when it was time to get up I barely had enough energy to get out of bed, my stomach was in knots and I had no appetite for breakfast. It had been nice being with Carmen over the weekend rather than being alone. But we were both so scared and stressed out neither of us had been able to give the other much comfort. As I watched a brilliant sunrise from the front window I wondered if it would be my last. I prayed to God that Erica would be acquitted, and I would be released from the pact. I prayed that if I did have to kill myself, God would forgive me.

Before I left, I lingered in the shower knowing it might be my last. It was weird because I had always taken all of life's pleasures for granted. Now I savored every minute I had left. Would I be strong enough to honor my solemn promise to Erica? Once I was dressed, I went to the dresser and opened the small tin box that held the cyanide capsules. I saw that one was missing. I hoped and prayed the guards had found it and wrestled it away from Erica. I knew though that somehow, she would find a way to smuggle it past them. I picked up a capsule and put it in my pocket and then gave the sign of the cross and asked for God's forgiveness for even thinking about taking my life.

After picking Carmen up from her hotel, we went directly to the courthouse. It was a bright, clear, sunny day which I thought was a good omen. A larger than usual crowd of reporters was there to ask me the inevitable questions. When we finally made it into the courtroom Webster escorted us into a conference room where we could wait for the jury's verdict. As I entered the room, I was hoping to see Erica, but she wasn't there.

"Won't they let Erica stay with us?" I asked.

"No, they have her in a holding cell up on the 7th Floor," Webster said. "They don't want to take a chance on her running again."

We waited all morning, but nothing happened. After

lunch, I called Suzie to see if there had been any phone calls as a result of the picture of Ralph that she had sent out on Saturday. She said the phone had been quiet. We continued to wait. There was no telling how long the jury would deliberate. It could be hours, days, or even weeks. I wondered what was going through Erica's mind as she sat alone in the holding cell knowing that at any moment her fate could be decided. It was cruel to make someone sit through such torture. I prayed for a quick jury verdict. My prayers were not answered. It was late in the afternoon when I decided to check with Suzie one more time.

"I've gotten some phone calls but you're not going to like what I have to tell you."

"What do you mean?"

"I know you just told me to send out Ralph's picture, but I figured we were out of time so perhaps I should send out everybody's picture."

"Everybody?"

"Right. I sent out pictures of not only Ralph but Arnold, Peter, and Joe as well."

"Really?"

"Yeah, and I've already got six phone calls. They all remember seeing Joe in the motel parking lot standing by his car. They said he was rather conspicuous because he was so well dressed and drove a red Corvette."

"Oh my God. I can't believe Joe is the one. It couldn't be."

"He had good reason. If you and Shirley Temple had been caught, there goes his securities license down the toilet."

"Maybe he was trying to protect me from getting disbarred and going to jail. He is my best friend."

"I'm sure he loves you, but I doubt he'd kill for you unless his own ass was in a crack."

"I can't believe he's the one. I've got to find him. See if you can locate him and get him to come down to the courthouse."

"Okay, boss."

While I was on the phone a message came that the jury had returned. We all jumped up and started to head for the courtroom. I took Webster aside and told him about the witnesses who saw Joe at the motel. He shook his head.

"It's too late," he said.

"Can't you ask the judge to recess the case for a few days while we check this out?"

"No, I said it's too late. If something comes of it we'll ask for a new trial."

"No, that will be too late," I replied.

"No, it won't. If Erica's convicted, they won't send her off to Huntsville for weeks. Don't worry."

"You don't understand, you can't let the jury announce its verdict," I said frantically.

"Get a hold of yourself, Rich. Come on. The judge will be pissed if we keep him waiting."

As I entered the courtroom, I noticed the gallery was filling up fast and the noise level was deafening. As I scanned the room, I saw Arnold, Ralph, and Peter. Joe was nowhere to be seen. It killed me that one of them might be laughing at Erica's predicament. I continued to look for familiar faces but never expected to see my mother and father as they took a seat in the gallery. Oh God, is this my punishment, I thought? Oh shit. Was I to commit suicide with my mother and father watching?

The door in the back of the room opened and a bailiff brought Erica in and seated her next to Webster. She looked at me and gave me an apprehensive smile. Her face was pale, and she was breathing heavily. I choked up seeing the distress in her face.

"Something's wrong with Erica," I said to Carmen.

"She's scared."

"I know, but she looks terrible," I said.

"She'll be fine once the jury finds her not guilty."

The bailiff stood up and said, "All rise!"

The turmoil in the courtroom came to a halt as the judge took the bench. He said something to the court reporter and then took his seat.

"You may be seated," he said. "Bailiff, bring in the jury."

The bailiff walked to the door to the jury room, opened it and the members of the jury walked in poker-faced and took their seats. I closed my eyes and prayed one last time for God's intervention. It was the moment of decision. As I opened my eyes I slid by hand into my pocket and felt for the capsule of cyanide. When I had found it, I pulled it out of my pocket and held it gingerly between my fingers. Adrenalin flooded my system. Could I take it? I didn't know. Then I looked at Erica and blew her a kiss. That was the agreed signal that we were both ready to take our lives. She cringed in apparent pain. I didn't understand why. Then she blew me a return kiss. I took a deep breath. There was no escaping death now if the jury found her guilty.

"Has the jury reached a verdict?" the Judge asked.

The foreman of the jury stood up and replied, "Yes, Your Honor, we have."

"The defendant will please stand."

Erica stood up slowly and took a deep breath. Then she coughed and glanced over at me. I was scared, I could hardly control my emotions. I looked at my parents and my mother gave me a sympathetic smile. God if she only knew what was about to happen. Tears welled up in my eyes. I felt the cyanide between my fingers and wondered how a tiny capsule could so quickly destroy human life. Fear consumed me as I recalled in graphic detail how the poison would work to kill me and the pain and suffering, I would have to endure before the end finally came. I wanted to run to Erica and wrestle away the cyanide from her grasp. I didn't want her to die nor was I ready to leave this earth with so little assurance that we'd be together in the afterlife.

"Bailiff, please bring me the verdict."

The bailiff brought the verdict to the judge and he read it. Without a glimmer of emotion, he handed it back and said, "Give it to the clerk to read."

The bailiff took the paper and handed it to the clerk. I fingered the capsule of cyanide preparing myself to swallow it quickly if that was to be my fate. She opened it up and began reading, "We the jury find the defendant, Eric Fox Coleman, not guilty by reason of insanity."

I jumped up and screamed. Carmen embraced me and we hugged each other wildly. I dropped the cyanide capsule on the floor and stomped on it. The crowd erupted in excited chatter. The judge shook his head and struck his gavel. Erica had done it. She was a free woman. God had forgiven us!

When I turned and looked at Erica, I expected to see her joyful face. But instead, her pale skin had turned blue, she was coughing incessantly and choking.

24
The Mishap

I jumped over the railing and ran to Erica, catching her just before she collapsed. Webster turned and looked at us, his face suddenly solemn. "What happened?" he asked.

"Get her an ambulance! She's sick," I screamed. "What's wrong, Erica? What did you do?"

She looked at me trying to tell me something, but she couldn't get it out. "The cyanide, where's the cyanide?" I asked frantically. She slapped the front of her dress with her hand and then contorted in excruciating pain. Tears were flowing down my face. A medic tapped me on the shoulder urging me to get out of his way. They pulled a stretcher up next to Erica and quickly lifted her up onto it. I followed them as they rolled her out of the courtroom and down to the hall to where an elevator was being held. The elevator went to the basement where an ambulance was waiting just outside the door. After they had loaded her, I jumped aboard and held her hand. She was almost unconscious. I couldn't imagine what was wrong with her until I smelled the pungent almond odor.

"Oh no! Oh my God no! She's taken the cyanide!"

"What?" the medic said.

"She's taken cyanide," I yelled.

"Are you sure?"

"Yes, can't you smell it?"

"Okay, I'll call it in and see what we should do."

One of the medics got on the radio while the other one

inspected Erica's mouth.

I looked at Erica and screamed, "Why did you take the cyanide? The jury acquitted you."

"There's no sign of cyanide in her mouth," the medic said.

"What?" I said very much confused.

Erica slapped at the front of her dress again and then began to shake.

"Do something. She's going to die!" I screamed.

The other medic got off the radio and said, "Okay, give her oxygen and start a sodium nitrate I-V."

Erica began to thrash, and she continued to hit her dress. I finally realized she was trying to tell me something.

"Oh my God," I said. "She didn't swallow it."

"Swallow what?" the medic asked.

"The cyanide pill. If she was convicted, she was going to take it. She had to hide it from the guards when she went through security."

"Seriously?" the medic asked.

"Yes," I replied and lifted the front of Erica's dress. The medic's eyes widened in realization as to what had happened.

"We've got to get it out," I pleaded.

"Okay," the medic said as he put on a pair of gloves.

A minute later he had extracted the pill and placed in a tray. I examined it and was pleased to see that it was mostly intact. Erica's distress had been the result of a small lesion at one end of the capsule that had allowed cyanide to slowly escape. When we got to the hospital, they rushed Erica into the emergency room. An orderly escorted me into the waiting room where Carmen was already waiting.

"Is she okay?"

"I don't know. She's unconscious."

"What's wrong with her?"

"Oh God, it's a long story."

"What is it, tell me?" Carmen screamed.

I told her about our pact.

"That's just like Erica," Carmen said. "It's always her way or nothing, I can't believe you let her talk you into such madness."

"I can't believe it either. I tried to resist her, but it was no use."

We sat impatiently in the waiting room for over an hour. Finally, a nurse came and told us they had taken Erica to a room. She said we should go up to the medical-surgical waiting room and the doctor would come to talk to us. By this time my parents, Webster and Suzie had made it to the hospital, so we all went up and waited. Finally, the doctor arrived and gathered us around to report on Erica's condition.

"She's stable right now. She's still unconscious so we don't know the extent of her injury. Fortunately, most of the cyanide didn't get out of the capsule otherwise she'd have died. It was good you realized what had happened when you did, Mr. Coleman. Another few minutes and the entire capsule would have dissolved."

"Will she be all right?" I asked.

"We won't know until she regains consciousness. Cyanide prevents the body's red blood cells from absorbing oxygen. It's possible she could have brain damage if the brain was deprived of oxygen for any length of time."

"Oh God, no." I moaned.

"Don't count her out yet, she might be fine," the doctor said. "We'll just have to wait and see."

"How long do you think it will be until she regains consciousness?" I asked.

"I have no way of knowing."

After the doctor was gone, I went over and stared out the window. My mother came over to me and put her arms around me.

"You must really love her," she said.

"Yes, more than you can imagine."

"I doubt that. I was young and in love once too you know."

"Hmm. ... I'm sorry I didn't call you and tell you about Erica sooner."

"I can see why you didn't."

"Can you forgive me?"

"Yes, but when she gets better, you've got to promise me that you'll visit us once in a while. I've missed you."

"What about Dad?" I said.

"It was hard for him to understand how you felt, but I think he's ready to forgive you. Why don't you go talk to him."

"Maybe later, right now all I can think about is Erica. I just pray she gets better."

"She will. You've just got to have faith."

After several hours, the doctor came back and told me I could go and stay with Erica. He said they had done all they could and now it was just a waiting game. I immediately went to her side. She was still rather pale, but some color had returned to her face. They were still giving her oxygen and an I-V was running. I took her limp hand in mine and rubbed it gently. I wrote love notes in the palm of her hand like she used to do to me. Then I ran my hand through her beautiful black hair and gazed at her smooth silky skin. I closed my eyes and thought back to the last time we had made love. She had been so incredibly alive and full of energy. I wondered if we'd ever make love like that again.

The next morning, the nurses woke me up and made me leave Erica's room while they bathed her. There was still no sign of her regaining consciousness, although I thought her nails had more color than they had the night before. I went back to the waiting room. Everyone had left except Mrs. Ramirez who was asleep on the sofa. I woke her up and suggested we go to breakfast. She wiped the sleep from her eyes and followed me downstairs. We went through the line, filled our plates, got some coffee, and found a place to sit.

"This is a good hospital," Carmen said. "Everyone is so friendly and helpful."

"Yeah. They have been really nice," I said.

"What are you and Erica going to do now that she's been acquitted?"

"Well, I've still got the lawsuit hanging over our head and I'm surprised I haven't heard from the bar association yet."

"What do think they will do to you?"

"I don't care what they do as long as they don't take away my license. If they suspend me awhile, I could live with that, but if I lose my license I would be devastated."

"What did you do?"

"I committed a crime called statutory rape for starters. Erica wasn't old enough to give her consent to sexual intercourse. If the DA wants, he could prosecute me for that, and then the bar would have to take some kind of action."

"But that was over a year ago. Do you think they would do anything about it now?"

"I hope not, but the fact that I was her trustee and had a duty to protect her won't sit well with the grievance committee."

"But doesn't someone have to complain? Who would complain?"

"Arnold, Martha's son. If Erica dies, then. ... Ah! Oh my God!" I laughed.

"What's so funny?"

"Erica's bond was revoked. Now, even if Erica dies, Arnold won't get a dime. I bet he was totally pissed when Erica left the country. I can't believe this. Arnold has no reason now to go through with the lawsuit or file a grievance. Oh, God. This is incredible. Oh, Carmen, Erica must pull through. She just has to wake up so I can tell her the good news."

After breakfast, I went back to Erica's room. There had been no change since I left, so I pulled up a chair next to her and turned on the TV. The morning news was just coming on.

"Coming right up, the startling end to the dramatic murder trial of Erica Fox Coleman," the announcer said. While several commercials were running, I took Erica's hand and brought it up to my face and kissed it. Then I pressed it firmly against my cheek. The odor of almond was gone, and Erica's sweet smell had returned. I smiled at her and then turned to look at the TV.

"Late yesterday, Erica Fox Coleman was found not guilty by reason of insanity of the murder of her aunt, Martha Collins. The Dallas jury took less than one day to decide that the long Fox family feud had created a virtual time bomb within Erica Fox that went off on April 3rd of this year when she fatally attacked Mrs. Collins. Just after the verdict was announced, however, Mrs. Coleman became violently ill and had to be taken to a hospital for treatment. The hospital lists Mrs. Coleman in critical condition apparently suffering from cyanide poisoning. There was no explanation given as to how cyanide poisoning occurred.

"In other news, Andrew Young resigned today as U.S. ambassador to the United Nations due to the recent controversy centering around his unauthorized meeting with a PLO representative."

"That's too bad, I liked Andrew Young. He's a good-looking guy," Erica said.

I looked at Erica and smiled. "You think? . . . Erica! You're awake."

"You're very observant."

"I can't believe this. How do you feel?"

"Hungry. Did I miss breakfast?"

"No, you've been eating constantly since you've been here."

"Oh really? I don't remember eating anything."

"It's been flowing through that tube in your arm."

"Oh, well I was thinking more of a waffle smothered in strawberries with lots of whipped cream."

"That does sound pretty good. I bet I could run over to IHOP and get that for you."

"Well, just don't sit there. Get going, I may starve to death before you get back."

"Okay, but before I go, how did your cyanide capsule get, ... you know?"

Erica grimaced, "Oh, God. I'm so embarrassed. I went to the ladies' room before they searched me that morning. It was the easiest place to hide it while I went through security. I guess in my haste, I stuck it in too far in and then when I tried to get it out, I couldn't find it."

I shook my head and said, "That was pretty risky. You almost killed yourself."

She nodded. "I know. ... Hey, was I dreaming, or did I get acquitted?"

"You were acquitted. You pulled it off, you little devil."

"Thank God," Erica sighed.

"I just realized since you forfeited your bond, Arnold has nothing to inherit now and no reason to pursue a grievance against me."

Erica laughed. "You just figured that out? Why in the hell do you think I took off to go see mama?"

"I thought you were pissed off that I wouldn't kill myself."

"I was but I still loved you and had to get you off the hook. If you hadn't come after me and reaffirmed our pact, I wouldn't have come back to Dallas."

"So, you intended to forfeit your bond?"

"Yes, it was the only way to get rid of Arnold."

"You gave up a million dollars just to save my ass?"

"Well, it's a cute ass," Erica noted.

"I can't believe you did that. I don't know what to say."

"Just say you love me."

"I do love you, but that million dollars was so important to you. I'm shocked you just let it go so easily."

"Who said it was easy? Giving up that money hurt me more than the cyanide."

I laughed. "You're something else."

"I know. You can thank me later. Right now, I'm more interested in that waffle."

"So now you're broke again?"

"That's okay, at least I have you."

I shook my head, still in shock over what Erica had done for me. Then I remembered.

"Hey, what about my bonus?"

"What bonus?" Erica asked.

"The bonus I got just about the time I became your trustee. I got a thirty-five-thousand-dollar bonus. It's been sitting in a cash management account. I forgot all about it."

"Really?"

"Yeah, and I've probably got fifteen thousand left from selling my interest in the firm."

Erica smiled. "Fifty thousand dollars, huh?"

"That's right."

"Well good, then what's the problem? Just do your magic. I'll give you a year."

"A year! Give me a break," I said.

"For a man as talented as you that should be plenty of time."

I shook my head and replied, "I'm going to go get your waffle now. I think the jury was right, you're a wacko."

The door opened and the nurse walked in followed by the doctor. While they were examining her, I went to the waiting room where everyone had returned.

"Erica's okay, she's awake and she's fine."

Mrs. Ramirez ran over, and we embraced. My mother started crying. Suzie and Webster stood up and hugged each other. Then my Dad came over and shook my hand.

"I'm happy for you son. You've been through a lot, and now you'll really appreciate Erica."

"Boy ain't that the damn truth. Thank you, Dad," I said and then began to choke up. "I'm sorry I upset you so much. You were always a great father."

"It was my fault. I should have realized your curiosity about your real father was only natural. I shouldn't have taken it so personally."

We embraced for the first time in several years. I looked over at my mother and she was crying tears of joy. I let go and smiled. It felt good to have a family again.

"Hey, I'll be back," I said. "I've got to run over to IHOP. Erica is hungry."

"You don't have a car," Dad noted.

"Oh, good point," I laughed.

"Come on. I'll drive you," he said.

25
Final Settlement

After Erica was acquitted, the judge put Collins vs. Coleman back on the civil trial docket. I told Michael before he ran up a lot of attorney's fees to call Arnold and see if there might be a settlement possibility. Since Erica's Trust was broke it didn't make much sense to fight over who was trustee. He asked me how much I could offer. I only had fifty thousand dollars left after forfeiting the bond and paying the attorneys. Erica was counting on me to parlay that money into another million dollars. After what she had been through, I certainly didn't want to have to tell her I needed that money to settle with Arnold.

I thought about borrowing what I needed for the settlement, but I didn't have any collateral and I doubted anyone would give me an unsecured loan for that much money. Unfortunately, I didn't have any rich relatives to go hit up, and most of my friends were just scraping by each month like I had been doing. Finally, I resigned myself to the fact that I was going to have to tell Erica the truth. I'd leave it up to her. We could settle the case or keep on slugging it out. It was Sunday night, about three weeks after the trial when I gave her the bad news.

"But we'll be broke,' she said.

"Pretty much but we'll be done with Arnold."

"You think he might take less?"

"I doubt it. The only reason he might settle for $50,000

is if Michael convinces him that's all I've got."

\"Shit, I hate being poor. It's scary."

"The practice is coming along. We'll get by."

Erica smiled and put her hands on my shoulder looking me in the eye. She shook her head. "Okay, as long as I have you, I'll be happy. . . . At least for a little while."

I laughed. "What does that mean?"

She smiled. "That means I'll give you a little extra time to make me rich since we're starting from scratch."

"Oh, thanks a lot," I said suddenly experiencing a strong jolt of deja vu. "You better give me about ten years."

She frowned. "Come on. Give me a break. I said a little extra time."

I didn't know whether Erica was giving me a bad time, or she was serious. It didn't really matter, the reality of the situation was it would be months, maybe years before we had any extra money to invest. My only concern at that moment was getting out of all the legal entanglements that still haunted us. The following day I was at the offices of Harper and Polk on an extension when Michael called Arnold. Michael and Arnold exchanged greetings. Arnold seemed dejected. Maybe he had already figured out he was fighting a losing battle.

"I wanted to talk to you about setting up some depositions," Michael said.

"Oh, right," Arnold replied.

"But before we do that you know we have an obligation under the local district court rules to try to settle this case," Michael said.

"I'm aware of that. Does your client have a proposal?"

"Well, as a matter of fact he does. We figure trying this case could run maybe twenty-five thousand dollars. Since no money was lost from the trust due to my client's acts and, in fact, the trust was quite profitable, about the best you could hope to do would be to have Richard removed as trustee and recover your attorney's fees."

"So, what's your proposal?"

"Well, my client would be willing to pay twenty-five thousand dollars in full and complete settlement of the case. This way we can all put this behind us and you'll have some cash in your pocket."

"Even if your client paid twenty-five thousand dollars, I couldn't take it. It would have to go into the trust. What good would that do me?" Arnold asked.

"You're right, however, as part of the settlement Erica has agreed to disclaim her interest in the trust. Since your mother isn't alive, that would mean you would be the beneficiary of the trust."

There was a pause and then Arnold asked, "Oh, so I'm the beneficiary but Richard Coleman is the trustee?"

"Well, that's your option. If you want Richard to resign, he will, but you may want to keep him on as trustee since he has such a good track record."

"That's all right. I'll invest my own money, thank you," Arnold said.

"Then we have a deal?" Michael asked.

"No, I'm afraid not. Coleman's not getting off that easy. I want a hundred grand, or I'll drag him through hell just to watch him burn."

"Come on, that's your mother talking. Don't prolong this senseless feud. Let's put this all behind us."

"My mother was murdered for Godsakes! You think $25,000 will make that go away?"

"This isn't about the murder, and I'm frankly not sure Erica did it anyway," Michael said. "I know she as much admitted it by pleading temporary insanity but that was a strategic move, we really don't know if she did it or not. What if she didn't do it?"

"That's bullshit. Of course, she did it."

"Okay, here's the deal," Michael said. "Rich and Erica only have $50,000 between them. That's all that's left. They're willing to give it all to you if you'll accept it. I'll be happy to give you an affidavit that they have no other assets. We'll even give you time to run an asset check if an affidavit isn't good enough."

Arnold thought for a moment, then he shook his head. "Okay, but I do want an asset check. I don't trust Rich or the Bitch. ... Let's just get this nightmare over with."

"Fine, I'll draw up the papers and have them delivered to you. Once you've completed your asset search and approved the settlement papers, we can finalize the deal."

"Good. I'll be waiting for them to arrive."

Within a week Collins vs. Coleman was history. It was painful paying my last fifty thousand dollars to Arnold, but that was better than a long-drawn-out legal battle. I was just glad to get it behind me. My last hurdle was the State Bar of Texas.

With all the trial publicity the local grievance committee notified me they were conducting an investigation into my conduct as Trustee of Erica's trust. Michael Harper agreed to represent me. After several weeks of negotiation, we agreed to a Public Reprimand and my agreement not to act as a trustee or in any other fiduciary capacity for a period of five years. It was all very humiliating experience but at least it was behind me.

My law practice did quite well once I was able to devote my entire attention to it. All the publicity I received from the murder trial, the settlement of the civil case and the grievance turned out to be less than devastating. The public seemed to have forgiven me for my transgressions in light of the unusual circumstances involved and the deep love that was evident between Erica and myself. To celebrate our victory, we had a delayed wedding reception at the Fairmount Hotel. Carmen, my parents and dozens of friends and acquaintances attended the gala affair. Erica and I danced all night in deep appreciation of the life we were beginning together.

When the guests had gone and we were enjoying one last round of champagne in our room, Erica handed me a thick brown envelope.

"What's this?" I said as I took it from her and examined it carefully.

"Open it," she laughed. "It's not a letter bomb."

I looked at her warily, wondering what she had in store for me. Finally, I opened the envelope. It was a small book, a savings book. I opened it. There was only one entry, a deposit in the amount of $50,000. I blinked to be sure I was reading it correctly.

"Just a little wedding present," Erica said with a smile. "Now I expect you to restore me to my accustomed standard of living."

I laughed and shook my head. "Where in the hell did you get $50,000?"

"It was easy. I sold my Porsche."

"You didn't?"

"You'll just have to drive me everywhere until you can replace it."

I put the bank book on the coffee table and took Erica in my arms. It was such a relief to be finally free. With Erica at my side I was the happiest man alive. I knew now there must be a God for only He could have engineered the miracle that had brought us from the brink of death into the glorious light that now engulfed us.

Epilogue

Somewhere in the Caribbean Sea, May 1982

After Erica was acquitted, the judge put Collins vs. Coleman back on the civil trial docket. I told Michael before he ran up a lot of attorney's fees to call Arnold and see if there might be a settlement possibility. Since Erica's Trust was broke it didn't make much sense to fight over who was trustee. He asked me how much I could offer. I only had fifty thousand dollars left after forfeiting the bond and paying the attorneys. Erica was counting on me to parlay that money into another million dollars. After what she had been through, I certainly didn't want to have to tell her I needed that money to settle with Arnold.

I thought about borrowing what I needed for the settlement, but I didn't have any collateral and I doubted anyone would give me an unsecured loan for that much money. Unfortunately, I didn't have any rich relatives to go hit up, and most of my friends were just scraping by each month like I had been doing. Finally, I resigned myself to the fact that I was going to have to tell Erica the truth. I'd leave it up to her. We could settle the case or keep on slugging it out. It was Sunday night, about three weeks after the trial when I gave her the bad news.

"But we'll be broke,' she said.

"Pretty much but we'll be done with Arnold."

"You think he might take less?"

"I doubt it. The only reason he might settle for $50,000 is if Michael convinces him that's all I've got."

\"Shit, I hate being poor. It's scary."

"The practice is coming along. We'll get by."

Erica smiled and put her hands on my shoulder looking me in the eye. She shook her head. "Okay, as long as I have you, I'll be happy. . . . At least for a little while."

I laughed. "What does that mean?"

She smiled. "That means I'll give you a little extra time to make me rich since we're starting from scratch."

"Oh, thanks a lot," I said suddenly experiencing a strong jolt of deja vu. "You better give me about ten years."

She frowned. "Come on. Give me a break. I said a little extra time."

I didn't know whether Erica was giving me a bad time, or she was serious. It didn't really matter, the reality of the situation was it would be months, maybe years before we had any extra money to invest. My only concern at that moment was getting out of all the legal entanglements that still haunted us. The following day I was at the offices of Harper and Polk on an extension when Michael called Arnold. Michael and Arnold exchanged greetings. Arnold seemed dejected. Maybe he had already figured out he was fighting a losing battle.

"I wanted to talk to you about setting up some depositions," Michael said.

"Oh, right," Arnold replied.

"But before we do that you know we have an obligation under the local district court rules to try to settle this case," Michael said.

"I'm aware of that. Does your client have a proposal?"

"Well, as a matter of fact he does. We figure trying this case could run maybe twenty-five thousand dollars. Since no money was lost from the trust due to my client's acts and, in fact, the trust was quite profitable, about the best you could hope to do would be to have Richard removed as trustee and recover your attorney's fees."

"So, what's your proposal?"

"Well, my client would be willing to pay twenty-five thousand dollars in full and complete settlement of the case. This way we can all put this behind us and you'll have some cash in your pocket."

"Even if your client paid twenty-five thousand dollars, I couldn't take it. It would have to go into the trust. What good would that do me?" Arnold asked.

"You're right, however, as part of the settlement Erica has agreed to disclaim her interest in the trust. Since your mother isn't alive, that would mean you would be the beneficiary of the trust."

There was a pause and then Arnold asked, "Oh, so I'm the beneficiary but Richard Coleman is the trustee?"

"Well, that's your option. If you want Richard to resign, he will, but you may want to keep him on as trustee since he has such a good track record."

"That's all right. I'll invest my own money, thank you," Arnold said.

"Then we have a deal?" Michael asked.

"No, I'm afraid not. Coleman's not getting off that easy. I want a hundred grand, or I'll drag him through hell just to watch him burn."

"Come on, that's your mother talking. Don't prolong this senseless feud. Let's put this all behind us."

"My mother was murdered for Godsakes! You think $25,000 will make that go away?"

"This isn't about the murder, and I'm frankly not sure Erica did it anyway," Michael said. "I know she as much admitted it by pleading temporary insanity but that was a strategic move, we really don't know if she did it or not. What if she didn't do it?"

"That's bullshit. Of course, she did it."

"Okay, here's the deal," Michael said. "Rich and Erica only have $50,000 between them. That's all that's left. They're willing to give it all to you if you'll accept it. I'll be happy to give you an affidavit that they have no other assets. We'll even give you time to run an asset check if an affidavit isn't good enough."

Arnold thought for a moment, then he shook his head. "Okay, but I do want an asset check. I don't trust Rich or the Bitch. ... Let's just get this nightmare over with."

"Fine, I'll draw up the papers and have them delivered to you. Once you've completed your asset search and approved the settlement papers, we can finalize the deal."

"Good. I'll be waiting for them to arrive."

Within a week Collins vs. Coleman was history. It was painful paying my last fifty thousand dollars to Arnold, but that was better than a long-drawn-out legal battle. I was just glad to get it behind me. My last hurdle was the State Bar of Texas.

With all the trial publicity the local grievance committee notified me they were conducting an investigation into my conduct as Trustee of Erica's trust. Michael Harper agreed to represent me. After several weeks of negotiation, we agreed to a Public Reprimand and my agreement not to act as a trustee or in any other fiduciary capacity for a period of five years. It was all very humiliating experience but at least it was behind me.

My law practice did quite well once I was able to devote my entire attention to it. All the publicity I received from the murder trial, the settlement of the civil case and the grievance turned out to be less than devastating. The public seemed to have forgiven me for my transgressions in light of the unusual circumstances involved and the deep love that was evident between Erica and myself. To celebrate our victory, we had a delayed wedding reception at the Fairmount Hotel. Carmen, my parents and dozens of friends and acquaintances attended the gala affair. Erica and I danced all night in deep appreciation of the life we were beginning together.

When the guests had gone and we were enjoying one

last round of champagne in our room, Erica handed me a thick brown envelope.

"What's this?" I said as I took it from her and examined it carefully.

"Open it," she laughed. "It's not a letter bomb."

I looked at her warily, wondering what she had in store for me. Finally, I opened the envelope. It was a small book, a savings book. I opened it. There was only one entry, a deposit in the amount of $50,000. I blinked to be sure I was reading it correctly.

"Just a little wedding present," Erica said with a smile. "Now I expect you to restore me to my accustomed standard of living."

I laughed and shook my head. "Where in the hell did you get $50,000?"

"It was easy. I sold my Porsche."

"You didn't?"

"You'll just have to drive me everywhere until you can replace it."

I put the bank book on the coffee table and took Erica in my arms. It was such a relief to be finally free. With Erica at my side I was the happiest man alive. I knew now there must be a God for only He could have engineered the miracle that had brought us from the brink of death into the glorious light that now engulfed us.

About the Author

William Manchee is a consumer lawyer by trade and practices in Dallas with his son Jim. Originally from southern California, he lives now in Plano, Texas. He is the author of the Stan Turner Mystery series inspired by many actual cases from his past. His other works include the Rich Coleman Novels and a science fiction series, the Tarizon Saga. He is also the author of the nonfiction book You Can Save Your Small Business.

THE STAN TURNER MYSTERIES
by William Manchee

Undaunted
Disillusioned
Brash Endeavor
Second Chair
Cash Call
Deadly Distractions
Black Monday
Cactus Island
Act Normal
Deadly Defiance
Deadly Dining
Deadly Blood

"...appealing characters and lively dialogue, especially in the courtroom . . . " (Publisher's Weekly)

"...plenty of action and adventure . . . " (Library Journal)

"...each plot line, in and of itself, can be riveting . . . " (Foreword Magazine)

"...a courtroom climax that would make the venerable Perry Mason stand and applaud . . . "
(Crescent Blue)

"...Richly textured with wonderful atmosphere, the novel shows Manchee as a smooth, polished master of the mystery form . . . " (The Book Reader)

"...Manchee's stories are suspenseful and most involve lawyers. And he's as proficient as Grisham . . . (Dallas Observer)

"...fabulous-a real page turner-I didn't want it to end!" (Allison Robson, CBS Affiliate, KLBK TV, Ch 13)

www.ingramcontent.com/pod-product-compliance
Lightning Source LLC
Chambersburg PA
CBHW020554310726
48979CB00008B/1217/J

* 9 7 8 1 7 3 3 3 2 8 3 9 5 *